BEHIND THE
RED DOOR

BEHIND THE RED DOOR

JACKIE BARBOSA

APHRODISIA

KENSINGTON BOOKS
http://www.kensingtonbooks.com

APHRODISIA BOOKS are published by

Kensington Publishing Corp.
119 West 40th Street
New York, NY 10018

All Kensington Titles, Imprints, and Distributed Lines are available at special quantity discounts for bulk purchases for sales promotions, premiums, fund-raising, and educational or institutional use.

Special book excerpts or customized printings can also be created to fit specific needs. For details, write or phone the office of the Kensington special sales manager: Kensington Publishing Corp., 119 West 40th Street, New York, NY 10018, attn: Special Sales Department, Phone: 1-800-221-2647.

Aphrodisia and the A logo Reg. U.S. Pat & TM Off.

ISBN-13: 978-0-7582-3458-2
ISBN-10: 0-7582-3458-9

First Kensington Trade Paperback Printing: June 2009

10 9 8 7 6 5 4 3 2 1

Printed in the United States of America

Acknowledgments

First and foremost, to my parents, who fostered my love of books and reading and always encouraged me to pursue my dreams, no matter how impractical or unattainable. If I wanted to fly, they were always there to cheer me on when I soared and to catch me when I fell.

Next, to my wonderful critique partners—Lacey Kaye, Darcy Burke, Erica Ridley, Janice Goodfellow, Emma Petersen, and Amie Stuart—who have taught me, supported me, and cheered me on every step of the way. Without you, this book would never have come into being.

I am also blessed to have made many friends in the romance writing community, all of whom have contributed in some way to my growth as an author. It would be impossible to list all of you here, but I am so, so grateful to each and every one of you.

Special thanks to Deanna Lee and Sable Grey, owners of Cobblestone Press, who published a little story called *Carnally Ever After*, which became the prequel to the novellas in this anthology. I can't thank them enough for their willingness to take a chance on me or for all their excellent advice.

No list of acknowledgments would be complete without a nod to my editor at Kensington Books, John Scognamiglio, who rocked my world with "the call," and my agent, Kevan Lyon, whose enthusiasm for my work inspires and humbles me.

And finally, but most importantly, to my children, who are patient and understanding when Mom says, "Not now, I'm writing," and to my husband, who has given me my own story-book ending.

CONTENTS

WICKEDLY EVER AFTER

1

_____

London, England—July, 1816

The blank paper, unblemished by so much as an inkblot, mocked him. The page as empty, it seemed, as his soul. Except that where the page was white, his soul was black. Or so his father, the mighty Duke of Hardwyck, was ever fond of reminding him.

Nathaniel St. Clair, sixth Marquess of Grenville, grimaced as he lifted the glass to his lips and took another deep swallow of whiskey. At least there was great amusement to be found in living down to the old man's expectations.

In fact, given his appalling lack of productivity this morning, Nathaniel could see no reason not to begin his pursuit of profligacy a trifle earlier than usual today. A visit to Brooks' for an afternoon at hazard, followed by a long night of fucking at the Red Door, appealed a great deal more than waiting for the arrival of the proper English words to capture the lyrical frivolity of Ovid's Latin.

What stopped him from following through on the impulse was not the sudden sting of conscience or a spontaneous flow of poetic verse, but the unexpected sound of tapping feet and voices in the hall outside his private study.

"I say, miss, I told you the marquess is not to be disturbed. You cannot mean to go in there." This squeaky protest came from one of the footmen, though Nathaniel would have been hard-pressed to remember the fellow's name even if he could have seen his face. The Hardwycks went through footmen the way other aristocratic families went through ready cash.

"I most certainly can," came the reply, calm and crisp and delivered in velvet tones Nathaniel would have recognized from the other side of a wall of granite.

The voice belonged to the Honorable Miss Eleanor Palmer, whose long, slender limbs and small, round breasts could claim no rival, either in his imagination or in reality. The only respectable lady Nathaniel had ever desired, she was also the one he'd always known he could never have.

For what would a proper, sensible Unmarried like Miss Palmer want with an inveterate wastrel like him? He came to his feet. His heart gave an oddly hopeful, arhythmic lurch as the doorknob turned.

He was about to find out.

Heedless of the footman who jabbered incessant objections at her heels, Eleanor marched into the surprisingly bright, airy study. She slapped the note from her former fiancé, the Earl of Holyfield, on the desk in front of the Marquess of Grenville and glared up at him. "What, may I ask, is the meaning of this?"

She cursed the bone-softening, knee-weakening heat that spread outward from her belly as she met his cornflower-blue gaze. No other man of her acquaintance had ever had this curious effect on her. It was most provoking. Straightening her spine, she did her best to adopt her most regal and imperious expression. She was here to dispel any notion that she might be remotely interested in accepting Grenville's suit, not to melt at his feet into an ignominious puddle of feminine longing.

What could Holyfield have been thinking even to entertain such an idea, much less commit it to paper in this letter to her father? Of all the unsuitable possible husbands for a bookish, reserved lady such as herself, the high-living, wild-loving Marquess of Grenville was surely the most unsuitable of all.

The marquess leaned down and plucked the letter from the desk. His long, elegant fingers bore several blue-black ink stains.

She ought to have known better than to come here. Perhaps she could forgive herself for having forgotten how tall and imposing a figure he cut, for few men had more than a few inches on her unusual height, but she could not excuse her failure to recall how preternaturally handsome he was. And surely it was unnatural for a man as dissolute and disreputable as Grenville to appear the very picture of robust masculine health. From the glossy sheen of his chestnut-brown hair, to the crystal clarity of his eyes, to the tightly corded musculature scarcely concealed by the close fit of his perfectly tailored coat, he exuded youthful vigor. In fact, with that lock of hair falling across his forehead as he scanned the missive, he more resembled a newly formed and wholly innocent Adam than the devil he was reputed to be.

His mouth quirked up on one side, Grenville looked from her to the letter to the footman, who stood behind her babbling incoherent apologies.

"Oh, do leave off fussing, er . . ." The marquess paused, his dark, straight eyebrows drawing together. "What's your name again, old chap?"

Eleanor could not suppress a smile at the words *old chap*. The doughy-faced youth could no more be characterized as old than a freshly baked loaf of bread.

The footman cleared his throat. "Beardsley, my lord."

Grenville nodded briskly. "You are dismissed then, Beardsley."

"As you wish, my lord." Beardsley sounded as though he'd swallowed a particularly sharp fish bone.

Her stomach dropped as Grenville's half-smile was replaced with a full grin. "You needn't fear I'll mention this lapse to my father. It shall be our little secret." Though he spoke to the footman, his gaze focused on Eleanor.

"Oh, thank you, my lord." The servant's heels clicked against the polished wood floor as he retreated. "And Beardsley?"

The sound of footsteps ceased. "Yes, my lord?"

Silence stretched out for several long, aching seconds as Grenville's gaze traveled from her face and over the length of her body with a searing intensity that left her breathless. And wanting—something.

"Close the door behind you."

Nathaniel studied Miss Palmer's delicate features as the footman beat his hasty retreat. The door clicked shut. She ought to be frightened, or at least alarmed, at the prospect of being trapped alone in a room with the notoriously amoral Marquess of Grenville. She ought to follow Beardsley out of the room as fast the long, slim legs concealed beneath the rose-and-cream-striped muslin of her day dress could carry her.

Instead, she stood her ground, meeting his regard with a steady gaze, her dark blue eyes sparkling with challenge and . . . was it excitement? The flush rising in her cheeks and the pulse fluttering visibly in her elegant throat suggested not fear, but interest. Perhaps even arousal.

How utterly unexpected.

"Surely, you do not expect me to remain here behind closed doors with you, my lord," she said at last.

He gave her a negligent grin and wiggled his eyebrows. "I most certainly do." When she opened her mouth to protest, he added, "What else is a gentleman to do when a young lady accosts him in his private study without benefit of a chaperone but protect her reputation by means of ensuring her privacy?"

"I came only to tell you I would not look favorably upon your suit, in the event your friend Holyfield has given you cause to think otherwise." The words came out in a rush, forced and a little breathless. She looked over her shoulder at the door. "And now I shall be going."

She extended her hand, a clear request for him to return the letter. He looked down at it, still clutched in his hand, and reread the passage that had brought Miss Palmer to his lair.

> *Despite my need to break our betrothal, I continue to hold your daughter in the highest regard and would not wish my perfidy to adversely affect her ability to make an advantageous match. To that end, I observe that the Marquess of Grenville is once again in the pool of Eligibles, and, further, I believe he would make an excellent husband for Miss Palmer. I am aware you do not hold him in high esteem, but I am of the opinion that a lady of Miss Palmer's faultless character could do much to temper his tendencies toward vice. Moreover, it cannot escape your notice that, should she marry Grenville, your daughter would one day be a duchess, a goodly step above the mere countess I should have made her.*

A small smile quirked Nathaniel's lips. He owed Alistair de Roche, who had absconded to Gretna Green just four days past with Nathaniel's former intended, a singular debt of gratitude. Lady Louisa Bennett had been his father's choice, after all, not Nathaniel's. If Holyfield hadn't done the ignoble thing and eloped with the girl despite their respective commitments to others, Nathaniel would have been sticking his head into the marital noose tomorrow morning.

Unfortunately, Holyfield's second act of magnanimity was destined to go to waste. No matter how well he thought Nathaniel and Miss Palmer might suit, her father, Viscount Palmer, would never consent to a match between his daughter and a man he referred to as Marquess of the Devil.

But then, Nathaniel wasn't particularly interested in the sort of union that would require paternal consent. Marriage was not on his agenda. However, she'd claimed it wasn't on hers, either. And she had come here alone. His cock twitched, stiffening at the thought.

Ambling round to her side of the desk, he crossed one ankle over the other and leaned against the corner, a deliberately indolent pose. Her eyes widened at his proximity, and her chest rose and fell more rapidly than before. *Excellent.*

When he stretched out his hand to return the letter to her, she stepped backward with a small gasp, then reached out to snatch the paper from him. He pulled it back toward his chest.

"Before I give it to you, tell me: why did you come alone?"

Her eyes narrowed, but her dilated pupils suggested she was more excited than annoyed. "I didn't. My aunt is waiting for me in the coach."

He made a mock frown. "I don't believe the venerable ladies of Almack's would consider a companion left out of doors to be any sort of chaperone a'tall."

"Aunt Eppie gossips," she admitted with a resigned sigh. "So I told her I'd come to return a parasol to Jane, and I'd only be a moment."

Nathaniel nodded. Jane, his younger sister, and Miss Palmer had become particular friends when they'd met in the queen's presentation queue two years earlier.

"I simply wanted to be certain you would not attempt to court me now that we are both free." She held out a hand, her expression pleading. "May I have the letter now? If I don't return soon, Aunt Eppie will wonder what's become of me and come after me."

Ah, but the moment was too delicious, too perfect to allow it to slip through his fingers.

"You must know I wouldn't dream of courting you, Miss Palmer. To do so would imply that I have honorable intentions toward you, and we both know I am not an honorable man." A slow smile curved his lips, one he knew was both wicked and beguiling. He turned and placed the letter purposefully on the desk behind him. "Which is why, if you want the letter, you'll have to come and get it."

"You can't be serious!" Eleanor exclaimed when she found enough breath to speak.

His smile didn't falter. "Of course, I'm not. I'm far too shallow to be serious. But even so . . ." He shrugged, indicating he didn't intend to back down.

Drat him, anyway! If it was a game he wanted, then it was a game she would give him.

She darted forward and to his left, determined to go around him to gain access to the letter. He uncrossed his ankles and mirrored her movement, blocking her with astonishing ease. She managed to pull up short before colliding with him and lunge to his right. Again, he foiled her, but this time, she wasn't able to halt her forward progress and landed tight against his chest. His heat and hardness and tangy male scent permeated everywhere their bodies touched, until it seemed she could taste him with her skin.

And, oh, he was delicious.

She ought to get away, ought not to stand there pressed against him in this near embrace. But the letter was right there behind him and once she had it, she could leave, her mission accomplished. She stretched her arms around the solid breadth of his torso, but he foresaw this gambit as well and gently grasped her wrists before she could reach her objective.

"I win," he said, the words delivered so quietly, she felt their rumble in his chest before she heard them issue from his lips.

Her eyes widening, she glared up into his face, intending to deliver some stinging retort or other, though she hadn't the foggiest notion what it would be. The impulse died in the hot intensity of his gaze, an expression she had never before seen on a man's face—at least, not directed at her—but recognized anyway: desire.

The broad smile he'd worn earlier had become smaller and a little pained. "I demand a forfeit."

"A forfeit?"

"A small one in exchange for the letter. Say, a kiss."

Her heart jumped into her throat and pounded there like a butterfly beating against a pane of glass, desperate for escape. Only it wasn't escape she wanted. Insanely, she pressed closer to him and tilted her chin upward. "Then do your worst," she whispered, "and be done with it."

He chuckled. "Oh, no. For you, Miss Palmer, nothing but the best will do."

Then his palms were on her cheeks, smooth and dry, and his lips touched hers, firm and warm and full of promise . . . and demand.

The effect of the contact was both instant and alarming. Heavy heat descended to her belly as if she were being filled with molten metal. The blaze spread from there outward to her fingers and toes. She didn't mean to hum with approval, but the sound vibrated from somewhere deep inside over which she had no control. His hands slid from her face to the back of her bonneted head, and he slanted his lips more urgently across hers, coaxing her mouth open.

He sucked at her lower lip, rolling it between his teeth, and she reeled with the sheer, mind-numbing pleasure of the sensation. His tongue flicked once, twice into her mouth, then slid all the way inside so that she tasted the sharp, pungent flavor of the whiskey he'd drunk mixed with a sweet, almost buttery essence on her taste buds.

He spread his legs, and her hips naturally settled into the space between them. With one hand, he continued to hold her head steady while the other coasted down her back to her buttocks. He cupped one cheek in his palm and pushed her tight to his groin, rotating his hips as he did. A thick bulge pushed insistently against her belly, and the soft flesh between her thighs responded with an instinctive rush of warm moisture.

In the one small corner of her mind that remained rational, she wondered how Grenville could evoke so effortlessly the sort of response she'd wished a thousand times to feel at even a fraction of this intensity for her former fiancé. But Holyfield's brief, perfunctory kisses had never made her feel as though she might ignite into a pillar of flame or melt into a river of hot wax.

They had never done anything at all.

Grenville lifted his head and thrust her abruptly away, though with regret rather than anger, she thought. He breathed raggedly, his cheeks were flushed with color, and as he turned to retrieve the letter from the desk, she saw that his fingers trembled.

"Here," he said gruffly, thrusting the paper toward her. "Go, before I think better of it."

Eleanor ought to take the letter and flee, but the molten ore pulsing in her belly seemed to have grown cold and hard in her feet. So instead of snatching the parchment from his hand, she stood there and stared dumbly at him for several long moments. In the ensuing silence, two equally dizzying thoughts impinged upon her slowly sobering brain.

First and most frightening, she wasn't incapable of passion, wasn't cold as she'd always believed. No one cold could be made to burn.

Second, the Marquess of Grenville was not nearly so amoral as he liked people to believe. He didn't want to let her go—that fact was writ in the taut lines around his mouth and eyes, in the tense sinews of his neck—but he was going to anyway.

And more fool she for wishing, however fleetingly, that he would confirm his reputation and thereby ruin hers. Aunt Eppie was waiting, and surely it had been much longer than ten minutes.

Her fingers at last found the will to take the letter from his hand.

"Thank you."

She was ready to break for the door when she saw he had picked up a book from the desk and was idly caressing its spine. A pretty volume, it was bound in dark blue leather with ornate gilt lettering spelling out the title and author. Close as she stood to him, she read the words easily.

And gasped.

"How did you come by that?" she demanded.

He looked up, his eyes widening. "This? Er . . ." He looked away, as if fumbling for an answer. As well he should, for the book he held was Clarence Mathews's translation of Ovid's *Metamorphoses,* and Eleanor knew the book was not due to be released by the publisher until early next month.

She knew because she had been counting the days until she could purchase it. No one had ever captured the voice of the Latin poets as beautifully or as accurately in English as Clarence Mathews. A fledgling translator herself, though of Greek poets rather than Latin, Eleanor admired Mathews above all others and considered his work the gold standard to which her own work might one day be held.

Grenville cleared his throat. "It is an advance copy. Mathews and I are friends."

Eleanor straightened, both surprised and excited. "Truly?" She frowned. "I have heard he is a recluse. However did you come to be friends?"

Grenville laughed. "Since I am clearly anything *but* reclusive?" He shrugged. "We've known each other since we were boys. You might even say we were raised together."

"Oh. Do you see him often now, then?"

A shadow of a smile passed across the marquess's lips. "Nearly every day."

The idea was born so quickly, she didn't think at all before the words popped from her mouth. "Could you introduce me to him? I am most anxious to meet him."

Grenville raised an eyebrow. "But, as you say yourself, he is a recluse."

Eleanor's shoulders slackened. "I am sorry. I shouldn't have asked."

He studied her, his forehead furrowing in thought. "No, no, it's quite all right. You admire his work then?"

"Oh, very much! He is the greatest translator and poet of our age. Ever, really." She couldn't help gushing, though it hardly seemed appropriate to speak so flatteringly of another man after what she'd just shared with the one she was speaking to.

For some reason she couldn't fathom, Grenville appeared . . . well . . . *pleased* by her enthusiasm. "He would be gratified to know that, I'm sure. And, as it happens, I believe he is seeking a proofreader for his next manuscript. Perhaps I could offer him your services?"

Eleanor couldn't believe her good fortune. She clapped her hands together. "Oh, yes, please, that would be splendid!"

"Excellent. But I should warn you . . ."

His eyes had taken on a devilish, predatory glint. An answering heat rose in Eleanor's breast and belly. She should put an end to her ridiculous fascination with the marquess this instant and walk away. The opportunity to read Clarence Mathews's work in advance was hardly worth the very real possibility that she might do something that would lead to the outcome she'd come here determined to avoid: marriage to the notoriously depraved Marquess of Grenville. The devil himself.

But she couldn't bring herself to leave, and she wasn't sure upon which man to blame her lack of willpower.

"You should warn me of what?" Her voice quavered, thin and reedy in her ears.

"You'll have to come here to get the pages. Alone. And I won't be responsible for what happens while you're here, should you be moved by what you've read to throw yourself at me."

"And why would that happen?"

He grinned again. "Mathews is translating *The Amores*. And I have every intention of using that to my advantage."

2

Clarence Mathews had wound up having a rather fruitful day after all. Nathaniel almost crowed with satisfaction as he patted the tall stack of pages he'd poured out with almost magical ease after Miss Palmer's departure.

Mathews, it seemed, had found his muse.

And she would be back. Tomorrow evening, if she kept her promise. Which she absolutely would not do if she had any sense of self-preservation. But of course, if she had, she would never have come in the first place.

The clatter of silver and plates across the hall from his study told him the dinner hour was upon him. He realized for the first time just how engrossed he had been in his work. The dying light of the setting sun was all that leaked through the sheer curtains over the room's one window and, were it not for the lamp he always lit when he worked, the entire space would have been shrouded in dusk. The tumbler of whiskey he'd poured shortly before Miss Palmer's arrival stood next to the inkwell where he'd left it, untouched in the ensuing hours.

Damn, but he had some work to do on his appearance before making his way to the dining room. He rose from his chair and crossed to look at himself in the oval, gilt-framed mirror that hung on the wall opposite his desk. Just as he'd feared—he looked sober as a judge.

He couldn't have his father suspecting he'd been doing anything other than boozing himself into a stupor all afternoon.

Silence descended on the other side of the door, an indication he had precious little time left to get himself in order. Certainly not enough to actually get rip-roaring drunk. And, oddly, he found the prospect of doing so didn't appeal to him in any case.

He wanted to remember each and every moment of his encounter with the delectable Miss Palmer with excruciating clarity. The taste of her lips and mouth, lemony sweet with a hint of spice. The softly rounded curve of her arse filling his hand. The vibrations escaping from her throat in a broken but unmistakable melody of pleasure.

In fact, he decided as he rumpled his hair and ran his fingers underneath his cravat to set it askew, he might not want to overindulge in alcohol for a very long time—not when the prospect of tasting the much more intoxicating Eleanor Palmer, inch by delightful inch, loomed so temptingly before him.

He ought not to seduce her, of course. It was very, very bad of him, far worse than anything he'd ever done to deserve his notoriety. He was not a despoiler of virgins. The women—and occasional men—with whom he frolicked had all been spoiled long before his arrival.

Which was probably why, he reflected as he ambled back to the desk to retrieve his whiskey, he found Eleanor so irresistible. She was so perfectly unspoiled, her responses as yet untainted by artifice or device, the reciprocity of her desire completely genuine. Like a long, cool draught of fresh water, he sensed she could quench the thirst inside him that always threatened to make him wither and blow away.

He dipped a finger into the whiskey glass and tilted his head back, allowing a drop of the liquid to fall into one eye and then the other. He blinked against the painful sting, but it should have the desired effect of reddening them. Lifting the glass to his lips, he downed the remainder in one swallow, just as the scratch on his door came to indicate that dinner was about to be served.

"Eleanor, darling, you must eat more than that or you'll waste away to nothing." Her mother's additional admonition, "and you haven't far to go," hovered, unspoken, in the air.

Eleanor looked up from her plate, around which she'd been pushing her creamed sole for the past quarter hour, and flashed her mother a guilty smile. "I'm sorry, Mama. I'm just a bit distracted this evening."

She punctuated her apology by forcing down a large bite of the fish. The heavy white sauce nearly gagged her, but she succeeded in swallowing, to her mother's obvious pleasure.

Neither her mother nor her father, nor even doting Aunt Eppie, had ever taken the slightest notice of how much Eleanor consumed—or did not consume—at meals before now. Had they done so, they would have noted that she could not abide the thick, oily gravies and sauces that their cook insisted upon slathering over every morsel that exited the kitchen at mealtimes. Eleanor's lady's maid had long ago learnt to summon up a plate of fresh fruit or raw vegetables before bedtime and after breakfast, and such treats accounted for the majority of Eleanor's diet. Without them, she might indeed have wasted away long ago.

Eleanor suppressed a surge of irritation at her mother's well-intentioned meddling. Ever since The Disaster, as Eleanor had taken to calling Holyfield's elopement with Lady Louisa Bennett, her parents watched her every move with dewy-eyed concern, treating her with the sort of delicate care typically reserved for the finest crystal goblets. Not for the first time, Eleanor regretted that she had so successfully feigned delight over her wedding to the Earl of Holyfield. Perhaps, if she had been less enthusiastic about the preparations, her parents would not have believed her so crushed by the demise of those plans.

Her appetite was even less vigorous tonight than usual, however, and to say she was distracted was no lie. First, there was her anticipation of Clarence Mathews's new book, which awaited her on her bedside table in all its leather-and-paper-scented splendor. But more immediately responsible for the peculiar fluttery twinge in her stomach and her accompanying loss of interest in food was the prospect of returning the book to Grenville—alone—and what was likely to transpire when she did. Permitting him to kiss her had been a mistake, but she hadn't anticipated the shattering effect the contact would have upon her. Agreeing to return was madness, she knew, nothing short of courting a repeat performance. Yet, shamefully—or perhaps shamelessly—she craved just that.

"Eleanor, you are not attending your mother." Her father's sharp reprimand cut through Eleanor's errant musings.

For the second time in as many minutes, Eleanor smiled awkwardly at her mother. "Yes, Mama?"

"I asked you how Lady Jane was holding up under the scandal." Lady Palmer frowned, her ethereal features displaying uncharacteristic signs of her age in the tight lines around her mouth and eyes.

"Lady Jane?" Eleanor echoed stupidly.

Her mother's pale eyebrows drew together. "Yes, dear. Eppie . . ."—here Lady Palmer cast an inquiring glance at her elder sister—"said you returned a parasol to her today and spent some minutes inside conversing with her."

Eleanor's face heated, and her already unsettled stomach plummeted. She should have remembered her purported reason for visiting the Hardwycks' household. That she did not was further evidence that she had no business whatever returning there

WICKEDLY EVER AFTER / 19

tomorrow night. She was a terrible liar and would give herself away before the week was out.

"This debacle cannot have improved Lady Jane's prospects this Season," Lady Palmer continued, appearing not to notice Eleanor's discomfort, "any more than yours."

Eleanor glanced toward Aunt Eppie, who watched her niece with shrewdly narrowed eyes. Eleanor often suspected her aunt, the widow of a poor country vicar, had a more astute understanding of human nature than her more worldly relatives would have credited.

"Now, Lucy," her aunt said, turning toward her sister, "don't you think it a bit soon to be discussing such things?" She looked back at Eleanor with a conspiratorial glint in her light gray eyes. "I'm sure Eleanor cannot be at all ready to consider another man's suit just yet."

Eleanor released a grateful sigh and felt some of the hot, red color dissipate from her cheeks.

To her left, her father cleared his throat. "Be that as it may, I'm sure Eleanor appreciates the necessity of getting back on the horse after a fall. Don't you, darling?"

A sharp pang of alarm flooded her chest, but she turned to look obediently at her father. "Yes, of course, Papa."

"Excellent." The viscount bestowed her with a fond, paternal smile. "Then you know we must show Society we aren't ashamed and you are not at fault in this affair."

"Which is why," her mother continued, "we have decided we shall attend Lady Chester's ball tomorrow night after all."

"Tomorrow night?" Eleanor squeaked in her horror. She had forgotten entirely about the ball—a much anticipated event on the London social calendar—but then, she hadn't imagined her parents would want to attend after all that had happened.

"I know it will be trying for you," her father said, "but we simply cannot hide our faces from Society and hope the talk dies away. You know as well as I that it will not."

Her mother nodded. "And it wouldn't hurt for you to consider other ... er ... husbandly possibilities. Lady Chester's nephew is available, you know, and doesn't need a well-dowered wife."

Eleanor nearly choked on her wine. Resigned though she was to marrying, for her parents could ill afford to continue supporting a spinster daughter and her chaperone on their tiny Hampshire estate's meager income, she knew better now than to accept the proposal of the next gentleman who, like Holyfield, was eager enough for the prestige of her royal bloodline to overlook the paucity of her dowry. In the end, her pedigree hadn't been enough to prevent him from running away to marry another woman.

This turn of events, however, was surely a blessing. Had she married Holyfield, they both would have been miserable. He would never have understood or accepted her bookish, solitary ways. Moreover, he wouldn't have been capable of fidelity, though he would have tried and hated himself for failing.

The outrageously handsome and socially sought-after Earl of Chester would be twice as bad on all these counts as Holyfield. Except, from what she had gleaned from Lady Jane about the man, he would neither attempt to be faithful to his wife, whoever she might be, nor feel remorse for his failure.

And the Marquess of Grenville would be the worst of them all.

No, this time, Eleanor wanted a man who shared her scholarly predilections, one who cared more for study and learning than for the pleasures of the flesh.

A man, perhaps, like Clarence Mathews.

She brightened at the thought. All she needed to do was determine whether he was married and, if he was not, persuade Grenville to provide not only Mathews's manuscript pages, but an introduction as well.

But the only way to do that was to meet him at the appointed hour tomorrow night. Which would mean slipping away from a ball at midnight.

The notion caused the corners of her mouth to turn up in amusement.

If Cinderella could do it, then so could she.

"Well, well, well," the Duke of Hardwyck drawled as Nathaniel took his appointed seat at the table. "To what do we owe the dubious honor of your presence this evening?"

Nathaniel lolled his head in his father's direction and stared at the fat old man with deliberately unfocused eyes. "I'm in mourning."

The duke harrumphed. "Don't pretend you're concerned about having bollixed up—"

The duchess gasped. "Hardwyck, really, you mustn't use such language in front of Jane."

Nathaniel looked at his younger sister, who sat across from him, and saw that despite her carefully neutral expression, her nearly translucent blue eyes sparked with amusement.

His father rolled his eyes at his wife. "Bollocks! Jane's probably heard worse from the gossips about your beloved son than she'll hear from me tonight." He turned his fierce glare back in Nathaniel's direction. "And even if you don't feel the least bit ashamed of what you've done to your mother and me, you might give a thought to what the scandal has done to your sister. Her prospects after three Seasons were thin enough before this. It's not as if she has your pretty face to fall back on, after all."

Out of the corner of his vision, Nathaniel saw his sister flinch, though her expression remained as blank as before. Sadly, she was perfectly accustomed to hearing these sorts of observations, not just from their father, but from many less-than-discreet gossips of the ton. Though Jane had an exceptionally keen wit and excelled in every aspect of feminine accomplishment, she was painfully plain, without a single facial feature that could be considered remarkable either for beauty or ugliness.

If she hadn't fallen head over ears for the Earl of Chester, whose taste in women was so fickle that he had never been known to keep a mistress for more than two months, she might have had a chance at making a happy union. As it was, whether she married the earl or not, there seemed every likelihood she'd end up in a marriage as unhappy as their parents'.

As unhappy as almost everyone's.

"Father, it is not Grenville's fault I haven't married."

The duke turned his scowl on his daughter now. "Indeed it is not. You are far too particular for a girl in your position. How many perfectly respectable suitors have you turned away now in the vain hope that Chester will come up to snuff?"

Jane's shoulders stiffened. "I'm not hoping—"

Nathaniel interrupted his sister's protestation. "Perfectly respectable suitors? Do you mean the Duke of Ponseby, who's sixty if he's a day and has managed to bury three wives in as many decades? Or perhaps you're thinking of Angus MacCreedy, who speaks a language that only distantly resembles English and probably hasn't bathed since he was born. And the last was Thomas Whitehouse, wasn't it, whose mother still has him in leading strings and who wouldn't know Shakespeare from Chaucer?"

"They're all titled, all single. Perfectly respectable."

"Ah, yes." Nathaniel lifted his wineglass, already filled by one of the footmen with what appeared to be an expensive Beaujolais from his father's extensive cellar, and tilted it in the duke's direction. "Just like me." He downed a large swallow of the liquid, mocking its excellence with the carelessness of his consumption.

Jane's posture relaxed as Nathaniel turned their father's abuse back on himself. Now, he had to keep it there.

"And I assure you, Your Grace, I am altogether broken up over my aborted marital bliss. That is to say, I shall miss pro-

foundly the additional thousand pounds in allowance my nup-
tials would have brought me. Not to mention the private town
house."

Hardwyck's countenance reddened until it nearly matched
the shade of the wine. "You're fortunate to have an allowance at
all, you miserable, sodden excuse for a son. I ought to cut you
off without a tuppence."

"Why don't you?"

Really, that was the question. It couldn't be because the old
son of a bitch actually nurtured some tender emotion for
Nathaniel. The duke had never paid a speck of attention to his
only son and heir when he was a child, unless it was to whip
him mercilessly for the slightest infraction. After the last beating, Nathaniel had realized there was no point in trying to gain
his father's love. There was none to be had. Far easier to fulfill
the duke's predictions of his son's certain fall into depravity
than to strive for approval he could never win.

"Please, darling," his mother pleaded, though Nathaniel
couldn't tell whether the term of endearment was meant for
him or her husband, "can't we have our meal without an argument?" She looked toward her duke, her light brown eyes turning puppy-dog round.

Darling was his father, then—not him.

Just as well. Of the two of them, she was the greater hypocrite. His father never felt a moment's regret for his violent
temper. His mother, on the other hand, apologized profusely
for her husband's behavior but did nothing to prevent it.

As usual, the duke ignored his wife's pleas for clemency. "If
I didn't have the power of the purse over you, I've no doubt
you'd be dead by now. And you're no use to me dead unless
you've managed to produce a legitimate heir first."

Ah, there it was. It all came down to that in the end.
Nathaniel was nothing more to his father than a stud horse, his
sole purpose to extend the family's bloodline and title into the

next generation. Once he bred a son in the bonds of holy matrimony, he might as well be dead as far as his father was concerned.

Yet another reason he had no intention of surrendering himself upon the marital altar. Once there, God would not provide a ram to be sacrificed in his stead. And if Nathaniel had once wished for Isaac's position as the beloved son, he'd since decided Ishmael had likely had the better bargain. A father who banished you was an improvement over one who was heaven-bent on destroying you.

And Nathaniel had no intention of breeding that characteristic into another generation.

"It is a shame, then," he slurred, working to match his speech to his appearance, "that Lady Louisa has better taste than her parents."

Hardwyck's lips curled into a feral smile. "And it is a great boon that Lady Chester has seen fit to invite you to her ball tomorrow night despite your utterly blackened reputation. I am sure there are still a few mamas and papas who can be persuaded to consider your suit."

Nathaniel grimaced into his wineglass. Unfortunately, his father's observation was all too accurate. No matter how many houses of ill repute he frequented, no matter how many prostitutes of either gender he fucked, no matter how much money he wasted at the tables or on drinking himself to a stupor, there would always be parents willing to send their daughters to the very devil in exchange for a title, particularly one accompanied by such deep pockets. The Hardwyck fortune was so expansive, even Nathaniel wouldn't be capable of bankrupting it in his lifetime.

Heaven forbid either his father or the ton's title-mad scavengers ever discovered the truth: that the debauched and damned Nathaniel St. Clair was also Clarence Mathews, scholar and poet. Oh, how the duke would crow to discover his son was something less than a complete scoundrel! And how the vultures would circle the corpse of his disgraceful reputation!

And then the import of his father's pronouncement struck him. Nathaniel narrowed his gaze upon his father, forgetting for the moment to appear inebriated. "Did you say Lady Chester's ball is tomorrow night?"

"Don't try to weasel out by claiming a prior appointment."

Never mind that it was true. A meeting he couldn't postpone without writing a note. A note that would reveal his handwriting . . .

"I swear by all that's holy I'll send you to Cranbourne Hall for the remainder of the Season if you don't make an appearance."

Nathaniel suppressed a shudder. Cranbourne Hall was one of the family's smaller estates, nestled deep in the Yorkshire countryside, miles in any direction from the nearest town on roads nearly always mired in mud brought on by the incessant rain. Unless Nathaniel wanted to add sheep to his list of unconventional sexual partners, Cranbourne was the last place he'd look to spend several months of his existence.

Especially not when his muse was here in London.

Somehow, he'd have to find a way to be two places at once. Or at least seem to be . . .

3

Escape from a crowded ball shouldn't have been this easy, Eleanor reflected as she descended the stairs from the Chesters' expansive townhome to the front drive.

When she'd complained of the stitch in her side, either her mother or Aunt Eppie should have insisted upon staying with her in the retiring room until she felt better. Instead, after seeing her comfortably settled and assuring her they'd return for her after dinner, the two women had put their heads together, giggled over some comment Eleanor had been unable to overhear, and departed without a second glance.

Pleased as she was not to have been forced to use the sleeping draught in her reticule, Eleanor was puzzled—and more than a little ashamed—by their behavior. They *trusted* her, and *this* was how she repaid them?

Slipping from the retiring room had been effortless. With everyone in the household, from guests to servants, occupied by the dinner service, there had been no one to spy her sneaking into the hall and down the long, grand staircase. She'd expected to encounter someone in the entry hall, at least, but that, too, had been deserted, the massive front doors open and unguarded.

Where *was* everyone? Really, the Chesters ought to exercise more caution! Anyone could walk in . . . or out.

As she reached the drive, she noted the coachman had managed to work the Palmers' understated black carriage to the front of the line just as she had requested. He'd been bribed to do so by a ridiculously small sum, a fact that made her feel even worse than before. No one should be so poor that her paltry pin money for a month would entice him to evil, least of all a decent man employed by her parents.

Several small groups of servants stood off to the sides of the drive, but none spared her the slightest notice as she made her way to the carriage. A young lady of quality might be on the verge of disgrace, but that was no concern of theirs, was it?

No, there was no one to protect her from herself.

She opened the carriage door and slid inside, preparing to rap on the roof to awaken the driver, who seemed to have dozed off while she'd been inside.

"I'd all but given up on you."

If she hadn't known instantly to whom that low, sardonic voice belonged, she would have done more than jump in surprise. She would have screamed in terror. Instead, she glared into the darkness at the shadowy figure seated opposite her. Fat lot of good that did when he couldn't see her face any better than she could see his.

"What are you doing here?"

"Waiting for you, of course." The marquess's indolent grin was evident in his tone.

Her eyebrows drew together ferociously. Or the expression felt ferocious, at any rate. "You are supposed to be waiting for me in your study."

"I got bored." Even in the shadows, she could make out his exaggerated shrug. "And I wasn't entirely sure you'd keep our appointment if left to your own devices."

Indignation swelled her throat. "I most certainly would—" She broke off as the full import of his presence at last registered on her befuddled brain. "How did you know I would be here?"

"In your family's coach, you mean? I confess it did not occur to me you might be so bold as to misappropriate another family's carriage for the ride to Hardwyck House." He leaned forward until his warmth radiated through her flimsy silk gown and straight to her skin. "Would you have gone that far to see me tonight, sweet Erato?"

Eleanor pressed back against the well-worn seat in an attempt to mitigate the unsettling effects of his nearness. The rocky, rumbling timbre of his voice stirred the same primitive twinge in the depths of her belly as his kiss had done, a sensation that interfered with both rational thought and justifiable irritation.

Just what did he mean by calling her Erato, muse of lyric and love poetry? How utterly absurd!

And terribly charming . . .

She fought to restore some measure of her former outrage. "Don't be obtuse. I meant: how did you know I would be here— at the Chesters' ball—this evening?"

"Ahhhhh," he breathed, as though he hadn't known what she was asking all along. Which she was quite certain he had. "While I should like to say that some uncanny force of Nature drew me to you, the truth is rather more mundane and a trifle demeaning to my manhood. You see," here he dropped his voice to a stage whisper, "my father insisted I put in an appearance tonight to repair my sullied reputation."

That sounded all too familiar. And yet . . .

"How is it I did not hear you announced or see you, then?"

"I arrived early and spent my evening in the card room." A flash of white hinted at a smile. "It is remarkable how losing large sums of money at whist can improve a man's standing in the eyes of his fellows."

Eleanor tried to scowl, but the corners of her lips turned up in spite of herself. "Then how did you know I was in attendance?"

"Your father enjoys playing whist. Alas, he's not very good at it, so I fear I did not rise much in his estimation."

Drat him, but his self-deprecating banter was disarming. Dangerous. He knew it, too.

She stiffened her spine. "You have not risen in mine, either, my lord. What sort of gentleman lies in wait in a lady's coach, scaring her half to death?"

"Were you frightened?" His voice dropped another octave, if that were possible, and before she knew what was happening, he was seated next to her, his thigh pressed tight against hers in the confined space.

Her breath seemed trapped inside her lungs. "Yes. No. That is, I knew it was you."

"So I do not frighten you, then?"

"No, of course not!" The pulse beating frantically in her throat, in her chest, between her thighs, said otherwise, but she refused to listen. Or look at him. Even in the dark, she knew it would be a mistake.

The devil himself could not be more tempting . . . or more dangerous.

His palm skimmed her jaw before turning her face gently toward his. He pressed his fingers softly to her lips as he bent in closer. He smelled of cigar smoke and, unreasonably, of lemonade.

"I should."

Even as his lips brushed hers, Nathaniel knew he should stop. Knew he shouldn't press her too far, too fast.

He'd deliberately avoided the Chesters' fine whiskeys and finer brandies, settling instead for tepid lemonade, determined to be in full possession of his wits when he met Miss Palmer this evening. He certainly hadn't planned to seduce her—not yet, anyway—but less than five minutes in her company had reduced him to little more than a carnal animal, all rational thought overruled by his hard, aching cock. He shouldn't think of her this way—his muse, his icon—but God help him, he wanted any part of him inside of any part of her like he wanted breath in his lungs. Tongue, fingers, prick. Mouth, cunny, arse. It didn't matter which or where as long as they were joined.

Ah, this was a terrible, unforgivable mistake. Her shoulders and spine stiffened when their lips met, every muscle tensed for flight. In seconds, he would lose her.

He clasped the nape of her neck with one hand, her waist with the other, sliding his tongue across the seam between her lips, desperate to forestall her escape for one more heartbeat. Then another. And another.

Her surrender was so surprising and so complete, he almost didn't recognize it when it came. One moment, she was pulling desperately away, and the next, with a soft, compliant sigh, the resistance drained from her limbs, and her mouth opened beneath his. His tongue swept aggressively inside, eager to take advantage before the opportunity was lost, before his brain caught up and realized she wasn't just letting him kiss her, but was kissing him back. With enthusiasm.

Lust sizzled behind his eyes: bright, blinding, and beautiful.

Freed of the obligation to prevent her from fleeing, he allowed his palm to skim upward from her waist to cup her gently rounded breast. Rather than shrinking away, as he'd half-expected, she gasped and pressed into his hand so that he could feel her nipple tighten and harden through several layers of fabric.

He lifted his head. "Eleanor, sweeting," he rasped, "I want to lick you here." He rubbed his thumb across the raspberry-sized nubbin of flesh to illustrate his meaning. "Will you let me?"

Her answer, in the form of a low moan and a nod, sent a fiery burst of jubilation through his veins. He made short work of the buttons at the back of her gown until the bodice gaped away, leaving her bare but for her chemise and stays. These he pushed aside until he could make out the soft swell of pale, nude flesh in the darkness.

Such tiny, perfect tits, just as he'd imagined, made for a man to lave and suckle. He dropped his head to do so, circling her nipple with his tongue before pulling it into his mouth.

Her breath quickened, coming in sharp, uneven pants. "Oh, my lord, please."

"Nathaniel," he commanded.

"Nathaniel," she murmured back. She threw her head back against the squab, arching into his mouth. "I feel so—"

"Good?" He rubbed his thumb across the other exposed nipple.

A sharp intake of breath.

"Yes."

A slow, shuddery exhale.

"No."

A groan.

"I don't know."

He lifted his head, knowing she felt the same, frantic craving for release he did. He couldn't have his tonight. However low and degenerate he might be, he wasn't a brute. She was a virgin, an innocent. And while virtue might be overrated, comfort was not, and there was precious little to be had in the Palmers' under-sized, underpadded coach.

But he could give her the pleasure he could not have himself.

He pressed the heel of his palm to the juncture of her thighs. "Do you feel aching and empty here, my Erato?"

"Yes," she whispered, her shame and uncertainty manifest in her tone.

Nathaniel grimaced. The only shame was upon Society for

instilling young ladies with the notion that a healthy response to a man's touch was a sign of moral turpitude.

He feathered his lips across her cheek and mouth. "Then I am truly blessed. And I would ease you, if you will permit me."

"I don't know," she repeated. "My mother told me what happens between a man and a woman, and I can't let you—" The words came out on an embarrassed rush of air.

He pressed a finger to her lips. "I don't intend to do that."

Though God knew he wanted to. To bury himself in her tight, wet pussy. His cock, already fully engorged, burgeoned more at the image of himself kneeling on the carriage floor, her thighs spread wide as he impaled her.

He cleared his throat. "Not here. Not now. I mean only to give you pleasure. May I?"

He saw his answer before he heard it. She bit her lip and nodded. "Yes."

Eleanor couldn't quite believe she'd just agreed to . . . well, to whatever it was she'd agreed to. She only knew that fire would consume her if he didn't extinguish it. Refusal was even more unthinkable, more impossible, than assent.

Who would have thought that the devil would tempt his victims with the very flames they had been taught to fear?

"Thank you," he murmured, brushing his mouth over hers in a kiss that felt almost reverent. He tugged her chemise and bodice back into place, the silk scraping tantalizingly across her sensitized nipples. "I wouldn't want you to take a chill."

How he could imagine she was in danger of that when every inch of her skin burned was a mystery. Or was, until he dropped from his place alongside her and kneeled in the narrow aisle between the seats. The sudden loss of his warmth brought a rush of cold air that made her shiver despite—or perhaps on account of—the heat pulsing in her veins.

And then she shivered for an entirely different reason as his hands closed around her ankles, sparking another burst of fiery anticipation. He coaxed her legs apart, his palms coasting upward with the rustling fabric of her skirts until he reached the inside of her knees.

"Lift your bottom," he rasped.

She ought to refuse. She ought to be mortified at even the thought of permitting a man who was not her husband—who would never *be* her husband—to touch her ankles, her calves, her knees, to say nothing of the places beyond. She ought to insist he unhand her immediately.

If she asked him to stop, he would comply. She was sure of it. But she didn't want him to stop. She couldn't bear to carry this heaviness between her thighs, a peculiar weight that made her feel full, yet empty, aching for something that lay just out of reach.

She raised herself off the seat, and he bunched her skirts up around her hips, exposing the gartered tops of her stockings and the loose cotton of her drawers. Shame, rather than longing, might have heated her cheeks if she'd cared about propriety.

He pushed her thighs wider, settling between them with a sigh that could only be one of satisfaction at having gained his objective. A shudder—half fear, half anticipation—ran down her spine, and her heart thudded wildly against her ribs like a prisoner desperate for escape. Except that she was running toward the force that captivated her, not away from it.

He parted the slit in her drawers, his fingers brushing across the damp, musk-scented flesh. She gasped and arched toward his hand, instinctively seeking greater contact, but he didn't comply. Instead, he bent his head closer and . . .

"You can't mean to . . ." she protested.

He chuckled, his breath warm and moist against her bared folds. "I most certainly can. I mean to lick and suck your pussy the same way I licked and sucked your tits. And you're going to like it even more."

Though unfamiliar with the words, she knew what they meant. Coarse, dirty words. Words men used with mistresses and courtesans. Wicked to say and wicked to do, and all the more thrilling for it.

A fresh, warm rush of moisture greeted the realization that she was going to permit him to do such an intimate, immoral thing. God, she would not only permit it, she would beg him if he did not.

He lowered his head and pressed his mouth to the curls, just above the spot where the throbbing ache was most concentrated. His tongue traced the outer folds of flesh, coming ever closer to, yet never quite touching, the spot where the rising tension told her she wanted—no, needed—his touch.

She squirmed beneath him, her fingernails digging into the leather upholstery so ferociously she feared she might leave visible marks. Her breath came in ever more jagged, uneven bursts until at last he gave her what she craved, dipping his tongue into the valley and stroking across the tiny, throbbing mound that marked the center of her existence. She heard someone whimper and knew distantly that the sound issued from her own lips, but the pleasure-pain built and built, a tower always on the verge of toppling, yet somehow managing to climb still higher.

Please, let it end. Please, let it never end.

As if he read her thoughts, he raised his head. "Stop fighting, Erato. The best is yet to come." He chuckled softly, as though he'd made a joke, before diving back into her pussy again and tonguing her with renewed vigor.

And then, it happened. So startling and beautiful that she cried out as the first, shattering waves of rapture burst over her, in her, through her. Nathaniel's hand came up to cover her mouth, muffling the sounds of joy she couldn't suppress as the fierce spasms peaked, crested, and then dwindled away to a luxurious, tingling ease that felt remarkably like peace.

Eleanor closed her eyes and leaned back against the squab, dazed and utterly puzzled.

The devil had just taken her to Heaven.

* * *

Damn!

He hadn't figured her for a screamer.

Nathaniel drew his hand across his mouth, and then pulled his handkerchief from his pocket. He dabbed the cloth gently against her pussy. They likely didn't have much time before someone came to investigate, and he couldn't leave her dripping wet.

He wasn't sorry, of course. It was difficult for a man to be anything but flattered when his lady cried out with pleasure. Particularly when he knew for certain her response was anything but feigned. But he would have been a damned sight more careful to dampen the noise had he imagined that a woman of such careful reserve and decorum in public could be capable of such unrestrained passion in private.

It was a marvel to behold, like watching an angel tumble from the remote reaches of heaven. And even more magnificent to be the man responsible for the fall.

His cock, still thick and unfulfilled, bulged against the fall of his pantaloons, insisting that now was the time to bury itself in her wet, warm cunny. Now, when she was slick and satisfied and the way would be smooth and easy for both of them.

Nathaniel steadied himself. *Easy, old chap. Not tonight.*

She remained motionless and silent as he finished the task of drying her and set the handkerchief aside. Though his eyes had adjusted to the lack of light some time ago, it was too dark for him to make out more than the outline of her features. He couldn't tell what she was thinking or feeling, and the realization left him curiously ill at ease.

It wasn't that he'd never wanted to bring a woman pleasure before. It was that he'd never before had cause to wonder how she would react after he did.

A rap on the carriage door interrupted any opportunity he might have had to find out. Eleanor gasped at the sharp sound and pulled at the bulge of skirts to push them back down to her ankles. Nathaniel did his best to assist her, though their hands bumped awkwardly in the darkness.

"I say, Miz Palmer, are ye all right in there?" The voice must belong to the Palmers' coachman, who'd been dozing in the driver's seat, no doubt lulled to sleep by his long, dull wait for Miss Palmer's arrival, when Nathaniel had slipped undetected into the carriage a half hour before.

"Yes, Mr. Fletcher, I'm quite all right." Despite her hasty efforts to set herself to rights, her voice was cool and steady. One would never guess she had just come in her lover's mouth, calling out with pleasure.

"Are ye sure?" The coachman's tone was diffident, and Nathaniel sensed he had one hand on the door handle, prepared to leap inside at the first sign that his mistress was in actual danger. "Ye startled me when ye screamed."

Nathaniel smiled. Mr. Fletcher had most likely been dozing all the time they'd been inside the carriage, then.

"I'm sorry. I'm afraid I felt something crawling on my leg and it gave me a fright."

An excellent explanation. Nathaniel found himself admiring the swiftness of her mind nearly as much as he admired the delicate curves of her body. Perhaps more.

A brief silence ensued as Mr. Fletcher seemed to consider this information. "Do ye still wish me to take you to Hardwyck House, then?"

"No, that won't be necessary. I've . . ."—here, her voice hitched slightly—"changed my mind."

"Oh." The coachman sounded a bit deflated. After a brief pause, he added, "I suppose ye'll be wanting yer two guineas back, then."

"No, Mr. Fletcher. Keep it as my thanks for your willingness to assist me."

"Why, thank ye, Miz Palmer, that's most gen'rous. And if ye be needin' anythin' else, just holler." This pronouncement was followed by the sound of gravel crunching as the coachman walked away.

Nathaniel levered himself from his position on the floorboard to the seat behind him, resisting the urge to rub his sore knees, though he'd scarcely noticed his discomfort before now. Eleanor didn't look at him, but smoothed her skirts with restless hands. He fancied her fingers might be trembling ever so slightly. He hoped. And waited.

"I can't imagine what came over me," she said after the silence had stretched long and palpable between them. She sounded as if she were apologizing, though whether to him or herself, he couldn't say. "You caught me by surprise."

Nathaniel chose to say nothing in response to this reproach. He could hardly deny his crime.

"I can assure you," she continued when he did not answer, "that it won't happen again." She leaned across the seat and retrieved something from between the edge of the upholstered cushion and the outer wall of the coach. She straightened and shoved it at him.

The Metamorphoses. He'd completely forgotten the purported reason for their assignation this evening.

She, apparently, had not.

He took the thin leather volume from her hand, allowing his fingers to caress the tops of her gloved hands. She snatched them away, but not before he felt her shiver in response.

She might be angry, but she was not immune. Achieving the ultimate pleasure had not cured her of her attraction to him.

"If Mr. Mathews wishes me to proofread his manuscript for him, then he may send it to me by courier or, if he prefers, deliver it himself. Do I make myself clear?"

Nathaniel half-grimaced, half-grinned. If she desired him half as much as she despised him, he could still win the game. "Quite clear. But before you go . . ." He reached inside his coat and pulled out a thick, tightly folded wad of manuscript pages, placing it on the seat beside her. "Here are the first fifty pages. I should warn you that Mathews's penmanship is virtually illegible, but I shall be happy to assist you in deciphering any problematic passages."

She huffed a deep breath, in and out. "Didn't you hear what I just said? I shan't be seeing you again. I am not some . . . some harlot to be used at your whim."

He raised an eyebrow, though in the darkness he knew she could not see it. "And of all men, I am the best placed to know it, am I not?"

She sputtered. "You took advantage of me. I wasn't expecting . . ."

"I know. I apologize."

That took her aback. "Really?"

He nodded. "I'm afraid I have no scruples whatsoever when it comes to taking advantage of devastatingly beautiful young ladies who happen to get into carriages alone with me."

"You were waiting for me!"

He shrugged. "It is all the same in the end, is it not?"

"No, it is not!" She rose from her seat. "I hope I never see you again!"

He grabbed her hand before she could break for the door and pulled her into his lap. She gasped and struggled, but went slack against him when he brushed his lips against the nape of her neck. He could almost feel the gooseflesh travel down her arm. His cock, hard and heavy with need, settled into the valley between her buttocks.

"You want me, Eleanor, and I want you. There is no power in Heaven or on Earth more powerful than desire. In the end, I will have you. As you will have me. You know as well as I that Eros cannot be denied."

She wrenched away from his grasp. "I know no such thing!"

A second later, the carriage door banged shut behind her.

Nathaniel sat in silence for some time after she left, waiting for the throbbing ache of arousal to subside.

She was right. She was not a harlot. And he could not bring himself to treat her as one. Not when everything about her stirred him, body and soul. With a sinking sense of impending doom, he knew what he must do.

He must marry Miss Eleanor Palmer.

Surprisingly, he could not bring himself to be sorry about the idea of marrying her. Spending the rest of his life in Eleanor's arms—and in *her*—sounded remarkably like Heaven. A place he'd never before dreamed of occupying.

But he was also going to make his father a happy man, and the knowledge twisted in his gut like the sharp, steely edge of a Frenchman's bayonet. He would never be good enough to suit his father. But he couldn't go on being bad enough to suit his own sense of justice.

Despite his worst intentions, there would be another generation of Hardwycks.

Damn!

4

Really, the fairy godmother had been wasted on Cinderella. Leaving the ball was the easy part. It was getting back in afterward that was the problem.

Eleanor crouched behind a large, stone vase at the bottom of the staircase leading back into the Chesters' town house. Two footmen in crisp red and blue livery, footmen who'd been nowhere in evidence when she'd left, flanked the open doorway. If she approached them now, they'd want to see her invitation, which she didn't have, and announce her arrival, which wasn't an arrival at all.

She should have foreseen this predicament. Her stomach pinched with a healthy dose of self-loathing. Had she really been so eager to read Clarence Mathews's work that she'd overlooked this simple practicality?

Or had she really been eager for something else entirely?

She shook her head to ward off the question. Preposterous! How could she have been eager to experience that? To allow a man to put his head between her legs and lick and lick until . . .

She shuddered involuntarily as heat curled anew where he'd touched her with his tongue.

Disgusting, she assured herself. *Horrifying. Mortifying. More.*

Ah, this was exactly why she must avoid Nathaniel—the marquess, she corrected, determined not to be trapped into thinking of him on such intimate terms—at all costs. He made her a base, immoral creature who cared only for vulgar, physical pleasure. A creature she hardly recognized as herself.

"In a bit of pickle, I see."

Eleanor jumped at Nathaniel's words, whispered so close to her ear that his breath wafted, soft and sultry, across her cheek and neck. She pressed a hand over her racing heart, but didn't turn to face him. "You shouldn't sneak up on a person like that."

"I didn't sneak." His tone was wounded. "You weren't paying attention."

That was true, but it didn't make her feel any better. "I told you I never wanted to see you again."

"True, but then, you can't see me as long as you keep staring at that vase, now can you?"

She wanted to stomp her foot in fury. Preferably on top of his. "Go away."

"And leave you alone out here the rest of the night? I think not." He moved alongside her and slipped his arm through hers. "Let's go inside, shall we?"

Eleanor couldn't stop herself. She whipped her head to look at him, aghast. "We can't go in together," she protested.

A slow smile spread across Nathaniel's features. "You're quite right. *We* cannot go in together." He jerked his head in the direction of the door and the footmen who guarded it. "But they don't know who *we* are, do they?"

"What? I—" But he was already propelling her along, and she couldn't find the will to resist.

When they reached the top of the stairs, the footman on the left stepped forward to greet them. "Good evening, sir, madam." He stretched out his hand. "Your invitation, please?"

Nathaniel extracted his arm from the crook of her elbow and patted the front of his dark blue coat as though he were looking for something. "I . . . um . . . ah . . . I'm sorry." He raised his palms and shoulders in apology. "My wife—"

His *wife?* Her heart pinched in an oddly pleasurable way. The word sounded so natural coming from his lips, she nearly believed it herself.

"—and I went out for a breath of fresh air. I'm afraid I must have left our invitation behind. If you'll call the earl, I'm sure—"

Call the earl? Was he mad?

"That won't be necessary, sir." The footman moved aside and gestured with one arm to indicate they should enter. "I believe you."

Nathaniel winked at her in triumph as they proceeded into the spacious—and deserted—entry hall.

"Now what?" she whispered, her gaze darting toward the open doors that led to the ballroom and dining hall. What if they were seen together?

"We go our separate ways. Unless . . ." He circled her wrist with one palm, the pressure gentle but insistent. His expression sobered.

Her heart hitched, as if it had accidentally become trapped between her ribs. "Unless?"

His cornflower-blue eyes, hopeful and a little uncertain, searched hers. "Unless you would consider making my little pretense a reality."

Eleanor breathed in sharply to quell the rising panic—or was it joy?—in her chest. "Are you asking me to marry you?"

He shrugged and gave her a disarming, lopsided smile. "Yes, I believe I am."

Pulse and respiration and even time halted. A sliver of a moment in which she almost said yes. Almost allowed her primal need to experience again what he'd done to her in the coach—and more—to overcome reason.

If she said yes, she could have pleasure. No, she could have ecstasy. But at what price? Every moment she spent in his presence, she lost a little more of herself—a little more of her reserve, her intellect, her single-mindedness. If she married him, she would vanish altogether, consumed by the same passions that drove him.

She stiffened her spine along with her resolve. "I told you yesterday I could never look favorably upon your suit." She tried to extract her wrist from his grasp.

He grinned, but there was no amusement in his expression. His grip on her wrist tightened almost imperceptibly. "That was before you came, screaming, in my mouth."

Heat suffused her cheeks. And her belly, damn him. "I told you that would never happen again."

"I know. But that would be a waste of a particularly delectable pussy."

She gasped, shocked and unbearably aroused by his words. "You can't say such things. Not here. Not now. Someone could discover us at any moment."

He looked around the empty hall in mock horror, as if taken aback by his surroundings. "You're quite right." He nodded toward the staircase and wiggled his eyebrows suggestively. "Perhaps we should repair to an upstairs room."

Desire unfurled inside her, as insidious and seductive as the serpent in the Garden of Eden. She worked to free her wrist in earnest. "You are mad, my lord."

He continued to hold her firmly, though he did not hurt her. "I am mad with desire for you, Miss Eleanor Palmer." He pulled her to his chest and dropped his head near the nape of her neck. "Marry me." His voice, deep and silken and virtually inaudible, caressed her skin like a slow, sensuous kiss, weakening her knees and her will at the same time.

"I can't," she whispered. "My father would never approve."

He shrugged. "We could elope to Gretna Green. It's all the rage these days, you know."

It was the wrong jest to make, for it reminded her not only of Holyfield and all the reasons he would have made the poorest of husbands, but of precisely what—of whom—she truly wanted in a mate.

"I could never marry you. We have nothing in common."

"Nonsense." He tugged her wrist downward and pressed her palm against the thick ridge at the front of his pantaloons. "We have this."

Involuntarily, her hand closed over that fascinating length of flesh, her fingers eager to explore what her mind refused to consider. When her mother had imparted the basic function and characteristics of this particular portion of the male anatomy, Eleanor hadn't quite believed her. But now, as the bulge stiffened and grew beneath her touch, she was forced to admit her mother had not misled her.

He groaned and ground his hips forward. She snatched her hand away, appalled by how easily he overcame her resistance.

"You've had this in common with scores of women—"

"More like hundreds," he interjected, his lips twitching, "but I won't quibble over numbers."

"Exactly! You never married any of them."

"None of them were you."

The bottom seemed to fall out of her stomach at the matter-of-fact sincerity of his tone. It would be so easy, so liberating, to yield to the passion and the pleasure he'd shown her. To give herself over to the wild, carnal nature she'd never known she possessed.

If only he weren't Nathaniel St. Clair, Marquess of Grenville, unrepentant seeker of every manner of vice, a man utterly without shame and equally without virtue. If only he were like Clarence Mathews: scholarly, poetic, sensitive, noble.

But two such disparate personalities could not be housed within the same person. The battle that raged within her every time she was in Nathaniel's presence was all the proof she required. The needs of the body or the needs of the soul: one must inevitably conquer the other. It was up to her to choose the victor.

Winning had never tasted so bitter.

Nathaniel needed a stiff drink and a soft whore. The trouble was, he wanted neither.

He wanted only the woman who'd just informed him, in no uncertain terms, that she would never marry such a foul and vulgar specimen of manhood as himself. Not when scholarly, high-minded fellows like Clarence Mathews were yet to be found in the world.

As he watched her flee up the stairs in a swirl of frothy white skirts, the temptation to shout out the truth almost overcame him, but he managed to hold his tongue. Not because he didn't want her to know who he was, but because she *did* know who he was, and the fact that he was also Clarence Mathews didn't change anything.

True, he was sometimes a scholar and a poet. Sometimes, he was the sort of man she admired. And on occasion, he was even the sort of man she would marry.

But he was *also* every bit as foul and vulgar as she believed. As his father believed. He enjoyed drinking and carousing and gambling and fucking.

Especially fucking.

He wouldn't apologize for it. And he wouldn't change. Not even for her.

She had to want *both* men.

He must play Orpheus to her Euridice. Except he would lead her into the underworld, not away from it.

5

Oh lucky ring, to touch my lady's hand:
Now envy for my gift hath me unmanned.
But if by Proteus's or Circe's witchy bent
I could transform into my present,
Then, whene'er her breasts I long to caress
by slipping my left hand inside of her dress,
I'll glide from her finger, though there I'd cling tightly,
and artfully fall into folds wrapped lightly.
Again, when I seal that secret note of hers,
lest sticky wax to dry gem adheres,
my lovely girl shall touch me to her moistened lips
and with her kiss the pain eclipse.
Plunge me in your purse, and yet I'll linger,
a clinging, shrinking ring upon your finger.
Wear me, drench your body in hot, showering pools
and let the falling water run beneath my jewels—
though, I think, your naked limbs would rouse my passion,
and, as that ring, I'd do my part in manly fashion.
         —Clarence Mathews's translation of Ovid's *Amores*

Eleanor's fingers trembled as she set the page facedown on her escritoire. No wonder the Emperor Augustus had taken exception to Ovid's writings and banished him to Tomis! And no wonder her brother's tutor, who'd agreed to teach her to read Latin and Greek only after she'd subjected him to months of relentless cajoling, had strictly forbidden her from reading any of Ovid's works other than the *Metamorphoses*.

Whene'er her breasts I longed to caress.

Eleanor's nipples tightened and puckered beneath the gauzy cotton of her night rail, just as they had done when Nathaniel had caressed them—and more—last night. Before she quite knew what she meant to do, she had cupped her breasts in her hands and was rubbing her thumbs across the peaks.

She gasped as desire stabbed down through her belly, directly to her pussy, surprised to discover that her own touch could affect her in such a way. She stroked her breasts—poor, insignificant little lumps of flesh she'd previously considered useless—and the ache between her thighs grew fiercer, hungrier.

Shocking. And shockingly good.

Plunge me in your purse . . .

She needed no explanation of that metaphor. Not when a musky perfume rose to her nostrils, reminding her of the place where Mama had told her she must permit her husband to put his male appendage. At the time, the idea had seemed foreign and unbelievable, but now, she craved to have the moist, slick cavity stretched, filled, completed.

Again, her hands traveled with a will of their own. From her breasts to her abdomen and then lower still, sliding beneath the knee-length hem and up again until her fingers found the naked folds of her womanhood, damp and hot and throbbing with arousal. She leaned back in the hard, wooden chair, spreading her legs a little wider to give herself greater access to this unexplored territory.

Delving between the creases, she slid her fingers farther and farther along the slit until she found the opening and slipped inside. First a single digit in experimental exploration and then a second, pushed in to the first knuckle and then all the way to the base.

A sigh of contentment escaped her lips, but soon the sensation wasn't enough. There had to be something more. Something like what she'd felt with Nathaniel.

He hadn't been inside her at all, instead concentrating his attentions on one small spot to bring her release, but her fingers pressed inside prevented her from accessing it. She began to withdraw, stopping on an indrawn breath when the palm of her hand rubbed across the very place that was desperate for contact. Her pleasure thickened and concentrated with the motion and, suddenly, she knew how to fulfill both needs at once. She drove her fingers back in, then pulled out again, pressing and rotating the heel of her hand against that most sensitive place.

Yes, that was it.

Closing her eyes, she repeated the action. In, out. In, out. Faster. Deeper. Her thighs grew taut; her heart pounded; her breath came in short, sharp pants. A wet, slapping sound accompanied each successive invasion, an erotic music that heightened her arousal and fueled her thrusts. She moaned softly as she felt the crest approaching, then clapped her free hand over her mouth to muffle her cry when the first, bright waves of release broke like the sun bursting from behind the clouds after a storm.

Beautiful.

Spent, she stared at the stack of as-yet-unread pages on her desk. She shouldn't read any more. Her cheeks flamed and her chest burned. Who—or what—was she becoming? She *must* stop now if she was to save herself.

But the pull of the poetry was too strong to resist. She picked up the next sheet and began to read.

* * *

"Maybe if I suck you a bit more, you'll be able—" The courtesan broke off at Nathaniel's warning glower.

He sat on the edge of the velvet-upholstered armchair next to the bed and pulled on his breeches. For the first time in his life, his cock had failed him. Never before, even at his most inebriated, had he failed to make wood at the appropriate time.

But tonight, despite being ridden hard by nearly a week of unrequited lust, his prick had simply lain there, limp and unresponsive. Even when he'd closed his eyes and tried to imagine it was Eleanor fondling his balls, Eleanor taking his cock into her mouth, he hadn't been able to rise to the occasion.

Because his senses knew she wasn't Eleanor. She didn't smell right, didn't taste right, didn't *feel* right.

Calliope sighed and stretched to a sit. "I suppose this means you won't be coming back," she said, reaching for the silk robe draped around the bedpost.

Nathaniel stopped in the midst of pulling on the first of his Hessians. Though her expression remained carefully neutral, there was no mistaking the disappointment in her tone.

"Probably not," he admitted.

"A pity." She slipped her arms into the garment, then ran the backs of her hands under her hair to free the blond tresses. "You're my best customer, you know."

"I know. I'm very reliable."

Whenever he came to the Red Door, he always asked first for Calliope. Of all the girls who worked for Madame Upshaw, Calliope best suited his taste in women. Tall and pale-skinned with small breasts, narrow hips, and long, slender legs, she was his idea of the perfect fuck. Or had been until Eleanor had burst into his study and into his heart.

Heart? That was getting a bit sentimental, wasn't it?

Maybe too much self-abuse made one soft in the head. He resisted the urge to look at his palms to make certain they hadn't sprouted hair. At least he was certain he hadn't gone blind.

Calliope smiled and shook her head as she tied the sash around her waist. "I don't mean it that way. You're not the only gentleman who prefers blond and bony—"

"You are *not* bony," he interjected.

She chuckled, but held up her hand to forestall further protestations on his part. "You are my best customer because you always give as much pleasure as you take. And therefore, I shall miss you."

Nathaniel's throat thickened, and so he merely nodded before returning his attention to donning his boots. Sentimentality apparently *was* caused by excessive wanking.

"You must love her a great deal."

He jerked his head up to stare at the pretty Cyprian, realizing that while he'd known her repeatedly in the Biblical sense, he didn't know her at all.

"No, I don't." The denial sprang reflexively to his lips. Love was for the lovable. Not for him.

Calliope raised her eyebrows.

For some inexplicable reason, he felt obligated to explain himself. "She's a lady. Unmarried. An Eligible. I have to marry her to fuck her, that's all."

The courtesan's lips formed a skeptical grin. "Perhaps. But that's not why you couldn't fuck me tonight."

Nathaniel shoved his foot hard into his boot. *Damn her, was she right?*

What he felt for Eleanor was more than simple lust, true. If it hadn't been more before he'd given her Mathews's pages the night of the ball, it was now. For when the pages had come back, they'd been notated with a combination of delightful praise and brilliant suggestions for improving the meter and sense of passages he'd struggled with. Ideas he'd immediately incorporated and expanded upon, so that now the work was many times better than he could have made it on his own.

Unable to countenance the thought of proceeding further

without her input, he'd sent her the next batch of pages by courier. They had returned, as superbly edited as the first.

Eleanor's body aroused him, but her mind completed him.

But that didn't mean he loved her. Just that he needed her. Which wasn't the same thing at all.

He stood and shoved his shirttail into his breeches, then donned his waistcoat and coat. His cravat he stuffed in his pocket. He had too much planning yet to do this evening to concern himself with tying it.

Eleanor had seen enough of Clarence Mathews. It was time for her to see *all* of Nathaniel St. Clair.

6

Eleanor looked up from her teacup to find the Marquess of Grenville lounging, arms akimbo, in the doorway to his sister's small sitting room. Clad in a dark green coat and buff breeches, he watched her with an expression that seemed at once satisfied and hungry, resembling nothing so much as a forest creature on the hunt.

And she was his prey.

Tension, thick and heavy, blossomed in her chest and belly. She ought to be looking for a likely escape route. Instead, she reached for the delicate china teacup on the table in front of her and lifted it to her lips.

As if she hadn't a care in the world.

She sipped the hot liquid, barely tasting the mellow flavor as it burned across her tongue and down her throat. "Someone will return any moment, you know," she said.

He smiled and shook his head. "I don't think so." His voice was as deep and rich as the sensation blooming at the juncture of her thighs. Straightening from his languid position against the doorframe, he uncrossed his arms. "My mother is much enjoying your aunt's unexpected company, and Jane is busy investigating the mysterious disappearance of the cucumbers that were meant for the sandwiches."

Eleanor's fingers trembled as she replaced the cup in its saucer. "You planned this," she accused, her voice calm despite her inner turmoil.

His smile grew a bit wider, a bit more predatory. "I take advantage of whatever opportunities life throws my way. As you well know."

She rose from the straight-backed Queen Anne chair, hoping she appeared regal and unaffected. Her stomach fluttered like a small bird trapped in the maw of a large cat, except that the feeling was pleasant rather than terrifying. "I thought I made myself quite clear the last time we spoke. I am not interested in anything you have to offer."

She marched purposefully toward him, prepared to push past him if he didn't step aside.

"Really?" He arched an eyebrow. "What if I offered you Clarence Mathews?"

She skidded to a halt, her slippers nearly sliding out from beneath her. "What?"

"I'm offering to take you to meet the great poet himself. If you're interested, of course."

If she was interested? Her heart thudded, its rhythm erratic. How could she be otherwise when her every thought, her every fantasy—both waking and sleeping—for the past week had been filled with Clarence Mathews?

A Clarence Mathews who looked alarmingly like the man standing in front of her.

If only she could banish Nathaniel St. Clair's image from her brain by replacing it with one of the real Clarence Mathews—a short, unimposing fellow with a balding pate and spectacles, perhaps—she might also put to rest the sleeping demon of desire the two men had awakened within her, one with his words, the other with his touch.

When she didn't answer immediately, Nathaniel shrugged and turned to leave. She grabbed for his upper arm to forestall him.

"Yes, I'm interested."

He smiled and nodded. "Very well. Come with me. You'll need to change your clothes."

Eleanor looked down at herself. Her light blue muslin gown with its dark blue printed flowers and puffed sleeves, while hardly formal, could scarcely be considered objectionable attire for making a social call. "Change my clothes? Whatever for?"

His eyebrows arched over clear, glittering blue eyes, and his lips tilted up into a devilishly handsome grin. "You can't visit a brothel dressed like a proper lady."

No proper lady would consider visiting a brothel at all, however she might be dressed. And yet, a mere two hours after this unthinkable idea had been proposed, Eleanor was poised to do just that.

Nathaniel made it all sound so easy. So harmless.

Clarence Mathews visited the Red Door, an exclusive and— Nathaniel assured her—tasteful brothel in Pall Mall, twice a month. Even a recluse required occasional female companionship, after all, although given the sensual nature of the text Mathews had been translating, Eleanor imagined he might be in need of such company rather more often than that. Moreover, Mathews never took callers at his home, so catching him in the brothel's drawing room this evening would be her one opportunity to meet him face-to-face.

If Mathews was there, Eleanor could introduce herself as his new proofreader, and perhaps persuade him to work more closely with her in the future. And if he was not, Nathaniel would bring her back to Hardwyck House straightaway. Either way, she would be none the worse for wear, and no one else the wiser as to her whereabouts.

And how, she had wanted to know, was the latter possible? She could hardly go missing at dinner hour without her absence being remarked.

Ah, but that part was the most elementary of all, Nathaniel had informed her with a chuckle. Then he had proceeded with arrangements so ingenious and yet so simple, Eleanor had been forced to admit—to herself, at any rate—that he had more intellect than she had previously been willing to credit.

Eleanor, it seemed, had been struck by a sudden stomach complaint. Although she was presently resting comfortably in one of the guest chambers, she was quite unable to travel home by coach and would therefore remain at Hardwyck House until the morrow. Aunt Eppie, after a brief visit to verify that the patient—who was, if the truth were told, a rather poor actress—was not in imminent peril, had been dispatched back to the Palmers' residence without a whisper of concern for her charge's safety or virtue.

Eleanor rubbed her spine against the seatback behind her as the coach jostled through London's cobbled streets. Though she wore her own soft muslin underthings beneath the rough, woolen dress Nathaniel had appropriated from the downstairs maid who now occupied the guest bed in Eleanor's stead, the fabric itched fiercely. How did servants abide such discomfort on a daily basis? Certainly, she intended to ensure her household staff—when she had them—were clothed in a finer class of material than the Hardwycks'.

Or, likely, the Palmers'.

The carriage lurched to a halt. Eleanor had studiously avoided looking at her traveling companion throughout their trip by staring out the window into the lamp-lit darkness of the city, though their knees had bumped together numerous times in the cramped space of the cabin. Now, she couldn't prevent herself from stealing a glance at him.

He was watching her. Studying her. Devouring her.

Lightning spiked between her legs as she remembered the last time she'd occupied a carriage with the Marquess of Grenville.

She snatched her gaze away, her cheeks hot with embarrassment . . . and something much worse.

However reckless and outrageous this business of visiting a brothel might be, it was absolutely essential that she meet Mr. Mathews tonight. Before she did something she would truly regret and wound up tied for life to entirely the wrong man.

Though she could hear the driver clambering down from his seat, Eleanor dared not wait a moment longer. She reached over and turned the handle to open the door. In her haste to escape the heat, she pushed with more force than she intended, and the door flew outward.

"Oy, 'ave a care for a man's nose," a gravelly voice intoned. The driver, no doubt. He must have caught the wildly swinging door, for it held steady on its hinges.

Under normal conditions, a lady would have allowed the driver to help her down, or for the gentleman accompanying her to exit and assist her to the street. But these were hardly normal conditions and, in her gray uniform and white mobcap, Eleanor hardly resembled a lady.

Maids got themselves down from coaches, when they rode in them at all. And so would she.

Pedestrians in all manner of attire—from the finely dressed ladies and gentlemen in silk and superfine to workmen in worn tweed and women wearing uniforms much like her own—crowded the well-lit street, each individual or pair or group intent on their own destination.

Eleanor felt, rather than heard, Nathaniel descend to the

sidewalk behind her. She surveyed the elegant beige facades that lined the street, each with multiple stairways and doors.

"Which one?" She asked the question without looking at him.

"The red one, of course," he answered, his arm snaking round her to point to a door just to her right.

It was, indeed, red. But for that distinction, however, it looked like any other door on any other street and certainly bore no outward sign to suggest what sort of establishment occupied the space behind it. For some reason, she had expected something more dramatic. Perhaps a large red arrow pointing down from the window above, with the words "Den of Iniquity" writ upon it in large, bold letters. Instead, the entry appeared completely innocuous. It might have been the door to a milliner's shop or a private residence or even to the National Gallery just up the street.

"You must come here often," she observed.

He emitted a sound that hovered between a chuckle and snort. "Not as often as I used to." His tone crackled like dry autumn leaves.

She spun to look at him, her eyebrows raised. "Why not?"

He shrugged. "I don't fancy the place as much as I once did."

"Really?" How many houses of ill repute *were* there in London? And how did gentlemen discover them when they were so well-concealed that the unsuspecting and untutored would never dream of their existence?

"Indeed. I fear I've found a more engaging, more challenging pursuit." He placed one hand on her lower back and pushed her gently toward the staircase.

As she obeyed the implicit directive, his palm traveled further down her backside, lingering just above the curve, the touch not intended to arouse desire, but to communicate possession. Hot awareness rushed down her spine to meet his palm. There was no doubt at all what—or who—was his new pursuit.

She ought to get back into the coach and insist upon returning to Hardwyck House. Immediately.

But her legs seemed to possess a will of their own, and already she was mounting the stairs to the landing in front of the innocuous red door.

And then she was following Nathaniel inside.

Eleanor could not have articulated how she fancied the drawing room of a brothel would appear, but the sight that met her eyes certainly did not meet her expectations.

A soft *oh* of delight slipped from her parted lips, for stepping into the large, lamp-lit room was like stepping back in time. A Corinthian colonnade lined all four sides of the rectangular space, creating a deep porch while leaving the center of the room free for a fountain, garden, and several bronze statues. Everywhere Eleanor looked, splashes of color caught her eyes. Rich reds, deep greens, and bright yellows frescoed on the walls. Shiny black, white, and blue tiles made up the mosaic floors.

The room was a near-perfect replica of the inner peristyle of a wealthy Roman's villa. Save for the fact that it was indoors rather than out, the place might easily have belonged to Ovid himself.

No wonder a man like Clarence Mathews came here. It must feel like coming home.

Beautiful women clad in lovely Grecian gowns, ranging in hue from white to gold to green to red, lounged on plush velvet divans between the pillars. Each wore her hair in classic fashion, laced through with pearls or gilt ribbon or flowers and vines. Eleanor touched the white mobcap concealing her own elaborate coiffure, absurdly embarrassed by her unembellished appearance.

There were men, too, also dressed in Grecian or Roman tunics that displayed broad swaths of well-muscled torsos and legs. She couldn't help admiring one particularly fit specimen whose costume, complete with a lion's pelt and club, was clearly intended to evoke Hercules. Another more scantily clad fellow with a slender frame and an especially youthful and handsome countenance might be Adonis, or perhaps Narcissus.

In fact, she might have just stepped into a fancy dress party conceived by a Society lady with a penchant for Classical detail, except . . .

The longer she looked, the more she saw that didn't quite fit her idea of a typical Roman villa. It began with the statuary in the garden. True, the characters depicted were familiar—the first pair was clearly Mars and Venus, the second Cupid and Psyche—but they were not posed in any sort of embrace Eleanor had seen in any textbook or on display in any museum.

Mars stood with his legs spread apart, his hips thrust forward, his expression one of intense concentration. He cupped Venus's buttocks in his hands while her legs wrapped round his hips and thighs, her head thrown back, her mouth open in a wordless cry of bliss.

As if that weren't shocking enough, Cupid and Psyche posed somewhat similarly, but in spoon fashion. Cupid held Psyche by her hips in front of him, impaled upon his shaft, the base of which was clearly visible where it rose from the juncture of his thighs. Like Venus, she wore an expression of rapture as she cupped her breasts in her hands, the thumbs caught mid-stroke in the act of caressing her own nipples.

Caught not just in any act, but *the* act.

A well-bred lady would look away. A well-bred lady would not feel this sort of excitement, this sort of anticipation upon seeing such vulgar images. Would not feel need blistering along her veins, urging her to replicate the scenes being played out in bronze—and, she discovered as she examined the room more closely, in the frescoes and mosaics.

The walls behind each pair of columns bore frescoes depicting an interaction between a pair—or sometimes more than a pair—of lovers. Lewd, lascivious interactions.

A woman kneeling before a man, his phallus in her mouth. A man reclining on his back with a woman straddling him. Two women sharing one man, one perched over his mouth, the other over his hips. A woman on her knees with one man's member in her mouth, while another thrust into her from behind. And perhaps most shocking of all, the same scene repeated, only this time with three men.

Awareness raised the flesh on the back of her neck and arms as she remembered the whispered gossip she had occasionally overheard between the mamas of eligible young ladies badly in need of rich and titled husbands. Rumors about the perverted tastes of the extraordinarily wealthy and fortuitously titled Marquess of Grenville, who enjoyed passing his time not merely with ladies of questionable virtue, but with men as well. *Disgusting*, they tittered under their breaths. *Repulsive. Depraved.*

Eleanor studied the image of the three men with greater interest. She didn't feel disgusted or repulsed. She felt . . . aroused.

Hot and slick and unbearably alive.

Her knees wobbled, and she swayed backward, hyperconscious of Nathaniel's warm presence just behind her right shoulder.

Heaven help her, she was as depraved as he was.

7

Nathaniel could pinpoint the precise instant when Eleanor surrendered to her surroundings. When she not only *saw*, but understood what she was seeing. The moment she ripened and softened like a sweet, juicy peach, begging to be plucked and devoured.

He watched her shoulders slacken, her knees weaken. He heard her breathing accelerate and smelled the faint musk of feminine desire. Her pussy would be damp. Her nipples would be hard. Every inch of her flesh must tingle. He knew her body's responses as well as his own, read them as easily as his mother tongue.

"May I assist you and your . . . companion, sir?" The proprietress of the Red Door, Mrs. Upshaw, rose from her divan near the door and approached them. She knew perfectly well who he was, of course, but her establishment prided itself upon protecting the identities of its patrons, so she maintained the polite fiction that she did not know his name.

Swathed in yards of bright blue and purple silk and wearing

a hat topped with a preposterous profusion of peacock feathers that swayed in counterpoint to her ample hips, Mrs. Upshaw more closely resembled a title-sniffing Society mama than a madam. Given her role as surrogate mother to her employees and matronly advisor to her customers, however, the effect was likely intentional.

Nathaniel inclined his head in acknowledgment of her greeting. "Indeed, madam, I hope so. My companion . . ."—he placed his hand on Eleanor's back, just at the curve of her waist, an unconscious declaration of possession—"is seeking to make the acquaintance of a certain gentleman. We believe he may be here this evening."

Mrs. Upshaw's sculpted eyebrows pinched together. "As I am sure you are well aware, we neither ask nor divulge the identities of our clients. I am at a loss to know how I can be of assistance to you under the circumstances." She surveyed Eleanor with a penetrating stare, taking in every detail with her shrewd eyes.

Eleanor, he noticed, did not flinch at the madam's perusal. Instead, she straightened her shoulders and met the other woman's gaze boldly.

Mrs. Upshaw returned her focus to Nathaniel. "How do I know this lady does not mean to entrap the gentleman in question by some ruse?"

Lady, eh? So much for that aspect of the ruse, such as it was.

It was the shoes—shiny and unscuffed—that gave Eleanor away. That and her unwavering pride. But only an astute observer like the madam would notice such things.

He hoped.

Nathaniel smiled his most charming, most reassuring smile. He begged the madam with his eyes, if not his mouth, to follow along with the charade. "I assure you, there is no ruse. She merely wishes to become . . . acquainted with the gentleman. And as I happen to know him myself, you need not divulge any information at all. I believe I will recognize him when I see him."

Mrs. Upshaw stroked her chin for a few seconds, then shrugged. "I suppose I can see no harm in it, and you have never given me reason to mistrust you." She gestured toward the drawing room. "As you can see, however, we have no customers downstairs at the moment, although a few have retired upstairs for the evening. You are welcome to use the peepholes to . . ."

"Peepholes?" Eleanor's tone carried disbelief and arousal in equal measure. She sagged into him, giving him a tantalizing whiff of clean, citrus scent mingled with the unmistakable aroma of feminine arousal.

She was nearly his, and he nearly trembled with anticipation. With anxiety.

If he bollixed this up, there'd be no second chance. Removed from the temptations of this place and informed of his perfidy, she would never permit him within a few hundred feet, let alone in her bed.

The madam's shoulders and well-padded bosom quaked with suppressed laughter, the swaying plumes on her hat emphasizing her amusement. "Why certainly, my dear. Some of our patrons enjoy watching nearly as much as doing, and most find the notion that their activities may be spied upon quite . . ." —she paused for a moment, no doubt searching for language suitable to a lady's ears—"stimulating."

"Oh." Eleanor's reply neared a whisper. From the angle of her head, he thought she was studying the frescoes again, trying to imagine them in motion.

Perfect.

Mrs. Upshaw smiled up at him, the twinkle again firmly evident in her eyes. She knew precisely what he was up to and had decided to aid him, thank the gods. Waving toward the hallway behind them, she retreated to her divan and reseated herself. "First

room on the left, third on the right, and sixth on the left are occupied. You know the way."

"Must we?" Eleanor whispered, turning to look at him with
wide, uncertain eyes. "Couldn't we just wait for him to finish
and come back down?"

"We could," he admitted, "but he might not come back down
until morning. It's not unusual for men to spend the night."

She worried her lower lip with dainty white teeth. "And if
he's not upstairs?"

"We come back down and wait a spell. If he hasn't arrived
within the hour, he isn't planning to visit tonight, and I shall
take you back to Hardwyck House without further ado."

Her eyes closed, and her mouth drew into a pucker—a pucker
that begged to be licked and suckled and nibbled like every
other inch of her slender form—as she considered this offer. If
she said no, then the game was over. Check, no mate.

As the silence gaped wide and rocky between them, he was
sure she would refuse. His heart pounded in his ears in time to
his silent plea.

Say yes, say yes, say yes.

"Very well," she sighed at last. She threw a surprisingly saucy
glance at Mrs. Upshaw, who had retrieved a book upon returning to her seat and now had her nose buried deep within it. "I
suppose I can't see the harm in it." It was only as he led her to
the stair that he heard her add under her breath, "Yet."

Despite her obvious misgivings, she mounted the stairs will-
ingly and climbed them with impressive alacrity. Whether she
was in a hurry to get this over or get it started didn't really matter. All that mattered was that every step brought her closer to
where he wanted her.

The staircase ended in a narrow hallway illuminated by small
oil lamps mounted between the doorways. He longed to pull that
ridiculous mobcap from Eleanor's head and display her flaxen

curls in the golden glow, but he knew he wouldn't stop there. He would run his fingers through the tresses to loosen them from their elegant bindings, until her hair flowed over her shoulders and down her back in a shimmering stream of light.

How long was her hair, anyway? Would the silky curls come to rest between the slender blades of her shoulders or at the inward curve of her waist, or would they reach all the way to her arse?

The rough woolen dress would be the next victim of the onslaught, an unwelcome interloper with no right to come between them. He wouldn't stop until she was naked and pliant beneath him, wouldn't stop until his cock was poised at her soft, moist entrance and she was begging him to fuck her now, please now.

Damn, he'd better make this fast, or he'd spill in his breeches before he'd even touched her.

The muffled sounds of enthusiastic couplings filtered into the narrow corridor: moans of pleasure, shouts of encouragement, the creak of well-worn bedsprings.

Nathaniel drew to a halt in front of the first door on the left. Eleanor stopped alongside him. His fingers trembled with suppressed desire as he reached for the tiny knob that slid aside to reveal the rectangular viewing window. Approximately four inches high by twelve inches wide, the peepholes were just large enough to allow two people to watch what took place inside, the beds carefully placed in each room to ensure their occupants would be visible through the open portal. Although there was, of course, no guarantee that the inhabitants would be using the bed.

Fortunately—or unfortunately, depending upon how one looked at it—the couple in this room had chosen to use the bed. Nathaniel recognized the balding, heavyset gentlemen pounding the red-haired Danae as Lord Thomas Preston, the magistrate for the district. The man inveighed in public against the sins of the flesh, but here he was anyway, probably getting his fuck for free in exchange for turning a blind eye to the establishment for another few days.

Bloody hypocrite.

But at least the unpleasant tableau had a calming effect on his libido.

He turned to Eleanor, who peered up at him through darkening eyes, and shook his head. "No. Not Mathews."

They proceeded to the next door. This time, the sight that met his eyes was considerably more arousing than the first. Though the woman with her large breasts and long black hair was not to Nathaniel's taste, she knelt in front of a lean, handsome young man who had likely come to divest himself of his pesky virginity. She sucked his cock rhythmically, one hand sliding up and down the shaft in concert with her mouth while she worked one or more fingers in and out of his arse with the other. The fellow's slack-jawed expression communicated both the depth of his astonishment at this treatment and the abject pleasure he took from it.

Nathaniel's cock sprang back to life. God, if Eleanor did that to him, he would surely die of rapture. He would wrap his fingers in her hair and thrust—

"Well?" Eleanor asked, her voice breathy and unsteady.

He slid the portal shut and stepped away. "No."

One more chance. Calliope's room.

He slid open the window and peered in. Calliope reclined on the bed as her client finished shucking his breeches and small clothes. He stood with his back to the door, but as he climbed onto the bed, his profile came into full view. Starkly handsome, with dark blond hair and deep-set eyes, the fellow looked familiar, though Nathaniel couldn't place him. Which likely meant Eleanor couldn't place him, either. And that was all to the good.

It was now or never.

Drawing back from the window, Nathaniel shook his head with feigned dejection. "That's not him, either," he sighed. He looked at Eleanor. Her pupils were deep ink-black wells circled by bright rings of indigo fire. She was close, so close to surrender.

But she must take every step by her own choice. He would not take her anywhere she did not want to go. Did not ask to go. "Would you like to go back downstairs and wait for him to arrive?"

And then, though he had long ago stopped believing in a benevolent deity, he prayed—not for salvation, but for complete corruption.

Hers.

Her father had the right of it when he called Nathaniel St. Clair the *Marquess of the Devil,* Eleanor thought. He was temptation incarnate, and she was powerless to resist the lures he set out for her.

What was more, she didn't want to. Even knowing she was being led down the path to damnation, she followed him. He might as well be the pied piper for all the will she had in his presence.

Had she ever truly believed that Clarence Mathews would be here tonight? Ever imagined that this excursion was anything more than a ruse? If she were honest with herself, she would admit the answer was no.

Had she ever even *hoped* that it was true? Or had she known all along and accepted the truth: that Nathaniel intended to corrupt her fully on this night, and she intended to permit it? To embrace it?

The answer scarcely mattered now. She vibrated with arousal, with curiosity, with need. Whether the cause was the erotic images she had seen in the drawing room, or the muted sounds of copulation seeping into the hallway from the rooms beyond, or her overwhelming attraction to Nathaniel himself, no longer seemed relevant. She had to know, had to see, had to experience what lay beyond that door.

Nathaniel watched her, his handsome countenance stark with hope, his lean frame taut with controlled desire.

The choice was hers. And she would burn either way.

She shook her head, but she couldn't say the words that would seal her fate. Instead, she moved toward the open window and looked in.

A tall, slender blonde woman reclined on a bed. As naked as God had made her, she fondled her breasts—which Eleanor could not help noticing were quite as small as her own—while an equally nude man with powerfully muscled shoulders and thighs kneeled between her open legs. He stared down at his fingers, which worked in unrelenting circles over that tender, magical bit of flesh with which Eleanor had so recently become acquainted. The muscles in the woman's legs flexed, and her eyelids fluttered. Then she shuddered, her hips lifting off the bed, grinding up into the pressure that brought her release.

Eleanor smoothed her hand over her stomach, toward the bit of flesh that pulsed and swelled between her own thighs. Oh, how she needed to be touched there. Worked there.

Nathaniel's hand came to rest on the curve of her back. Her gaze snapped to his face. He was watching the couple, too.

"He's about to fuck her, you know," he murmured.

Fuck. The word prickled over her skin, hot and forbidden. Her knees wobbled as the tension in her belly grew tenfold.

"Look."

She did.

The woman still reclined on the bed, but now the man had positioned his hips so that his erect phallus bobbed just above the blond curls at the juncture of her thighs. He took his shaft in one hand and rubbed the rounded tip along the seam of female flesh until he found the entrance he sought. The lean muscles of his backside bunched as he released himself and grabbed the woman's hips with both hands.

Eleanor shivered as though chilled, a perverse reaction to the searing heat of the blood racing through her veins, pounding in her ears. As though she were a participant in, rather than an observer of, the scene playing out before her eyes. Traitorous, treacherous eyes that couldn't look away.

He plunged forward with a sure and certain grace. The woman murmured something unintelligible and arched upward, grasping his buttocks in her hands to guide him forward. To assist the invasion.

And then the two of them began to move, pushing together, rocking apart in a rhythm Eleanor instantly recognized as the one she had discovered when she'd put her fingers inside and . . . oh God . . . fucked herself with them.

Only now, that would never be enough.

"Do you still want Clarence Mathews?" Nathaniel whispered at her ear.

She turned away from the window and leaned her head against his shoulder. He smelled of whiskey and spice and arousal. Or maybe the arousal was hers. She couldn't be sure.

She shook her head as his hand came up to caress her neck, cup the base of her skull. Hot tentacles of longing slithered down her spine.

"No," she admitted. She inclined her head toward door. "I want you to do to me what he's doing to her."

Nathaniel's eyebrows lifted. "You'll have to be a little more explicit than that, Erato. What exactly do you want me, Nathaniel St. Clair, Marquess of Grenville, to do to you?"

Eleanor swallowed hard, her throat thick as porridge and

dry as parchment. She wasn't sure she could say the words. But if she didn't, he might not . . . And that she could not bear.

She took an unsteady breath and forced out the words she knew he wanted to hear. "I want you to fuck me, Nathaniel St. Clair. Please."

8

Eleanor sighed with relief as Nathaniel's lips brushed against her forehead like a prayer. "I thought you'd never ask."

He swept her up in his arms as if she weighed no more than a figment of his imagination, cradling her against the solid warmth of his chest as though he feared she would evaporate like the muse he'd named her. Three strides down the hall and he reached a door that was slightly ajar. He nudged further with the toe of his boot and carried her inside.

Into the room and into the paradise of his kiss.

Sweet, nibbling kisses danced around the edges of her lips like tiny question marks. Asking *are you sure* and pleading *say yes* and begging *let me in.*

She opened her mouth to the onslaught and kissed him back with the only word that lived inside her. *Yes, yes, yes.* His answer was fierce and demanding, a deep, tonguing, rough response that left her breathless and boneless, unable to do more than cling to his neck and return the favor, measure for measure, until they both panted and trembled with need.

In a corner of her mind, she registered the sound of the door clicking shut and the warmth of a blazing fire in the hearth, though its heat was inconsequential compared to the flames leaping and dancing beneath her skin, through her bones, into the very marrow of her being.

He allowed her feet to slip to the floor. "Show me how much you want me, Erato." His tone was rough, almost grim, and he searched her face with a bright blue gaze, at once demanding and vulnerable. "Take off your clothes."

She opened her mouth to object that she couldn't possibly disrobe without assistance, but closed it again. She wasn't wearing one of her own elaborate gowns, but a simple dress fashioned for a maid who must of necessity dress and undress herself.

A novel concept.

Her fingers trembled as she located the rough black buttons that secured the gray bodice. She couldn't look at him as she undid the fasteners one by one, afraid she would either lose her confidence or rip the dress in her haste to remove it, if she could see his expression. Only as the last one came free and the fabric fell away from her shoulders did she lift her gaze from the floor.

He was nude.

How had he undressed so quickly?

Her heart fluttered ineffectually, like a butterfly pinned to a display board. She recalled the day she'd confronted him in his study and thought he looked the part of Adam, a newly formed creation into which God had just breathed life. Now, as she allowed her gaze to sweep unabashedly from the thick curls of brown hair on his head, to the taut musculature of his shoulders, chest, and abdomen, and down to the tighter near-black curls at the juncture of his thighs, she understood for the first time why the Bible said God had made man in His image.

Man was beautiful. Or more precisely, *this* man was beautiful. If God looked like Nathaniel St. Clair, every woman on Earth would get herself to a nunnery, eager to be His bride.

The shaft of his manhood, springing up from his loins, gave her pause, though. It seemed larger—thicker and longer—than she had imagined. She stared, trying to recall if the man she'd seen through the window had been quite so . . . alarmingly endowed, and decided he had not.

Nathaniel was a tall man. Perhaps he was larger in this respect than the average man as well.

Something in her expression must have communicated her apprehension, because Nathaniel said, "Don't worry, Erato. I won't do anything you don't ask for."

She sucked in her lower lip and shook her head, a wave of uncertainty nearly swamping her resolve. Could she really do this?

"I don't know what to ask for," she whispered.

He took a step closer and reached out to touch the mobcap that still covered her head. "You could start by asking me to help you get these clothes off." He gestured toward his own nakedness. "You've fallen a bit behind, I'm afraid."

"I've never undressed myself before," she admitted.

"Then now is a poor time to start." He grinned and affected a small, courtly bow that made her giggle. "May I be of assistance, my lady?"

His voice lowered an octave on the words "my lady." He was in earnest now. If she said yes, she would be his lady, now and forever.

Her throat felt dry and tight, but there was no denying the arousal that pulsed in her blood, tingled on her skin, and flickered between her thighs.

"Yes, please."

"Yes, what?" he prompted.

"Yes, help me undress, Nathaniel."

His lips brushed her forehead again. "I thought you'd never ask."

Nathaniel couldn't get the ridiculous maid's garb off her quickly enough. Whatever had possessed him to costume her in such a fashion? His lady should wear silks and satins and fine, soft muslins in bright, rich hues, not rough, gray wool.

That was, when she wore anything at all. If he had his way, he would keep her in bed for days on end wearing nothing but her soft, velvety skin and covered only by the hard, hot length of his body.

Dress, shift, drawers, and cap soon lay in a drab heap on the polished wooden floor, leaving her in stockings, garters, and the shiny leather shoes that had given away her status to the much-too-perceptive madam. Although he'd undressed her in his mind a thousand times before, although he had touched and tasted her breasts and her cunny, seeing her near naked in the firelight—the culmination of his fantasies—kindled a primitive, possessive emotion in the center of his chest that felt strangely like . . .

No, don't examine it. Don't think. Just do.

He could see she was fighting the urge to cover herself, her shoulders tense and her eyes wary as he skimmed the length of her long-limbed, slender body with his gaze. As if she feared he'd find her lacking.

As if. From her pert, teacup-sized breasts to the concave plane of her belly to slim legs that took forever to reach from her narrow hips to the floor, she was flawless.

He should say something to put her at ease, but his tongue stuck to the roof of his mouth. What did a man say to a goddess? He couldn't think of a single, solitary thing, so he did instead what any right-minded man would in the presence of divinity: He got down on his knees and worshipped her.

First with his lips, pressed gently to the dewy skin of her abdomen, just above her navel. Then with his tongue, tracing a line to the dark golden curls at the apex of her thighs. And then with his whole mouth, working into the crevice between her legs, finding her sweet, delicious center. There, he licked and suckled until she moaned with pleasure, spreading her legs wider to allow him greater access, all hesitation and embarrassment forgotten.

Soon, her knees began to tremble, and she clasped his head for support. "Please," she managed to say between panting breaths, and he knew—though she couldn't find the words—that she was asking him to take her to the bed, for her legs could no longer hold her upright.

He rose from the floor and scooped her up in his arms. Carrying her to the bed, he seated her on its edge and set about removing her shoes, stockings, and garters, tossing them all into the same heap with the remainder of her clothes. When he had finished, he coaxed her gently back until she reclined against the velvet-cushioned pillows and then he stretched out alongside her.

His cock rested against her thigh, hard and heavy with lust, while his heart swelled with a deeper longing he refused to name.

Propping himself on one elbow, he trailed his fingers from her collarbone over her breasts and down to the prominent peaks of her hip bones. Gooseflesh followed the path of his touch, and her limbs trembled. When he met her gaze, he found her pupils dilated but her eyes wide and startled instead of heavy-lidded with desire.

He feathered her silky blond hair away from her brow. "Are you anxious, Erato?"

The shiny, pink tip of her tongue darted out to wet her upper lip, a sensual gesture that wreaked havoc on his already tenuous self-control. "A little," she admitted, her voice tremulous and hoarse. "My mother told me it might hurt the first time."

Nathaniel smiled and nodded gravely. "I've heard that, too. Though not, I confess, from my mother."

An adorable little frown creased her forehead. "You mean you don't know?"

"Not from personal experience, no. I fear I am just as anxious as you are."

Though it hardly seemed possible, her eyes grew even wider. "You? Why?"

He looked down into her uncertain features, and a fierce surge of tenderness swept through him. "Because I wish only to give you pleasure, but know I may give you pain instead. And because this fellow," he reached down and pumped his shaft to emphasize his meaning, "is a bit too eager to get inside your sweet little pussy to listen to reason."

Her gaze followed the path of his hand to his cock, and she gulped. "Are most men so . . . large?"

Ridiculous as it was, Nathaniel couldn't suppress his masculine pride at being judged *large*. But though a part of him wanted to claim exceptional prowess in this arena to impress her, he suspected she would be more worried than impressed if she believed he was significantly more endowed than the average man. And so he settled for the truth.

"I am larger than some and smaller than others, but not exceptionally so."

"Ah," she sighed, apparently reassured. "I thought you were much bigger than the man we saw in the other room."

He grinned. "I may be. But it's probably more a matter of proximity."

She nodded.

"A proximity I'd like to increase, if you're willing." He slid his palm from his cock across to her hips, and then down to cup her mons.

She nodded again, and he saw her pulse pounding in her throat, heard the hitch in her breath as he slipped one finger between the slick folds of her sex. Anxious she might be, but she was eager, too, the wetness of her pussy demonstrating her readiness as clearly as his throbbing erection demonstrated his.

"Then ask for what you want, Eleanor."

She swallowed hard and whispered, "Fuck me, Nathaniel."

He was over her and between her legs in one swift movement. Without being asked, she spread her thighs wide, parting the glistening petals of her flesh so he could see every glorious detail, from the tender pink bud of her clit to the tiny opening below. Jaded as he was, her faith awed him, and he trembled every bit as much as she did as he rubbed his cock over and down the exposed seam of her pussy several times. She shivered and arched upward each time he found her entrance with the head of his shaft, but each time, he held back.

"Please," she gasped the third time, "now."

"I thought you'd never ask," he muttered, and in one slow, deliberate motion, he entered Heaven.

9

_____

Eleanor blinked, astonished.

Nathaniel's thick, hard length was seated to the hilt within her, yet she felt no discomfort. Oh, there had been a brief twinge of pain right at the beginning, but it was nothing compared to what she had expected, especially when she'd seen just how *big* Nathaniel was.

But to her amazement, it didn't hurt at all. To the contrary, the sensation of being stretched and filled was lovely.

And not enough.

Nathaniel leaned over her on his palms, his eyes closed, his face a taut mask of restraint. He held back, she realized, because he feared *she* was in pain. When nothing could be further from the truth.

Driven by feminine instinct, she rocked her hips back and forth, imitating the rhythm she'd inadvertently discovered with her fingers. In response, he groaned in protest and dropped his head forward until his forehead rested against hers.

"Keep going," she urged, twisting her fingers into the thick, curly locks at the nape of her neck. "I want more."

He lifted his head and searched her eyes with an intense gaze. "Are you sure you're ready?"

Eleanor pulled his face closer and kissed him with all the certainty and passion she possessed. That was all the answer he seemed to need. His mouth melded to hers as he began to move within her, out and in, his body creating the same subtle friction she'd found with her fingers.

Only this . . . this was so much better. So much fuller, so much richer, so much stronger. She tilted her hips upward to meet his thrusts, her fingers clutching at his hair, his shoulders, his buttocks as he rode her, faster and surer, deeper and harder. The sounds of their coupling—the *slap, slap, slap* of skin against skin, the grunts and sighs of effort, of pleasure expanding and building—aroused Eleanor so powerfully that she could scarcely breathe, her heart pounding wildly so she was sure Nathaniel must feel it, too.

"Oh, please . . . uh . . . oh, please." Alternating between sobs and whispers, she strained toward the release that lay just out of reach while he alternated between tormenting her and soothing her with kisses and licks and nips as his mouth traveled from her lips to her earlobes to her neck to her nipples.

"Do you like my cock fucking your pussy, sweet Erato?" he rumbled wickedly near her ear.

She groaned brokenly, grinding her hips to meet his downward thrust, the dirty, forbidden words pushing her closer to the edge.

"Say it," he urged. "I want to hear you say it."

Her face flamed, but she was already so hot everywhere else, she scarcely noticed. "I . . . like your cock . . ."

He plunged in hard, stealing her voice.

"Like you fucking . . ."

Again.

"Fucking my pussy," she finished at last.

"Good girl," he murmured, tugging at her earlobe with his

teeth. "You were made for this, Eleanor. Made for fucking. This is who you are. You know that now, don't you?"

She was so desperate for the salvation of release, she couldn't process the implication of his words, and so she assented without thought. "Yes, yes, please."

"Thank God," he whispered.

He adjusted the angle of his thrusts ever so slightly, so that his shaft now stroked a particularly sensitive place inside her she hadn't known existed. Pleasure swelled and peaked as he pounded her, his pace fast and furious but mated to her own frenzied need.

There was nothing ladylike, nothing reserved about her now. She writhed beneath him, riding the crest higher and higher until the first wave of ecstasy erupted at her core. Gasping, she dug her fingernails into the taut muscles of his shoulders and sobbed as the world seemed to come apart in the kaleidoscope of rapture.

Swooping down, he captured her mouth in a kiss that was simultaneously sweet and fierce. He thrust into her again— once, twice, three times—then shouted, his back and arms shuddering as his cock pulsed inside her like a second heart.

A heart he gave her in exchange for the one he now owned.

Nathaniel fully intended to confess and beg Eleanor's forgiveness for concealing his identity—just as soon as he could find the wherewithal to speak. And he certainly would have done so, had Eleanor's stomach not chosen that precise moment to emit a low but unmistakable rumble. Chagrined, Nathaniel realized that dinner was one part of his scheme he hadn't thoroughly considered. He should have foreseen that they'd both be in desperate need of sustenance after the vigorous bout of lovemaking he'd hoped for, and he should have planned accordingly.

Eleanor's cheeks flushed a lovely shade of pink, and she pressed her hand to her lips as if the offending sound had issued from her mouth rather than her belly. "Oh, dear."

After the total abandonment with which she had just shared the most intimate parts of her person with him, her embarrassment at this small lapse in her body's etiquette was endearing.

He chuckled and dropped a tender kiss on her pretty little nose. "It is no wonder you're hungry, Erato. I did deny you your supper, after all. Not to mention the cucumber sandwiches that were meant to accompany your tea."

She shook her head, her lips twisting into a wry smile. "I'm almost never hungry. But now," she pressed her hand to her abdomen as her stomach growled again, even more audibly than before, "I'm positively famished."

"I believe I shall take that as a compliment." He wiggled his eyebrows suggestively, and Eleanor let out a peal of laughter that warmed him in a way that was not at all erotic. The strangeness of this might have worried him, if he hadn't had more pressing issues to attend to.

Rising from the bed, he retrieved his breeches and shirt from the floor. The brothel was home to more than two dozen people. Surely it had a kitchen that prepared meals.

"I'll go and find us something to eat," he said as he pulled his stiffly starched shirt over his head.

"Shouldn't we be going?"

His head popped through the neckline. "Going? Where?"

She had wrapped the red coverlet around her torso and clutched it tight above her breasts. One shoulder rose slightly, causing a tantalizing swell of soft, white flesh to peep above the richly colored fabric. "I thought . . . well . . ."—she nibbled at her lower lip, and he envied her teeth their perpetual proximity to that deliciously tender bit of flesh—"that we would be going to Gretna Green tonight. After . . . this."

He stepped into his breeches and padded back to the bed. Leaning over, he brushed his lips across her forehead. "Not on an empty stomach, sweetheart. But I have to admit, I had in mind to apply tomorrow for a special license so I can marry you properly. You deserve better than an anvil wedding." He straightened and grinned down at her. "You do have the dress already, I imagine."

"Yes, but . . ." Her brow furrowed.

"But?"

"Papa will object." She gazed up at them, her soft blue eyes filled with worry. "You know how he dislikes you. He might say no. And then I should have to tell him . . ." She closed her eyes and shuddered.

Poor darling. He couldn't blame her. As much as he wanted his father to know of and despise his every transgression, Eleanor must want her kind and loving father to remain ignorant of even her slightest fault. And sleeping with the ton's most notorious rake—in a brothel, no less—would hardly qualify as a minor sin.

He smoothed his hand over her hair. "If you want Gretna, then Gretna it shall be. But not until morning. 'Tis a long way to Scotland, and such a trip should not be attempted without a proper meal and good night's sleep."

And a better night's loving. He still had plenty yet to show her—about Nathaniel, about Clarence, and most importantly, about herself.

Eleanor waited until Nathaniel gently closed the door behind him before she rose from the bed and ducked behind the screen on the opposite side of the room to use the chamber pot. After what she had just permitted—nay, participated in—it was ridiculous to be so modest, but she simply couldn't bring herself to walk naked across the floor to indulge in such a crass bodily function with him there.

She supposed she should be grateful another, equally urgent bodily function had intervened on her behalf. Her stomach roared again, and she shook her head in disbelief. She couldn't remember when she had ever been so hungry.

Never before had she been so aware of her body, of its needs and desires. Her mind, her intellect had always taken precedence over the corporal. She ate and drank and slept because she needed to, not because doing so gave her any particular pleasure.

Nathaniel had changed her in a fundamental way. Her body, its joys and pleasures, mattered to her now. She could never go back to the ascetic, abstemious existence that had once suited her so well.

She would never really be Eleanor Palmer again. And she didn't know whether to be glad or sorry.

After completing her toilette, she retrieved her shift from the floor and donned it. Then, to keep herself from descending into a torrent of doubt and uncertainty, she set about tidying the room, separating her maid's garb from Nathaniel's gentlemanly finery. When she reached the dark green coat, she shook it to smooth the wrinkles and laid it carefully over the back of the red velvet upholstered armchair that sat before the fireplace.

As she put it down, a white square fell out of the breast pocket and fluttered to the floor. She stooped to recover it, expecting to find it a handkerchief, but instead discovered it to be a folded sheet of paper.

Even before she began unfolding it, she knew she should not. Nathaniel might now be her betrothed in intention if not in law, but that hardly bestowed upon her the right to read his personal notes or correspondence. But some premonition tickled at the back of her neck and drove her to open it and find . . .

Dear Holyfield,
  I trust this brief note finds you and Lady Holyfield well and happy. You will both be pleased, I think, to hear that by the time this reaches you, I shall have made Miss Eleanor Palmer my lady wife.

You were right, my friend. I do believe she may temper
my tendency to vice.
Yours sincerely,
Grenville

As a child, Eleanor had once fallen from her horse. She never forgot the sensation—the shock of her breath being torn from her lungs, and the gasping pain of trying to recover it.

She felt that now.

Nathaniel's handwriting was the same as Clarence Mathews's.

Nathaniel St. Clair—the debauched and dissolute Marquess of the Devil—*was* Clarence Mathews.

There was no denying it. The evidence was irrefutable.

Her vision blurred, and her head spun. She dropped the note to the floor.

All along, he had lied to her. Allowed her to nurture her fantasy of a noble, scholarly poet when nothing could be further from the truth.

Oh, how he must have laughed at her behind his hand when she gushed over Mathews's poetry, when she praised Mathews's superior morals and intellectual skills. He must have found her quite silly and ever so amusing. And how much fun it must have been for him to string her along, to seduce her, all the while knowing the truth.

How long had he planned to keep the secret? Another day? A week? A month? The rest of their lives?

Her chest burned as though her heart were being torn asunder and, at the same time, ripped from her chest. Tears stung the corners of her eyes and swelled the back of her throat.

Why hadn't he told her? What possible explanation could there be for such dissemblance, other than that it amused him to make a fool of her?

To think she had been on the verge of marrying him. Of confessing that she loved him.

But she was nothing to him but a great jest.

A bitter laugh escaped her lips. A great jest, and a remarkably easy fuck.

Her gaze darted warily to the door. How long did she have before he returned? She couldn't begin to guess.

She had to move quickly. For there was no way she could face him, no way she could bear to listen to him attempt to justify his behavior. She must leave this place. Now.

With all the speed she could muster, she put on the maid's dress and buttoned it up the front despite trembling, angry fingers. With no time for drawers, stays, or stockings, she shoved her bare feet into her cold leather boots and laced them tight. Her hair she braided roughly before shoving it up under the mobcap.

Once she was respectably clothed, at least to outward appearances, she took a deep breath and prayed she wouldn't find Nathaniel in the hall. Opening the door, she poked her head out and breathed a sigh of relief. The hallway was deserted.

It wouldn't do to go out the way they had come in, however. If she were to flee by the front stairs, she might well encounter Nathaniel or someone else who would ask questions. But she reasoned that even a brothel must have a servants' passage, and after she crept into the hallway, she found it easily enough—a narrow doorway tucked between two rooms. She ducked inside and followed a winding stairwell down several floors to a door that led, mercifully, to the street.

The night was still young for London's populace, and the street was well-lit and crowded with pedestrians and carriage traffic. No one spared a second glance at a maid emerging from a nondescript doorway and ascending to the street. Her appearance would cause no remark whatsoever.

Stopping on the sidewalk, she looked to her left and right to gain her bearings. It was fortunate that Palmer House was situated only a few blocks from Pall Mall in the fashionable St. James district. Her parents could have sold the townhome and pocketed a tidy sum, given its fortuitous address, but her father maintained that the sale price would scarcely offset the cost of letting other lodging in London during the Season, when decent accommodations were at a premium. Eleanor had often wondered whether that was strictly accurate, for she knew many families no wealthier than her own who seemed to manage, though they were forced to take up residence in somewhat less advantageous neighborhoods. But now, she was grateful for her Papa's stubbornness, for it meant she could easily walk home.

How she would get in was another problem entirely.

And then, perhaps, she would let herself cry.

10

Trying to drink oneself to death wasn't nearly as entertaining when one actually hoped to succeed, Nathaniel decided as he downed another finger of whiskey. His stomach turned over in revolt as the burning liquid settled in a hard, hot lump.

It had been a week since he'd returned to the room at the Red Door with a plate of creamed sole and asparagus only to discover that Eleanor had vanished. At first, he thought it some sort of game, but then he'd seen his note to Holyfield, which he'd planned to post in the morning, on the floor and realized the awful truth.

He'd rushed to the street in his breeches, shirt, and bare feet in the hopes of catching her, drawing bemused stares and shocked gasps from passersby. She was nowhere to be seen, however, and he knew instantly where she'd gone—home.

At first, he was furious. How could she leave without giving him a chance to explain? If she only understood *why* he had concealed his identity, surely she would forgive him.

He awoke early the next morning, prepared to go to her parents' house and beat the door down if necessary to see her, but as his valet brushed his coat to remove the lint, the fallacy in Nathaniel's reasoning suddenly struck him smack in the mouth. What could he say to her that would make his deceit acceptable?

With a sinking sense of certainty, he knew the answer. *Nothing.* His lies weren't like lint, insignificant specks of dust, easily swept aside if not ignored outright.

All these years, he'd told himself he was only playing at being the wicked wastrel, had nurtured the secret belief that some streak of nobility hid within him. He'd always chosen his playmates carefully—women and men as bored and jaded and impervious to injury as he was. And when he immersed himself in his poetry, he *felt* like a respectable, decent man.

But now, he could no longer lie to himself. He had taken his amusement with an innocent who not only didn't know the rules, but had no idea it was a game at all. He'd had more than a dozen opportunities to tell her the truth, to let her choose whether or not she wished to play. He hadn't done so.

And the reason he hadn't was obvious. He was *exactly* the man he'd thought he was pretending to be. As black-hearted a blackguard as his father had always maintained. Maybe worse.

He lifted the crystal decanter from the table beside his armchair, removed the stopper, and poured another finger of the golden liquid into his glass.

At least he was certain Eleanor had made her way to her parents' home in safety. When he'd realized he could no more appear on her doorstep and request an audience with her than he could hope to spend the afterlife in any place but the deepest levels of Hell, he'd sent Jane round to the Palmers'. The butler had told Jane that Miss Palmer was resting comfortably in her room after returning unexpectedly the night before, but would not be accepting visitors for a day or two due to her illness.

He raised the glass to his lips, then shook his head and set it back on the table. The liquor only seemed to exacerbate his pain, not relieve it, and it would be years before he could consume enough to actually do himself in with an excess of the stuff.

Not that he actually *wanted* to die. No, what he really wanted was to relive the past two weeks and make right everything he had done wrong. Hell, he'd relive his entire life to set things right, if that's what it took. He'd work twice as hard to be the moral, upstanding heir his father had always wanted as he'd worked to be the antithesis.

He replaced the stopper in the decanter and rose from his chair. It was past time to stop wallowing in self-pity. He couldn't change the past, but he could try to be a better man from now on. He wasn't entirely sure what that meant, but he knew where he had to start.

With his father . . .

Nathaniel scratched on the door, his chest burning at the ignominy of being reduced to requesting entrance to his father's library. He was the man's son, not some common servant.

"Enter." The duke's gruff voice sounded from within.

Nathaniel turned the knob, threw open the door, and stepped inside.

His father didn't look up from the ledgers he was reviewing. When Nathaniel didn't speak, the duke waved his hand in irritation, his gaze still firmly fixed on the long columns of figures that enumerated the Hardwycks' obscene wealth down to the minutest detail. "Yes, yes, what is it now?"

Nathaniel straightened his shoulders. He didn't know what it was about his father that always made him feel like a ten-year-old boy on the verge of another beating for some childish transgression. Never mind that he could now put the old man on the floor with a single swing of his fist. "I've come to apologize."

Hardwyck's eyes nearly popped out of his head as his gaze snapped up to his son. "What?"

Nathaniel closed the door with a resounding thud and took two more strides into the room so that he stood square in front of the massive, mahogany desk. "I wish to apologize for being a miserable excuse for a son, and to promise to do better in the future."

The old man gaped, his heavy jaw slack with disbelief, then sputtered, "What—Why—I don't believe it."

Nathaniel shrugged. "Believe it or don't. It's of no consequence to me. I merely wish you to know that I regret having caused you and Mother so much pain and worry." The words left a bitter taste in his mouth, for he wasn't really sorry that he had hurt his parents, but instead that in doing so, he had destroyed his own chance at happiness.

Selfish to the last, he was.

He pivoted on his heel and made for the door. No sense spending any more time than strictly necessary in the evil old goat's presence.

A heavy hand on his shoulder stopped him in his tracks. Surprised, he spun to face his father, who stood directly behind him. He would never have guessed that such a fat, elderly man could move so quickly.

Even more astonishing, his father's silver-blue eyes, normally cold and emotionless as ice, were glassy with . . . tears? What the hell?

"All I ever wanted was to keep you safe. To see you reach manhood."

Was this supposed to be an apology? If so, it was damned weak.

Nathaniel set his jaw. "Only because you need me to carry on your precious bloodline. Tell me, did it ever occur to you I might have *wanted* to do the job if you'd cared half as much about me as you do about my prick and where I put it?"

The duke's ruddy complexion went sallow as the blood drained from his face, though whether he was more shocked by the coarse words, or the harshness of the tone in which they were delivered, Nathaniel couldn't say.

Heaving a slow, ragged breath, Hardwyck removed his hand from Nathaniel's shoulder and pointed toward the deep armchairs that sat near the fireplace. "Sit down, son. It's time you knew the truth."

Nathaniel scowled. "The truth?" As if he needed to hear all the reasons he was an unworthy son now. Hadn't he heard them all his life?

His father nodded. "Sit."

Though Nathaniel's stomach knotted with disgust at the prospect of having his faults catalogued in excruciating detail, he did as he was bid. If he could bear the loss of Eleanor—his muse, his love—he could stand whatever criticism his father was about to dish out. It couldn't be worse.

The duke took the seat next to Nathaniel and stared into the low fire that burned in the hearth for a moment, before turning to fix an earnest gaze on his son's face. "Have you ever wondered why there are no portraits of you as an infant?"

Nathaniel blinked. What a peculiar question!

And yet, now he thought of it, it was rather odd. There were christening portraits of all the Hardwyck heirs going back several generations, as well as family portraits that included every St. Clair baby ever born. Every baby except him. But if it had ever crossed his mind to wonder why—and it hadn't—he would have assumed it was just another indication of how much his father had despised him from birth.

He shrugged and shook his head.

"It's because, when you were born, you weren't the heir. You had an older brother."

Dumbfounded, Nathaniel gaped as his father in disbelief. "I had what?"

The duke sighed, and his eyes took on that glassy shine of tears again. "Your mother and I had a son the same year we were married. Henry David Frederick St. Clair. We doted on him, partly because he was our first child and partly because your mother had trouble conceiving and carrying until you were born when Henry was almost eight years old. We let him get away with all manner of scrapes and horseplay, never imagining . . ."

Hardwyck choked back a sob, and Nathaniel felt a curious and unwelcome well of sympathy rise in his breast.

"When you were a little over a year old, Henry fell from a tree and broke his neck. He died the following day, and you became the heir."

Nathaniel's heartbeat roared in his ears as the memory of the last—and most brutal—beating he had suffered at the old man's hands crashed through his brain. He'd been climbing a tree. It was something his father had expressly forbidden him to do at least a hundred times, but Nathaniel was twelve and high-spirited and couldn't see the harm in climbing trees. He would never forget the steely glint in his father's eyes or the ice-hard tones of his voice when he'd commanded his son to get down . . . now, or the biting sting of the lash with which the duke had delivered his punishment.

No wonder he had never been able to please his father. His childish pranks and pratfalls weren't evidence of some innate brand of wickedness in his character. His father hadn't hated his only son; he'd been terrified of loving another child to death.

He looked at his father, huddling in the oversized armchair, and saw not a monstrous tormenter, but a shrunken, broken man who hid his fears behind a mask of cruelty.

There could be no forgiveness, of course. No matter the cause, his father's transgressions were inexcusable.

But they were *his father's* transgressions. Not his. And that made all the difference.

11

Like unto the gods is he,
That man who sits across from thee.
His face is near enough thine own
To hear thy voice's dulcet tone,
And thy shining laughter, too,
So that envy runs me through.
For while I gaze upon you two,
I bid my every word adieu.
My tongue is frozen by desire,
Beneath my flesh, a subtle fire.
Blinded. Stunned. The sound of thunder
Tears my ears and heart asunder.
Sweat breaks out and, chilled, I shiver,
As though immersed in Hades' river.
My color drains, like dead grass drying,
And I fall slack, one breath from dying.

—Sappho, trans. Eleanor Palmer

Eleanor set down her pen and reread the lines she'd just committed to paper. It was the best verse translation she had ever done, capturing almost word for word the original Greek text in rhymed English couplets.

But her success brought her no satisfaction. A month ago, she would have been gleeful at such an achievement. Today, the accomplishment left her empty and unfulfilled.

She placed the new page atop the growing stack of translations she had done since arriving last week at Auxleigh Manor. Soon, she would have enough to submit for publication. If she was lucky, she could earn a sufficient income from sales of her work to support herself and Aunt Eppie, for marrying now was out of the question.

She could never permit another man to touch her as Nathaniel had. It would be a form of sacrilege.

Her vision blurred. By now, Nathaniel had likely forgotten her, moved on to another woman. If she'd stayed in London, she would have tormented herself, desperate to avoid him yet secretly straining to catch a glimpse of him at the opera or the theatre or some other ton event he might deign to attend.

Better to be here in the wilds of Northamptonshire, where the foolish hope that he might come to her could not prey upon her. She ought to have given him a chance to explain. Perhaps he hadn't been making sport of her. Perhaps he'd had a good reason for concealing his identity. She'd been too quick to judge, too quick to take offense. Now, it was too late.

He hadn't come to her in London, though she'd waited a week and prayed he would. He certainly wouldn't come to her here.

And without him, she couldn't come at all. For all that her body ached and burned with longing, she'd lost the capacity to bring herself pleasure. Hard as she tried, wicked as her thoughts had become, she wanted more than her own fingers—wanted his hands and lips and tongue and cock, needed him to kiss and caress and fuck her.

Her pussy throbbed, begging for release, and Eleanor pressed the heel of her palm between her thighs to quell the rising tide. Not that it was likely to do any good.

A brisk knock on the door made her snatch her hand away, her heart pounding irregularly with embarrassment.

"Come," she called, and then her cheeks flamed hot as another blistering bolt of desire pierced her. No subtle fire for her.

The door opened, and Mr. Covey, the butler, stepped into the library. He held a square of paper between his fingers. "A footman just delivered this for you, Miss Palmer."

Eleanor squelched the tiny flare of hope that sparked in her breast as the butler brought the letter to her. It could *not* be from Nathaniel. If she even entertained the notion that it might be, she would be sorely disappointed to discover a note from her parents or, perhaps, from Lady Jane, inquiring after her well-being.

"Thank you, Mr. Covey," she said as he handed her the note, her fingers trembling only a little. She turned it over, and her heart flipped over as the scribbled lettering on the front came into view.

"I must say, if the fellow hadn't told me it was for you, I'd never have known," Mr. Covey remarked, his expression censorious. "I can scarce make out the script at all."

Laughter bubbled up in her throat, wild and exuberant, making her cheeks hurt with the effort to suppress it—for the source of the butler's complaint was easily discernible. The letter was addressed in the scrawled hand she'd come to know so well:

Miss Eleanor Palmer, Auxleigh Hall, Northamptonshire

Joy warred with apprehension as she broke the seal on the note, unfolded it, and read:

My dearest Erato,

There are no words sufficient to express the depth of my regret at having deceived you. Though I dare not hope you will give it and know I scarce deserve it, I humbly beg your forgiveness. You hold my heart in your hands.

I anxiously await your answer.

Nathaniel

He awaited her answer. Could that mean—? "Is the footman waiting for a response, Mr. Covey?"

"Yes, miss. I left him in the entry hall. Shall I wait for you to—"

But Eleanor was already passing by him and heading for the door. By the time she reached the hall, she had broken into a dead run.

She skidded to a stop on the white-and-black-tiled floor of the large foyer. Her heavy breath echoed in the sparsely furnished space, most of the more expensive pieces having been sold off in the past several years to cover her brother's Oxford tuition. The room was deserted.

Disappointment twisted her lips into a frown as she turned back toward the library. The butler strode toward her.

"He's not here, Mr. Covey."

"I'm sorry, Miss. He said he would wait."

Eleanor sighed. So much for her foolish idea that Nathaniel himself had come. He'd not only sent a servant in his stead, he hadn't even chosen a reliable one.

Well, she couldn't take the same chance. There was only one thing to be done.

"Mr. Covey, order the coach made ready. Aunt Eppie and I will be returning to London this afternoon."

Eleanor opened the door to her bedchamber and rushed to the wardrobe. Aunt Eppie had been taken aback by her niece's sudden decision to go back to London, but had agreed readily enough. Now, there was no time to be lost in packing. As late as it would be when they made their departure, they would not arrive until the day after tomorrow. That seemed an impossibly long time.

Grabbing an armful of gowns, Eleanor turned to toss them on the bed. And stopped cold.

For reclining there, in all his leanly muscled, naked splendor, was Nathaniel St. Clair.

Her mouth dropped open, and the dresses fell to the floor in a multicolored heap. "How—what are you doing here?"

Nathaniel propped himself up on his elbow and gestured at his nude body. "I think it should be obvious I am waiting for you."

Likely, she should have been angered by his audacity, by his complete disregard for propriety and convention. But that was Nathaniel. When had he ever cared for what people thought of him or what the rules told him he could or couldn't do?

And wasn't that quality one of the reasons she loved him?

Laughing, she threw herself into his welcoming arms. "This is becoming a habit, you know."

"I told you I was a man who believed in taking advantage of his opportunities." He chuckled and pulled her tighter into his embrace.

She snuggled her face tighter to his bare chest, not quite believing he wasn't a figment of her imagination. But his unmistakable tangy musk in her nostrils and the radiant heat of his flesh against her skin convinced her he was real. If her fantasies had been half as vivid as this, she wouldn't have been so miserable these past weeks.

Lifting her head, she looked down into his chiseled features and frowned in mock reprove. "You're very confident of yourself, my lord. Did you really think I'd forgive you so easily?"

He traced a finger along her jaw. "I had hopes. Have you?"

"Forgiven you? Yes. Though I'd still like to know why you didn't tell me. Why you let me believe I had to choose between you and Mathews when you're the same person."

Nathaniel brushed a stray curl back from her forehead and shook his head. "I never meant you to choose. I only wanted . . ." He paused and gave a small harrumph of self-reproach. "It sounds ridiculous now even to my own ears, but I thought if you knew I was Clarence Mathews, you'd want me for the wrong reasons. That you'd marry me only for what's up here . . ." He pointed to his temple. ". . . and not for what's down here." Taking her hand, he guided her fingers down between his legs.

She wrapped her fingers around the smooth length of his cock. He sucked in his breath as she squeezed gently. His shaft stiffened perceptibly at the simple touch, causing an answering twinge between her thighs.

"It doesn't sound ridiculous at all," she admitted with a wry smile. "The Eleanor Palmer who came to visit you in your study was terrified of her baser needs. And Nathaniel St. Clair awakened every one of them."

His fingers reached for the buttons at the back of her muslin gown. "And now?"

"Now, Eleanor Palmer knows there's nothing base about love."

"And do you love me, Eleanor Palmer?"

Her chest swelled with emotion, so powerful she feared her rib cage would crack, and she nodded. "Oh yes."

His eyes searched hers, as if probing for some tangible proof of her claim. "I am a man of strong appetites, Eleanor. I enjoyed living up to my reputation for wickedness and debauchery. It gave me great pleasure. But I will gladly give up all but one of my vices for you. You have only to agree to join me in the pursuit of that one vice for the rest of our lives."

She grinned down at him. "As long as the vice you're referring to involves this . . ." she murmured, tightening her grip around his cock, "I suggest we get started right away."

He grabbed both sides of her bodice and pulled it apart, sending buttons flying. They clattered to the polished floor like tiny hailstones. "I thought you'd never ask."

As she rose to her knees to help him divest her of her gown, a troubling thought niggled at the back of her brain. "Nathaniel?"

At her querying tone, he stopped in the midst of baring her breasts. "Yes, darling?"

"Is it true, what they say?"

He raised an eyebrow. "Probably. What do they say?"

"That you . . ." Her cheeks grew flame-hot as the images painted on the walls at the Red Door came unbidden to her mind. The shocking, tantalizing pictures of men fornicating with other men. She swallowed hard, and her voice dropped to a choked whisper. "That you carry on with men as well as women."

His eyes widened, and he brushed the backs of his knuckles over her cheek. "Would it concern you if I said it was?"

She bit her lower lip as the ache in her belly intensified. There was no denying the idea—in the abstract—didn't trouble her at all. To the contrary, it aroused her.

However, the notion of Nathaniel with anyone but her caused a bitter taste in her mouth. She knew she could satisfy his need for a woman. But if he needed men, too—that she could not fulfill.

She took an unsteady breath. "Only if you'll miss that. If it means I won't be . . . enough for you. I couldn't bear it if . . ."

His expression sobered, and he pulled her face down to brush a sweet, reassuring kiss across her lips. "I love you, Eleanor, and when I marry you, I shall promise to forsake all others 'til death do us part. And I will mean it, but if you cannot trust me to do that, the sex of my previous lovers hardly matters."

Her heart soared at his obvious sincerity. She did trust him, though doing so seemed to defy all logic.

And yet, perhaps it made perfect sense. For where most men revealed their faults to their wives only after the wedding vows were spoken, Nathaniel had concealed his best qualities and dared her instead to love him, warts and all

She pressed her mouth to the sensitive spot just below his ear, and he shivered. "Yes, I trust you. I believe I've always known I could trust you."

"Really?" Laughter rumbled in his chest. "That was very foolish of you. I could have done you serious harm, you know."

Eleanor shook her head, her love for him stretching even broader and wider than before. "But you didn't. You could have, but you didn't. When you let me leave your study that afternoon, I knew there was a streak of goodness in you, even if you didn't. And I wasn't wrong. But as much as I love your goodness, I love your wickedness even more." She rolled her hips across the hard ridge trapped between their bodies. "So, don't stop being wicked."

Like a drowsing cat roused to action by a rustle of leaves in the bushes, Nathaniel moved with astonishing speed. The fingers of one hand twisted into the hem of her chemise, pulling it up around her waist, while the other slid into the opening in her drawers to find her slick and ready. "If there's one thing I can promise, it's that I'll always be wicked for you."

And then he rolled her beneath him and showed her just how wicked he could be.

SCANDALOUSLY
EVER AFTER

1

London, England—July, 1816

"Are you prepared to make a choice for the evening, sir?"

Calliope detected a hint of diffidence beneath the impatience in the madam's tone and wondered at it, but couldn't tear her gaze from the gentleman to whom Mrs. Upshaw's words were directed. A new client, he was making his fourth circuit of the Red Door's voluptuously appointed sitting room—prowling, really—examining each of the available ladies with a level of scrutiny that bordered on obsessive. As if he were assessing their prospects not as bedmates for the night, but as partners for a lifetime.

The thought made her shiver, though whether with fear or anticipation, she wasn't sure.

Certainly, it wasn't his rugged good looks or fine manners or expensive attire that affected her. Years of working in London's most exclusive brothel had rendered Calliope proof against the charms of the handsome, cultivated, wealthy gentlemen who frequented the place. She might be a better class of whore than those who walked the streets or plied their trade in the squalid cribs around the docks, but she was a whore nonetheless. And whores knew better than to allow themselves to imagine a future of any kind.

Of course, they weren't *all* handsome and cultivated, she reminded herself, a tiny smile tugging at the corners of her mouth. The only requirement for bringing one's custom to the Red Door was ready cash, and plenty of it. A few hours with Mrs. Upshaw's girls came dear, but customers came anyway and didn't complain. Calliope's smile grew a little wider and stronger at the double entendre.

At just that moment, the gentleman stopped in front of her divan. Their eyes met, and the smile died on her lips. Irises the color of thunderclouds ringed bottomless black pupils, and within their depths, a storm raged. Hot. Hungry. Haunted.

Her heart and stomach constricted as those eyes pinned her, trapped her in their steely embrace. Yet she didn't flinch, didn't blink. He challenged her to look away, to show distaste or fear, but Calliope was too proud—and too foolhardy—for that.

After several long, tense moments, he broke the connection and flicked his gaze to Mrs. Upshaw.

"This one," he said, nodding toward Calliope. His voice was a contradictory mixture of gravel and satin—the tone rough, the accent refined. "For a week."

Calliope let out the breath she hadn't been aware of holding in a surprised rush. *A week?*

"A week?" Mrs. Upshaw's scandalized words echoed Calliope's thoughts. "I'm sorry, sir, but such an arrangement is out of the question. I simply cannot dedicate one of my . . ."

The madam trailed off, for as she spoke, the gentleman removed the bulging coin purse from his waist and crossed to where she stood near the sitting room's entry. When he reached her, he upended the pouch's contents alongside the book that rested, open and facedown, upon her divan.

"A week. Day and night. Take it or leave it."

Mrs. Upshaw's tongue darted out to lick her bright red lips, a combination of excitement and avarice sparkling in her shrewd eyes at the bounty laid out before her. Though Calliope could not count them from her vantage, there must be at least fifty coins there, all of them gold guineas. As much as the house as a whole earned in a week.

Her heart pounded furiously against her ribs. A week. Day and night. Why? Men frequented places like the Red Door for variety, not constancy. Even her "regular" customers sampled the wares of the other girls.

Uneasy awareness prickled the back of her neck, made her palms damp. She recalled the madam's slight hesitation when speaking to him, the turbulent sea of emotion that swirled in his eyes. He might be a gentleman in the technical sense of the word, but he exuded a raw, barely leashed energy unlike anything she'd ever encountered. Curiosity leapt inside her like a cat pouncing on a ball of string, the need to unravel the mystery as involuntary as breathing.

Mrs. Upshaw looked from the pile of coins to Calliope, her slightly raised eyebrows communicating the question. *Yes or no?* The madam never forced her girls to accept a client, and she wouldn't now, even with a moderate fortune riding on the decision.

As if there could be any real doubt . . .

Calliope raised her chin a notch, and Mrs. Upshaw smiled. "As you wish, sir." She bent down and scooped the coins into a tighter pile. "Calliope will show you upstairs."

Calliope rose from her divan in the languorous, elegant fashion she'd been taught in emulation of a fine lady's manners. Catching the gentleman's turbulent gaze, she tilted her head toward the doorway that led to the stairwell and her room. His nostrils flared and his eyes widened at the sight of her, for once she stood, the true transparency of her gown was readily apparent, and he could now make out the lines and curves of the body he had purchased with expert precision. And he liked what he saw.

The familiar thrill of pursuit thrummed to life in her belly, and her tongue darted out to moisten her drying lips. She reveled in the moment when a man revealed, through the smallest of spontaneous reactions, the power she wielded by simple virtue of being female.

And this was a man worth having power over.

She allowed her hips to sway a trifle more than usual as he followed her, aware that her friends watched her with a mixture of envy and relief. For though they would have liked to be the ones to earn a cut of that bounty, none of them wanted to commit to a week with a stranger who might or might not have "proclivities."

But the former Callie James—born in the Seven Dials and raised on the streets of London—could handle anything. Unlike her companions, she hadn't fallen from higher circumstances into this life. Instead, this life had raised her up, made her more than the daughter of a ragpicker and a scullery maid could ever dream.

The sounds of coitus were easily distinguishable when they entered the narrow hallway.

"Is it always like this?" From the way he grumbled the question, she assumed he meant the noise level, though it wasn't something a customer had ever complained oft before. If anything, they seemed to like it, the guttural cries and deep moans whetting their appetites for their own impending satisfaction.

She drew up in front of her room. "In the hallway, yes. Inside the rooms, no."

"Good." With that gruff, monosyllabic answer, he reached for the knob and opened the door. "After you."

Once they were both inside, he shoved the door shut behind him with a loud thud. Calliope turned to face him, preparing to ask what he would like her to do first. Most men chose to be sucked, although a few skipped right to the main event. She preferred the ones who enjoyed a bit more preamble, as she found the fucking considerably more pleasurable when she'd had a chance to work up to it, and sucking cock excited her.

She thought sucking *this* man's cock would excite her even more than usual.

"Strip and get in bed," he ordered, his voice flat as he opened the buttons of his dark blue coat.

She suppressed a sigh of disappointment. So he was one of those who went straight for the crotch. A pity, that.

The filmy white gown came undone by two simple fasteners at her shoulders and slid to the floor around her feet. Nude, she stepped out of the frothy white circle and crossed to the bed. She sat on the edge and watched in silence as he undressed.

The removal of his coat revealed the outline of well-defined biceps, a trim waist, and an undeniable bulge beneath the fall of his buff-colored breeches. Already, she approved.

He unwrapped his snowy cravat and draped it over her armchair, then unbuttoned and took off his waistcoat, a tastefully brocaded dark blue silk that matched to perfection the hue, if not the fabric, of his wool coat. Next, the shirt came off over his head, and Calliope couldn't hold back a sharp intake of breath.

A long, deeply puckered scar ran diagonally across his finely muscled torso, from a spot a few inches above his navel to just below his left nipple. Her chest grew tight in sympathy for the pain that wound must have caused when it was fresh. This man, now so physically hale and hearty, had once been very close to death.

For some perverse reason, the thought brought the sting of tears to the corner of her eyes.

How absurd! She blinked rapidly to banish the sensation. Whores didn't grow sentimental over their clients. Especially ones they hadn't even fucked yet.

If he heard her gasp, he didn't acknowledge it. Instead, he sat on the chair and pulled off his boots. When he was done, he stood and, still wearing his breeches and stockings, crossed to the mantle where a large lamp provided most of the light for the room. He blew out the flame, leaving only the small fire burning in the hearth to provide illumination.

"Lie down." He stalked back to the bed, his muscular frame seeming even more impressive as he towered above her in the flickering glow.

Irritation flashed through her. *Do this, do that!* Never had she been so ordered about in her life, not even as a scullery maid. Most men were more polite that this, even with prostitutes.

"You're still wearing your breeches," she objected. Of course, he didn't have to take them off to fuck her, but usually . . .

This was all so odd, so unaccountable.

He raked a hand through his hair. It was the color, she thought, of beach sand. Or what she imagined beach sand would look like, for of course she had never been to the shore.

"Let me worry about that. Just lie down." He didn't sound angry. He seemed more resigned than anything.

What harm could it do? She swung her legs up off the floor and reclined onto the pillows.

"Under the blankets. And scoot over."

When she had done so, he climbed in beside her, leaned back, and closed his eyes.

As the seconds ticked by, Calliope's bewilderment grew. He made no move to touch her. He did not ask her to touch him. In fact, he did nothing at all but recline there, his rough-hewn features softening slightly with each passing moment.

Finally, she could bear the suspense no longer. "What now?" she demanded.

He cracked an eyelid and rolled a dark gray eyeball at her. "Now, we go to sleep."

Sleep? In the name of bloody Christ on a biscuit, he *had* to be joking. Surely no man, not even a wealthy one, would pay fifty guineas to actually *sleep* with a woman.

But he certainly didn't seem to be in jest. His eyes closed again, and he shifted his upper body against the pillow as if to get more comfortable. Before long, his breathing evened out, and the tension leached out of his face.

Calliope stared at the ceiling, dumbfounded. Just what sort of madman had she tied herself to for the next seven days?

2

Cannon fire. Confusion. Men shouting, calling out, screaming. The acrid smell of gunpowder and smoke and blood. So much blood.

Jack jerked awake, heart pounding, bathed in icy sweat. It took him a few seconds, as it always did when he awoke from one of these nightmares, to get his bearings. His pulse slowed as he realized where he was. The brothel. In bed with the gorgeous blonde harlot who'd been bold enough to look him in the eyes and hold his gaze.

Few people could.

She still slept. Which meant he hadn't humiliated himself by crying out before he woke.

And judging by the deep red glow of the embers in the fire, he'd been out for hours, longer than he'd managed in a single stretch for weeks.

He looked over at his bed partner. Calliope. Certainly not her real name, but it suited her nonetheless. He could imagine a man being moved to poetry by her beauty.

A man other than him, of course. Lieutenant Colonel Jack Prescott was accustomed to spouting commands, not verse.

He tossed off the blankets and rolled gently off the bed. The room had cooled considerably, and he crept closer to the hearth before he stripped off his damp clothing. His pulse slowed as the nightmare-induced panic began to subside, but what came next would be worse.

The names. The faces. The last words of every one of the men he'd sent to certain death. All 278 of them.

He folded himself to a sitting position on the rug in front of the fireplace and waited for the show that played over and over in his mind to begin.

But inexplicably, it didn't.

Instead, his thoughts turned to *her*. His lips twitched as he recalled her consternation when he'd ordered her not to service him, but to sleep.

It hadn't been easy. He was honest enough with himself to admit he wanted her. Watching her sway up the stairs without grabbing a generous handful of her arse had been an exercise in self-denial the likes of which he hadn't experienced since he and his men had been dug in behind enemy lines with nothing to eat for a week but stale bread and beans.

But he hadn't come for sex. He'd come for sleep, something that had persistently eluded him since resigning his commission two months ago.

At first, he thought the memories were keeping him awake, the dreams that caused him to sleep only in brief, fitful snatches. But then the real reason dawned on him. He had become so accustomed to being surrounded by his men—in barracks or tents or holes in the ground—he could no longer sleep alone.

Once he realized what he needed was a bed partner, the solution had seemed obvious. Hire one. And where better to find such a companion than a brothel?

The possibility that he'd want to do something *other* than sleep hadn't occurred to him. Not that he was normally immune to the charms of beautiful women, of course, but he expected his bone-deep exhaustion to win out over lust for at least a few days, if not the entire week.

He glanced over at the bed. Her hair spread out across the pillow like ripe wheat. Her lips bore the reddish-pink tinge of a sweet, fresh apple set against the creamy hue of her skin. The upper half of one breast, the color and size of a peach, peeked over the top of the blankets. She was a banquet, and he'd more than paid for the privilege to feast.

Nor was she likely to object if he woke her. It was said that Madam Upshaw had only three requirements for the girls she hired. First, they must be beautiful. Second, they must be intelligent, capable of maintaining a conversation with a gentleman should that meet with his desires. Third, and most important, they must like to fuck.

His cock twitched and stretched. He'd seen genuine interest—equal parts curiosity and desire—in her indigo eyes earlier this evening. If he crawled into the bed and slipped his fingers between her thighs, he was sure she would be wet and ready for him within minutes. And when he sank into her, she would moan with pleasure and wrap her legs around him and arch to meet his every thrust until . . .

He jerked from his fantasy as he caught himself listing toward the floor.

God, he was tired. And for this one night, the ever-present ghosts seemed content not to haunt him. His eyelids felt like a dead man's, coins pressed upon them to hold them down.

Dry again and warmed by the heat from the crackling embers, he forced himself to his feet and stumbled back to the bed.

Indulgence in sexual pleasure was for men who slept each night in peace and awoke each morning with a clean conscience.

Not for Lieutenant Colonel Jack Prescott, soldier, commander, and agent of death.

He floated on a cloud of erotic sensation. Wet heat engulfed his cock. *Pussy or mouth?* Mouth, he decided drowsily as a tongue circled the glans, then stroked down along the underside of the shaft.

His hands fisted in thick, silky hair, guiding the head up and down to elicit the greatest pleasure. Strands of it escaped his fingers, brushing against and tickling his thighs.

Thick, liquid desire curled up inside his balls. Fuck, he was going to come.

Why couldn't he have dreams like this more often? He hadn't had dreams like this since he'd been a randy—and distinctly virginal—youth. And they'd never been this vivid. Hell, even his nightmares weren't this real . . .

He struggled from the fog of slumber. This was no dream. His fists curled in real, wheat-blonde hair, and he was thrusting his cock between the lush, apple-red lips of the most accomplished mouth he'd ever had the privilege to fuck.

His mind rebelled. He hadn't asked for this.

But his body was well ahead of his sleep-addled brain, fully engaged in the act and determined to finish with or without his blessing. She fondled his tightening balls, then pressed two fingers against the tight band of flesh below the sacs. As if she'd pulled a trigger, the expert touch catapulted him into orgasm.

He grabbed her head tight to hold her steady as he came in long, wrenching spurts that lifted his hips from the bed, pushing his cock to the back of her throat. His breath shuddered out in deep, violent pants at the exquisite intensity of the pleasure.

So good. Unbelievably fucking good.

He was dimly aware that he was giving her no choice but to

take his seed, but he couldn't let her go, couldn't stop driving into the warm, welcoming embrace of her mouth.

Damn it. *This* was why he couldn't be with a woman, shouldn't be with a woman. He was a beast, a brute who forced others to his will.

With a grunt of self-loathing, he released her head and dropped his arms to his sides. And then dug his fingers into the mattress when she kept right on suckling and swallowing. When it was over, she lifted her head and gave the head of his cock a last, savoring lick before sliding up to stretch out alongside him with a sigh that sounded curiously like satisfaction.

He rolled up onto his side to look down at her. "Why did you do that?"

A small, enigmatic smile touched her lips. "You seemed to need it." She lifted her shoulders in a shrug, her eyes wide and guileless.

The gesture drew his gaze to her delectable breasts. This close, they reminded him even more of a pair of peaches than before. Round and firm, covered in golden, velvety skin. Would they taste as sweet as they looked? His mouth watered, and a jolt of lust spiked through his gut. God, how could he want more when she'd just sucked him through an orgasm that should have left him weak and sated for days?

What the hell was wrong with him?

Jack prided himself on his self-control, especially when it came to women. Officers who thought with their pricks instead of their brains inevitably got themselves—and everyone else— into trouble. Like the commanding officer of the regiment who'd fallen for a pretty peasant girl in Brittany, only to discover she was passing information to the French. That hadn't ended well for anyone.

"The only thing I need is sleep," he said, his rising irritation making his tone harsher than he intended. "If I want anything else, I'll tell you."

She rose up on one elbow, her half smile broadening into a grin. "I assure you, sir, you told me in the most emphatic terms what you needed." She laid her hand over his penis, which rested, still semierect, against his abdomen. Semierect became considerably more erect in a matter of seconds.

"When a lady wakes up with one of these . . ." Her fingers traced along the sides and grazed the head, and he bit the inside of his cheek to stifle a groan. ". . . poking her arse . . ." She wrapped her palm around him and squeezed him gently but firmly.

Like a good soldier, his cock snapped instantly to full attention. *No, bad soldier!* The admonition did no good, however. His shaft pulsed in her grasp, ready and willing for combat.

". . . she knows precisely what the man attached to it needs." Her eyes met his, her indigo irises reduced to slivers around deep, dark pupils. "What she wants to know is whether he is man enough to admit it." She said the words with just enough cheek, enough playfulness, that he couldn't take offense.

And what she was doing with her hand. . . . Already, another climax threatened to erupt, and she'd only just begun.

He emitted a muffled curse. Why the hell was he resisting this? He wasn't in the military any more. He could fuck any woman he pleased. And right now, this woman pleased him.

God, how long had it been since he'd really enjoyed being with a woman, savoring all the tastes and textures of a woman's body, reveling in the soft sounds of her pleasure? He closed his eyes. Since before the war. So long, he could scarcely remember what it was like.

Maybe she was right. Maybe this was exactly what he needed.

But this time, he would do it *his* way.

3

_____

For a heart-stopping second, she wondered if teasing this man hadn't been a rather grave mistake. No sooner had she spoken the words than she was pinned beneath his hard-muscled body, wrists trapped above her head in a steely grip, gaze captured by a pair of storm-darkened eyes. Her breath stuck in her chest. Perhaps he was not just troubled, but violent.

But then she caught it—a glint of humor beneath the dark edge of pain and hunger—and her heart thudded against her ribs with relief. She wasn't in danger . . . yet.

"And what _he_ wants to know," the man who loomed above her teased, dark and possessed of a devilishly carnal grin, "is whether the lady in question knows what she is letting herself in for."

And then he shifted slightly, dipped his sandy head, and sucked her left nipple into his mouth. As if echoing the thunderstorm in his eyes, lightning arced from her breast to her pussy. He laved and nibbled the first bud until it was pebble hard, then repeated the procedure on the other nipple until she was aching and breathless and . . . needy.

It wasn't supposed to happen this way.

Calliope was always in control, even when she pretended otherwise. Ever since she'd sucked her first cock, she'd always gained her pleasure from giving it, from knowing she could make the strongest, most powerful man weak with lust . . . lust for her, the rag-and-bone picker's daughter.

But this man . . . Oh, sainted Mary Magdalene, he made her forget to be Calliope. Made her forget everything except the tumult that followed in the wake of his lips, his teeth, his tongue. Her pulse hammered helplessly in her throat and beneath his tight grasp on her wrists. Throbbing, wet heat flooded her pussy, and she writhed and squirmed under him, though whether she was trying to gain escape or get closer, she wasn't sure.

She couldn't let this happen. Oh, she could let him fuck her. But these tantalizing flicks of his tongue at her breast and the sweet caress of his fingers as he traced each protrusion of her rib cage were too intimate, too . . . affectionate. As if he cared about her pleasure rather than simply taking his own.

No, this had to be stopped. Before every barrier she'd constructed to separate her soul from her body fell beneath this tender assault.

Push him and he'll break.

"Oh, please, sir," she moaned, "fuck me now. I can wait no longer."

A chuckle rumbled deep in his chest, and the sound raised goose bumps on her flesh. He lifted his head and looked up at her, his mouth turned down at the corners in mock reproof.

"Now, now, you started this. 'Tis hardly fair to give a man a taste to whet his appetite and then deny him the satisfaction of his meal." He broke eye contact and let his gaze slide suggestively down the length of her torso to rest on the tumble of tawny curls between her thighs.

Alarm rippled up her spine as she recognized his intention. He wanted to do to *there* what he'd done to her breasts. Lick her, tease her with his teeth and tongue. The thought made her pussy clench and her clitoris throb with arousal, but her stomach skittered nervously.

She'd already lost control, and she'd never regain her equilibrium if she let him pleasure her like that. As if she were something more to him than a mere vessel on which to achieve his own release.

But she could hardly say no. If this was what he wanted to do, then it was her duty to accommodate him. All she had to do was remember she permitted it for him, not for herself, and she would be safe.

"I would never wish it to be said that I allowed a man to go hungry," she replied, her voice sounding throaty and tremulous to her ears.

Though just a few hours ago, she would have deemed him devoid of a sense of humor, his eyes fairly twinkled with it now. "Ah, then you are a wise woman."

"Wise?"

He wiggled his eyebrows. "You know the route to a man's heart is by way of his mouth."

It was a jest, of course, but the bottom dropped out of her stomach nonetheless. She didn't want his—or any man's—heart, only their cocks and the money they paid for her services. But something about this man tugged at her in ways she didn't want to acknowledge, made her almost wish he could love her.

Oh, what rubbish was she thinking? She was addled because he had bought her for a week and paid so much. And perhaps because he was a bit more handsome, considerably more compelling, and a great deal more skilled than most of the men she bedded. It had been a long time since she had been with any man who wanted more than a quick suck and fuck. The irregularity of the situation was making her strange and sentimental . . . that was all.

She had no more time to consider the ridiculousness of her responses, because he released her wrists and slid his body down between her legs, forcing her to spread them wider to accommodate the breadth of his shoulders. Settling on his elbows, he ran his palms up along the sensitive flesh of her inner thighs. His callused skin, like his stormy eyes, belied his gentleman's facade, and she wondered again at the contrast, but quickly abandoned all thought as the gentle abrasion of his touch raised goose bumps in its wake.

She trembled as his fingers reached her core and brushed over the soft folds. His breath teased her, made promises he didn't seem in any hurry to keep. Instead, he grazed her labia with tantalizing strokes of his fingertips, each time venturing closer to her aching clitoris until she had to bite her lip and clutch the sheets to keep from begging.

Please, touch me. Lick me. Make me come.

She held back the words, but not the sob of frustration that welled in her throat. He raised his head just enough to meet her eyes, and she gasped at the blatant hunger she saw in their depths. Primitive and predatory, as though he intended in truth to devour her. Her heart thudded a precarious rhythm, fueled by a dizzying combination of lust and apprehension.

He ran his thumb down her slit, then parted her lips with both hands, exposing the hot, wet center of her to the cool air. "Ripe and juicy as a summer peach," he muttered thickly. "Are you as sweet as you look, *mignon?*"

She hadn't been sweet since she was fifteen, but it didn't matter. His gaze never left hers as he lowered his mouth and delivered a long, savoring lick just where she wanted it. Her cunt convulsed at the contact, already so close to climax from mere anticipation that this single touch was nearly enough to throw her over the edge.

"Mmmm." The appreciative murmur rumbled from his chest. "Better than the finest fruit."

He dropped his gaze and buried his face deep in her pussy. And, oh God, devour was the right word for what he did to her then, because she was swallowed whole by the intensity of sensation as he swirled her clitoris with steady, certain strokes of his tongue. His movements were precise and unerring, as if he knew instinctively how much stimulation would be too little or too much.

Her breath left her in short, sharp pants, "Ah, ah, ah," like little puffs of steam escaping from under the lid of a boiling teapot, but the release of air did nothing to relieve the pressure that built beneath his mouth. And then there was nothing she could do to hold back the storm that raced through her as her climax burst over her.

He grabbed her hips and pulled her pussy tight to his mouth, sweeping his tongue across her clitoris again and again as she came, so long and hard the pleasure mingled with pain. Hot tears stung in the corners of her eyes and she arched and twisted beneath him, desperate for more, desperate for respite. But even when the shuddering had ceased, he didn't end his assault, and before she had time to think how strange this was, she was coming again, the climax emanating from someplace deep inside her she hadn't even realized existed.

A place that might be very close to her heart.

Sweet Mary Magdalene. She was in so much more danger than she'd ever dreamed possible.

4

Jack lifted his head and wiped his mouth with the back of his hand. A profound sense of peace descended over him as he looked down at the woman he'd just finished pleasuring. Her face was flushed, her respiration rapid and shallow, her pink-tipped nipples still pebbled and rosy in the aftermath of arousal, her hair spread out around her like a fallen angel's halo.

How long had it been since he had done something considerate for another human being, with no thought either of consequence or recompense? Since forever, it seemed. Since the day he bought his commission and became the commander of men, demander of sacrifice.

For once, he would be the one to make the sacrifice. A small one—insignificant in the scheme of things—and yet, the idea held powerful, potent symbolism for him. A break with the past. A new beginning.

Giving without taking.

Levering himself up, he stretched out alongside her, pulling her to him until her head rested in the cradle of his shoulder. Her hair flowed across his skin like fresh spring water, bright and refreshing. He ignored the pulsing ache of his cock, the near bursting fullness of his balls. Closing his eyes, he simply reveled in the musky sweet scent of her skin, in the quiet satisfaction of holding a beautiful woman in his arms.

He might have drifted off to sleep in short order if her fingers hadn't snaked down his abdomen and wrapped around his cock. Damn, but she was a persistent little thing. He grabbed her wrist, extracted himself from her grasp.

She heaved an exasperated sigh. "I do not understand you at all, sir. You have paid a fortune for my body, yet you do not avail yourself."

"I assure you, I have availed myself to my satisfaction."

"Nonsense," she retorted. "You are hard as a poker."

Cracking an eyelid, he fixed her with the single-eyed stare that stopped the petty skirmishes amongst his men as quick as gunshot. "The condition is hardly permanent. I expect I shall survive."

Unlike his battle-hardened men, she didn't flinch, refused to look away. She met his stony-eyed gaze dead on, without a hint of fear or hesitation. "I never said you would not. I simply do not understand why you choose to suffer when 'tis clearly unnecessary."

Without even realizing it, she had found the knife and twisted it inside his gut. "The only thing I am suffering from is lack of sleep."

"When men wish to sleep, they generally do it in their own beds. And they certainly don't pay to do it with a whore in a brothel."

It was his turn to flinch. For no reason he could fathom, he didn't like to hear her refer to herself as a whore. And perhaps that was why his next words tumbled from his lips. "I can't sleep alone."

She was silent for so long, he wasn't sure she had heard him. Or that, if she had, she was so stunned by his cowardly admission, she couldn't think of anything to say. Perhaps she was so appalled, she was trying to contrive a means to escape from their bargain.

Just when he was certain she would castigate him for his childish fear of the dark or monsters beneath the bed, she draped her arm across his chest and snuggled in tighter to his shoulder. "Then you shan't."

He blinked in surprise, but breathed his relief. She wouldn't leave him to face his demons alone. He tightened his arm around her and held her close, fiercely grateful for her acceptance. Although why the approval of a prostitute, even an obviously educated, expensive one, should matter to him, he couldn't say.

"There is one thing, though," she murmured drowsily after several minutes had passed.

"Mmmm, what is that?"

"Your name. If we are going to spend a week together, I don't think I can go on calling you 'sir.' "

Combing his fingers through her silken hair, he chuckled sleepily at her entirely accurate observation. "Prescott. Lieu—no, *Mr.* Jack Prescott."

5

Callie woke to a crick in her neck and a loud rumble in her belly. Judging by the insistence of her hunger, she had overslept the breakfast bell by quite some time.

Prescott sprawled beside her, his jaggedly cut, compelling features relaxed in sleep to a near boyish quality. At some point during the night, they had drawn apart from their initial embrace, and had wound up face-to-face, his arm draped over her waist, her leg thrown over his hip.

Her stomach protested again, louder than before. Prescott didn't stir at the sound, but if she didn't extract herself soon, she would wake him. At first, she hadn't believed him when he said he couldn't sleep alone, for he had not exhibited so much as a hint of weakness since the moment she had laid eyes on him. But then she'd remembered the haunted, hollow look in his eyes and knew it must be due, in some measure, to lack of sleep. A condition she ought to have recognized before, having suffered from it herself during those first lonely weeks on the streets before Mrs. Upshaw had found her and brought her to safety.

And if that was the case, she should leave him in peace while she went down to the room for breakfast. She could get herself a quick bite and bring him something to eat when she returned. She wouldn't be gone long.

After easing her leg from atop him, she lifted his arm and wriggled her way out from underneath. Sliding off the bottom of the bed, she crept behind the screen to use the chamber pot, wincing as the sound of water hitting porcelain seemed to echo in the small room.

To her relief, he still slept soundly when she came out to don her gown. On any other morning, she would have gone down-stairs in a more traditional day gown, not her working dress, but she didn't want to open the squeaky wardrobe drawer and risk waking him. The girls who were still in the dining room would tease her relentlessly and Harvey, the still pimple-faced adolescent footman who waited the morning table for them, would blush to his ears at the sight of her.

She tiptoed to the door and slipped out into the hall, sparing one last glance for the sleeping man in her bed before she closed it softly behind her.

When she entered the dining room, nine pairs of eyes set in nine of the loveliest faces in London snapped up from half-eaten plates of food, half-drunk cups of coffee, and half-read morning papers. And that was peculiar, for it was exceedingly rare for the entire upstairs staff—as Mrs. Upshaw was fond of calling her Cyprians—to take the morning or afternoon meal together. Normally, the girls came and went as they pleased, with the footmen serving fresh food from the kitchen when they arrived and clearing up after them when they left. Breakfast was served between half-past nine and eleven in the mornings, lunch from two until half-past three. Only dinner was served in sit-down fashion, and that for the simple reason that everyone had to be done eating before customers began arriving at nine.

Even more peculiar, the entire assembly studied her with rapt attention. At first she wondered at this, but when young Harvey's cheeks bloomed like a red, red rose at the sight of her, she remembered she wore her evening gown.

Shrugging to herself, she took the empty seat between Niobe and Europa, and nodded to Harvey, who promptly disappeared through the swinging door to fetch her plate.

Leda—nee Miss Lucy Craddock-Jones, who had found her way from a pampered upbringing in Berkshire to the Red Door by way of an unfortunate liaison with not one, but two of the family's grooms, both of whom she had been entertaining when her father returned early from his morning ride after his horse had thrown a shoe—was the first, as usual, to find her tongue. "Well, well, well, here is Sleeping Beauty at last. And none the worse for wear, it would appear. I told you she had come to no harm, that he wasn't the sort for that."

"You did not think so last night," Electra, the Red Door's newest hire, shot back. So new, she introduced herself as Elizabeth to customers half the time and rarely remembered to respond to her new, more ethereal appellation. "You were just as afraid of him as the rest of us."

Leda crossed her arms over her ample breasts. "I was not."

"You were until you saw all those bright, shiny coins," Phoebe, whose real name actually was Phoebe, retorted before popping another piece of scone in her mouth. "Then your eyes all but tumbled out of your head."

Daphne, the only Cyprian who had worked for Mrs. Upshaw longer than Callie, rolled her eyes. "All our eyes did, Phoeb. That was a right fortune." Her expression turned dreamy. "Enough to retire on."

"Which is precisely the problem, if you ask me." Niobe had come to work at the Red Door only recently, but she had a long and storied history in London's exclusive brothels. Nancy Hewitt, as she'd once been known, had shagged more members of Parliament and ministry heads than the rest of them com-

bined. After a short stint as the mistress of a politically powerful but financially deficient minister of state, she'd returned to
the trade for better pay and living conditions. "What did he
want in return for that bounty?"

Callie swallowed hard as everyone turned and regarded her
with eager, expectant gazes. Though Mr. Prescott had done nothing to suggest she ought to keep his insomnia a secret, her conscience rebelled against revealing the truth. What had passed
between them last night was private. Intimate. Special. And she
wanted to hold it to herself like a map to buried treasure.

Nothing that transpired between the girls and their customers
was ever kept secret. For eight years, Callie had shared her every
thought and impression about every man she'd ever taken upstairs, and her sisters had done the same. An entirely sensible
practice, since clients seldom chose the same girl every night.
Whoever took a new customer first was practically bound by
convention to provide details of their encounter so that the
next girl he hired would know what to expect, what to offer.

But then, Prescott had hired her for a week, hadn't he? She was
under no obligation to give them any details until her time with
him was over. A sharp pain pierced her heart at the thought. When
their time was over. As it would be. As she knew it must be.

Europa nudged Callie with an elbow. "Aren't you going to
tell us?"

She bit her lip. "Well, I . . ." Damn, she had to give them something. "Just the usual."

Thetis arched an eyebrow in her characteristically French way.
"The usual, eh? Tell us, at what time did he leave?"

"He didn't," Callie admitted slowly.

"You mean—?" Maia gasped.

Calypso finished, "He's still upstairs?"

Now, nine pairs of eyes fixed upon her with nine times more
curiosity than before. Men rarely spent the entire night at the
Red Door, and when they did, it was usually an accident brought

130 / *Jackie Barbosa*

on by an excess of drink or, in a few cases, opium. Jack might have seemed odd to them all last night, even intimidating, but he had certainly not appeared intoxicated.

A leaden weight plummeted to the hollow pit of Callie's stomach. Hollow because she hadn't had a chance to take a bite from the plate of eggs and sausage Harvey had placed in front of her at some point when she hadn't been paying attention. And now, having admitted he had stayed the entire night, she would never escape their plaguing questions until she'd answered every last one.

"Oh, poor Callie, did he fuck you all night long?"

"Are you very sore?"

"No wonder you were late to breakfast. You must be exhausted."

"How many times?"

"Don't you hate it when they just pump and pump you and can't come?"

"When that happens, I always let them play backgammon with me," Daphne put in conversationally. "'Tis better to take it in the arse than have them go on 'til dawn."

"Enough!" The barrage ceased instantly at the sound of Mrs. Upshaw's commanding voice from the doorway. She glided into the now silent room in a near deafening rustle of taffeta skirts. "Do none of you recall that the gentleman purchased the right to Callie's company for a week, *day and night*? And that every moment she sits here fielding ridiculous questions from you jabbering flibbertigibbets raises the chances that she will be missed?"

Callie gasped in alarm. What if he woke, found her gone, and claimed she had violated their agreement? Would he demand his money back? That would be disastrous—for her, for the Red Door, and for all the girls at Harlowe House who depending on the brothel's profits for their education.

Hastily, she vacated her seat. "I'm sorry, Mrs. Upshaw, I wasn't thinking when I came d—"

"Sit down, child," the madam said with a wave of her hand and a benevolent smile. "I didn't mean to worry you. I only meant to silence this gaggle of gossips so you can eat your breakfast in peace and return before he awakens. They can pester you for details after you've fulfilled your promise."

Cowed by this reproach from the woman all of them considered a surrogate mother, no one said another word as Callie hastily polished off her meal. When she was done, she bid the assembled company a good morning and started out into the hall when she remembered . . .

"Harvey?" she said, turning back round to face the servant.

His wide-eyed gaze traveled up from the apex of her thighs to her face rather than the other way 'round, and then his face purpled when a quirk of her lips told him she had caught him at it. "Y-yes, ma-am?"

Poor child. He couldn't be much past seventeen, if that, and was undoubtedly an innocent in both body and spirit. How Mrs. Upshaw had ever chosen to hire him when he was so patently unqualified to work in a house of ill repute was beyond her. Privately, Callie suspected nepotism. There was something of a resemblance between them in the shape and color of his eyes. One of these days, she might take pity on the poor boy and initiate him into the secrets of the flesh, if only to save him from his own embarrassment.

Hoping to ease his discomfort, she bestowed him with a friendly smile and a wink. It wasn't as if she objected to being ogled, after all. "Would you please have a plate made up and brought to my room?"

The miserable young man nodded, his expression brightening ever so slightly. "Of course, ma'am."

After thanking him, Callie departed the dining room and

started up the back stairs. Two sets of staircases led to the floor on which the bedrooms were located—one from the parlor which was used by clients and one from the private rooms which were only used by the servants and the girls who lived in the house. Of course, this did not account for the Red Door's entire staff, for Mrs. Upshaw always kept two or three male demimonds— as she preferred to call them; "prostitute" was such an ugly word—on staff to serve the needs of clients with more eclectic tastes. None of the men lived at the house, however, for Mrs. Upshaw deemed their presence detrimental to her girls' collegiality, but instead took private lodging in the neighborhood.

Even so, when Callie opened the door from the back stairway and into the corridor, her first thought when she heard a distinctly male voice cry out was that Ganymede, Hercules, or Diomedes must be entertaining a customer. Only when that cry was followed by another, this one clearly not of pleasure but of anguish, did she realize where the sound originated.

And from whom . . .

6

Cannon fire. Confusion. Men shouting, calling out, screaming. The acrid smell of gunpowder and smoke and blood. So much blood.

And the faces. Oh God, the faces. And names.

Henry Thomas Wright. Richard David Jacoby. George Crenshaw. Michael McInerney. Isaiah Wil—

"Mr. Prescott, Mr. Prescott, wake up." A cool, dry hand caressed his sweating forehead. The voice and touch of an angel. " 'Tis only a dream."

If only it _were_ just a dream. But no, every image, every sight, sound, and smell was excruciatingly, agonizingly real.

Even so, he managed to claw his way from beneath the heavy rubble of sleep, threw off the crushing weight of memories he wanted nothing more than to forget.

Yet it was his curse, his burden to carry them.

His eyes fluttered open. She perched on the bed beside him, her unblemished brow furrowed with concern as she bent over him. The blaze burning in the fireplace lit her golden hair from behind with an ethereal glow. Her diaphanous white gown—

the same one she'd worn last night—had come undone at the shoulder and gaped away to reveal the curve of one perfect breast.

Calliope. His pulse steadied, his panic eased, his rigid muscles relaxed.

His angel was a whore. Or his whore an angel. He wasn't sure which.

Her features softened with relief. "Thank heavens you're awake." She straightened up, thereby depriving him of the lovely view. A pity.

"I'm sorry if I frightened you," he apologized, still gathering his fractured wits. Returning to the present after reliving the past so vividly was always like being pushed through a brick wall from darkness into bright light.

"Oh no, not at all," she assured him breathily, refastening the closure at her shoulder. Another pity.

And she was lying, too. She *had* been frightened. Her averted eyes told him as much.

But it wasn't his crying out in distress that had frightened her. As he shook off the last of the nightmare-induced confusion, he realized the source of her fear.

She had left him alone. Had gotten out of the bed, donned her gown, and left him. And when she had returned, he had been in the grips of his familiar, nightly torment.

Perhaps, after his admission last night that he could not sleep alone, he should be angry that she had left him, but instead, he was profoundly relieved. The memories hadn't seen fit to persecute him until after she had gone, which meant his conjecture had been accurate.

He couldn't sleep alone. But he *could* sleep, unmolested and undisturbed, if she stayed with him.

"Thank you," he murmured, clasping her upper arm in one hand. It was then he noticed the scratch on her cheek. It was red and raised, but not bleeding. "Did I do that?" he asked, brushing the injury with his thumb.

"Yes. But it's nothing," she assured him quickly. " 'Twas an accident, not done apurpose."

"Nonetheless, it must have hurt. And for that, I am sorry." He levered himself up to a sitting position. "When did you leave?" He posed the question in as neutral a tone as he could muster. If she thought he was angry or upset, she might be less than honest in her answer.

An answer he needed to know.

She folded her hands in her lap and stared at them for a second, before lifting her gaze to his again. "Perhaps twenty minutes ago. A half hour at the most. I was hungry, and you looked so peaceful that I went down—"

He pressed two fingers to her lips. Soft, plump, berry-ripe lips he suddenly wanted to lick, to kiss, to suckle with his own. A thought that manifested itself in a rush of blood from his brain to his cock.

Damn it. Not now.

"Don't apologize," he said, forcing away the vibrant image of flipping her underneath him, lifting her skirts, and plunging inside her. "I didn't intend to keep you from your breakfast."

"But last night, you said 'day and night.' I forgot. I shouldn't have left without waking you. Without asking your permission." She looked back down at her hands, which lay perfectly motionless just over her mons.

Right where he wanted to be. God, if she was trying to distract him from whatever irritation he might harbor against her for her desertion, his throbbing erection would be an excellent measure of her success.

"You would be within your rights to claim I breached the agreement," she finished, her tone dejected.

Hell, he knew he was a monster. Responsible for the deaths of hundreds of men, half of them on a single ill-fated day. But no one save his superior officers was aware of what had happened at Waterloo, and no one ever would be.

Why, then, did she fancy him so cruel as to renege on their agreement simply because she'd gone for a bite to eat? After what had passed between them in this bed last night, shouldn't she have more faith in him than less? On the other hand, the better people got to know him, the more reason they seemed to have to scorn him.

He sighed in resignation. "I did not intend my words to be taken quite so literally. You are not an indentured slave. When I said I wanted you day and night, I meant only to ensure you would not be engaged by another man in my absence." Placing his fingers beneath her chin, he tilted her head up. Her eyes were like shards of the sky in the south of France on a clear October day—bright, clear, sharp. "You didn't seem frightened of me last night. You are now. What has changed?"

Aside from the fact that she had just found him raging in his sleep like a madman, his reactions so violent he had hurt her, however inadvertently.

"I'm not frightened *of* you. I'm frightened *for* you." She shook her head. "When I came in and heard you . . . saw you like that . . . I knew I shouldn't have left you alone."

Jack stared at her, speechless. Of all the emotions he had imagined he might inspire, sympathy was at the bottom of his list, just above love and right below admiration. Pity he expected. Disdain he took for granted. And instead she offered compassion and comfort.

Angels did, indeed, come in the strangest forms.

He opened his mouth, though to what purpose he wasn't entirely sure, but was prevented from saying whatever it was that was about to fall out of his mouth—something no doubt entirely ill-advised—by a sharp rap on the door to the chamber.

"Oh," Calliope said, jumping to her feet. "That will be your breakfast."

"My breakfast?" he asked as she rushed to the door and opened it.

She murmured something unintelligible to the person in the hall. When she turned back around, she held a tray bearing a plate laden with food and a small silver pot with a steaming spout. She kicked the door shut behind her with the bare heel of her foot.

"Of course. You didn't think I would have breakfast and leave you to go hungry, did you?"

In all honesty, the question hadn't occurred to him one way or the other, but as she walked toward him, the mouthwatering aroma of eggs, sausages, and—yes, it was coffee in that pot—assailed his nostrils. He was hungry. Famished, in fact.

But his need for sustenance went well beyond food. He was far more starved for the touch, the tenderness, the kindness of another human being. For the warmth and passion and, yes, love of a woman.

No, not any woman. *This* woman.

7

One would never suspect from the speed and precision with which Jack Prescott cleared his heaping plate that he carried not one spare ounce of flesh on his sinewy frame. Callie only knew because she inspected every visible inch of his body—surreptitiously, of course—as she went about her normal morning routine while he ate.

As she brushed her teeth and hair and washed her face, she examined the smooth, elongated ridges of his biceps and triceps from her vantage at the mirror. While she selected a shift, stays, and lavender day gown from the wardrobe, she admired the rippled definition of his pectoral and abdominal muscles. And when she took the selected items of clothing with her behind the privacy screen to change, she marveled at the corded musculature of his calves and thighs . . . at exactly the moment he finished eating and set the tray on the floor.

Revealing another muscle entirely.

She couldn't prevent herself from taking an audible breath at the sight of his penis. His was undoubtedly the most aesthetically pleasing male organ she had ever seen—and she had seen a great many. Perfectly proportioned from the base of the thick shaft all the way up its impressive length to the velvety soft tip, it jutted from its nest of tawny curls, proud and predatory as a lion.

If he were any other man, any other client, she would have known exactly what to do. Would have dropped her clothes to the floor, climbed onto the bed, and straddled his lap. Would have ridden him until he groaned and shuddered and took the Lord's name in vain.

But with Mr. Jack Prescott, she wasn't sure. When he'd been in the same condition last night, he hadn't wanted to fuck her. Perhaps he'd simply been too exhausted. Or maybe he just didn't want her because she was a whore. Whatever the reasons, for the first time since she'd learned to suck cock in a dark corner of the scullery, she didn't know what a man wanted of her.

It was disorienting.

Worse yet, her pussy throbbed and dampened with primal longing. Bloody well ached to have that lovely cock inside her, stretching her, fucking her until this strange, new void was filled.

That was alarming.

"Thank you." He spoke the words with genuine gratitude. As if he wasn't saying them merely to be polite. "You didn't have to do that."

She shrugged. "Of course, I did. I couldn't let you go hungry. 'Tis nearly noon."

Swinging his legs off the bed, he got to his feet. His cock bobbed up and down, waving at her, beckoning to her. She licked her drying lips as liquid heat flooded her belly. He was impossibly attractive, frighteningly compelling.

"I didn't mean for the food," he murmured. His stormy-hot eyes pinned her in place, frozen and melting at the same time. He advanced on her slowly, strengthening her impression of him as a large, lithe cat on the prowl.

ment, and then "Oh!" as he captured her mouth with his.

Oh God, he was kissing her. Kissing *her.*

She had been kissed only once before. A sloppy, awkward affair delivered by a young man she'd briefly imagined she might marry, the experience had been more than enough to change her mind about kissing and marriage. Both, she decided, were highly overrated.

Her first instinct was to squirm away, to avoid the shocking intimacy of mouth upon mouth, but surprise and curiosity held her in place. For there was nothing sloppy about the gentle but insistent pressure of Jack's firm, moist lips, nothing awkward about the way he tipped his head to one side and molded his honeyed, humid mouth to hers. This kiss was heavenly, divine . . . and wholly profane. His mouth stroked, suckled, teased, cajoled, and she was squirming now, but for greater contact, for better purchase, not less. Erotic sensation surged inside her. She parted her lips, and his tongue swept eagerly inside. He tasted of coffee, of longing, and of loneliness so powerful and persistent, it made her chest ache.

She wanted this. Wanted him. Wanted his tongue in her mouth, his cock in her pussy. Wanted every inch of their bodies clinging together in the sweaty, feverish pursuit of ungodly pleasure . . . and a reprieve, however brief, from the perpetual isolation of being who they were.

"Come back to bed with me?" he whispered against her mouth.

He was under no obligation to ask; she was his to use as he pleased. Yet he waited for her answer as if her consent mattered. As if *she* mattered.

Yes, oh yes, she wanted to shout, but sentiment so thickened her throat, she couldn't speak. She nodded instead.

Clasping her hand in his, he led her to the bed. In charged silence, he unfastened the clasps that held her gown in place. The fabric whispered against her hypersensitive skin on the way to floor, causing her to shiver despite the fire that seemed to radiate from every pore in her body.

His hands, cool and dry compared to her own overheated flesh, skimmed over her bare arms, trailing goose bumps in their wake. "Lie down."

She stretched out on the bed, and Jack joined her, but when

she reached out with the intention of taking his beautiful penis in her hand, he stayed her attempt by grasping her wrist.

"No. I want to make love to you, not be serviced by you." He rolled atop her, pinning her beneath his deliciously solid weight. The head of his cock slipped effortlessly along the slick folds of her sex to rest at her entrance. In a single thrust, he would be inside her, but he shook his head when she pushed her hips upward impatiently. "Let me love you the way a beautiful woman should be loved." His eyes bored into hers, intense, greedy. "The way you deserve to be loved, Calliope."

Her stomach lurched oddly. To speak of love was silly, impulsive. Men didn't love women like her. Oh, the young and uninitiated sometimes imagined they did, but only because they confused a willing pussy with love. But Jack wasn't young—at least not *that* young—and no man who could use his mouth as he did could be considered uninitiated.

She knew the truth, understood reality. By love, he meant intercourse. Nothing more or less.

But for just this short time, she would suspend her belief in reality and embrace the fantasy.

She met his eyes, unblinking. She wanted this man, this moment, as she had never wanted anything in her life. And she wanted it to be as real as it could be. A beautiful memory she could take out and examine whenever she felt lonely or unloved.

"It's Callie," she corrected.

His eyebrows drew together. "Callie?"

"My name. Calliope is Mrs. Upshaw's invention. I'm just plain Callie James."

His features, drawn harsh and tight with need, softened as he released a short burst of laughter. He smoothed her hair back from her face, traced a long section that cascaded along her neck and over her shoulder to curl just above one nipple. A tremor of desire followed the path of his hand, so fierce that tears stung the backs of her eyelids.

"Trust me, Callie James, when I say there is nothing plain about you. And nothing plain about what I plan to do with you now."

8

Jack had, indeed, begun with very elaborate plans for how he would make love to her, but with his cock nestled at the slick, hollow entrance to her pussy, he felt his vaunted self-control slipping dangerously from his grasp. Her surrender was complete, unconditional. He could ride her fast and hard, with no thought to her pleasure, and she would be right there with him. Hell, maybe even a little ahead of him.

But a quick and dirty fuck wouldn't do. Not when she had gifted him with a small, secret piece of herself that he was sure no other man had ever shared. For all he knew, a thousand men might have had her body; only Jack had her name, her trust.

Unfortunately, Calliope—Callie, he reminded himself—was no help at all. Her hands coasted down his back, grabbed handfuls of his arse. She shifted beneath him, impatient, eager. "Please, Jack," she whispered, her breath hot against his neck, "I need you inside me."

Last night, her pleas for him to fuck her hadn't swayed him. He'd been resolute, in command. Today, they affected him like an avalanche . . . swamped him, buried him, crushed him. Because today, her need felt as real, as potent as his.

Why deny her what he craved?

Seizing her wrists, he pulled her arms up over her head, causing her back to arch. Her gorgeous, raspberry-tipped breasts brushed against his chest as he drove his cock into her wet, welcoming cunt. She gasped at the sudden invasion, and pure male pride swelled his chest as he felt her inner muscles stretching, straining to accommodate his length, his girth.

She closed her eyes and whimpered softly, and his first thought was that he was hurting her with his rather formidable size. He was well aware that he was more generously endowed than most men, and he'd learned long ago that with most women, he must go slowly and carefully at first. But then her pussy contracted around him, squeezing him so tight he thought for a brief second he might lose consciousness as blood rushed from his brain to his balls. Again and again, spasms racked her, squeezing his cock like a fist, and the truth struck him like a gunshot.

She's coming. From nothing more than having his cock buried inside her.

God almighty, but she was unbelievably responsive. Uninhibited. Abandoned. Magnificent.

In that moment of insight, all hope of finesse was lost. He fucked her with all the subtlety of a forest fire, wild and uncontained. And she was a raging conflagration herself, spreading her legs wider to accept his frenzied thrusts, clutching at his hips and buttocks to help him drive deeper, returning his hungry, possessive kisses with a fervor that made him dizzy.

She sobbed his name against his mouth as she came a second time, her angelic features lighting up in pure unholy exultation. The musky, pungent perfume of their coupling and the erotic sound of his cock plunging repeatedly into her ripe, succulent sex pervaded the room.

But touch and scent and sound weren't enough anymore. She gave a little moan of frustration as he withdrew from her, but when he caressed her and said gruffly, "Roll over," she smiled and nodded.

Once on her stomach, she lifted her hips and spread her thighs, baring glistening pink lips and the tight, tiny rosebud of her arse to his view. Kneeling between her legs, he explored the delicate flesh there with his mouth, from clitoris to pussy to her puckered rear entrance, reveling in her hot, spicy flavor and her soft, sweet sighs of pleasure. When she was trembling with renewed need, close to yet another climax, he lined up with her lush, luscious pussy and sank slowly back inside. The sight of his shaft thick disappearing inside her combined with the sharper, steeper angle of penetration made him damn near delirious with pleasure, but he wasn't done.

Not nearly.

The muscles of her abdomen jumped with anticipation as he slid one hand down her velvety smooth skin and through the curls below until he found the tender bud of her clitoris. She hummed her approval as his fingers set a steady rhythm in time to the long, even thrusts of his cock.

Impending orgasm gathered in his balls with the ferocity of storm clouds skidding across the sky, colliding and expanding until he could no longer contain the tempest. He closed his eyes and clenched his jaws, desperate to hold out just a few seconds longer for her to join him. Hunching over her back, he buried his face in the curve of her neck and teased the silky skin beneath her ear with his lips. She moaned and turned her head, allowing their mouths to meet in a deep, drugging kiss.

God, he loved kissing her. Loved it even more, perhaps, than fucking her, although it was difficult to be entirely objective in this assessment when he was buried balls deep in her cunt and on the verge of going off like a loaded twenty-four-pound cannon. There was a shyness, an innocence to the way her lips followed his lead, cautious, hesitant. As if, for all her experience in the ways of men and fornication, she had never been properly kissed before.

Her tongue slipped between his lips, an abrupt foray he had neither initiated nor expected. The surprise alone was enough to push him over the edge into the climax he'd been holding desperately at bay. As he surrendered to the shuddering spasms that claimed him, he felt her mouth move under his.

"Thank you," she whispered as she stiffened and came right along with him.

And he thanked the God he'd long since stopped believing in that he'd found her.

Jack's skin twitched as Callie absently traced the ridged edges of his scar. Though the disfigured flesh was virtually insensate, the unblemished skin on either side was not.

"That tickles," he growled, grabbing her hand to stop the path of her fingers before she got any nearer his navel and forced him to double up with laughter.

Her expression grew instantly contrite. "I'm sorry. I didn't know. I was only wondering . . . how did it happen?"

He grimaced at the memory. "I was young and foolish and found myself on the wrong end of a Frenchman's bayonet. The only reason he scraped me with it instead of running me through was that he was as young and foolish as I was."

"You were lucky to survive," she observed quietly, burrowing her head back into the hollow of his shoulder.

She was right . . . and dead wrong. He had indeed been lucky to survive the wound. Lucky that the tip of the bayonet had failed to pierce any vital internal organs. Lucky that he had lapsed swiftly into unconsciousness when the whiskey-swilling surgeon sewed his skin together with stitches so uneven they would have shamed a nine-year-old girl into hiding her sampler. And lucky that the wound hadn't festered and putrefied like so many other men's, killing with slow, ruthless efficiency.

But if he hadn't been so lucky, he wouldn't have lived to cause the deaths of 278 men.

"Is that what you were dreaming about? Nearly dying?"

He couldn't contain a bark of bitter laughter. "No. I only wish it were."

Her brow furrowed with concern. "What is it, then?"

"It doesn't matter." He turned his head and pressed his lips against the top of her head. "It was merely a nightmare. Nothing of import."

"It matters to me," she said solemnly, propping herself up on an elbow. Her sharp, probing eyes cut through him as surely as any bayonet. Laid him open and vulnerable.

Jack sighed. He'd never told anyone. In part because the nightmares and insomnia were a relatively recent phenomenon, and in part because no one would believe he wasn't mad. There was nothing normal or natural about his freakish ability to recall every name, every face, every voice, every incident with razor-sharp precision. For him, the past and the present differed only in substance, not in form.

No, he had no intention of telling her the source of his anguish, and yet he heard himself say, "I dream about all the men I've killed."

Her eyes widened. "The enemies you killed in battle?"

He snorted with self-derision. "That would make for a rather short nightmare. Commissioned officers rarely participate in direct combat, and when they do, it's usually a matter of self-preservation. In a decade and a half, I was only forced to take up arms to defend myself seven times." And each of those seven incidents was scorched into his brain, the face of each of those French soldiers as vivid in his mind as if they stood before him.

But he hadn't known those men's names. Hadn't known the

names of their wives and children or childhood sweethearts. Hadn't heard their hopes and dreams for the futures they'd never have.

Hadn't sent them out to die.

"Then who . . . ?"

He pressed his fingers to her lips. "My friends and comrades. The men who had the misfortune to fall under my command and died as a result."

"But . . . surely you don't blame yourself for their deaths. You didn't kill them. The French did." She searched his face for reassurance. "Didn't they?"

"Mostly. A few of them died when a nearby rifle exploded or misfired. But by and large, they were killed by enemy fire."

"Then their deaths are not your fault. They are the enemy's fault."

"I know. But I cannot dismiss my responsibility. I sent them into those battles. I asked them to make the ultimate sacrifice, while I made none at all."

She nodded slowly. "They were your men, your brothers. You didn't want any of them to die. But that is not the reason you have nightmares, is it? There's something more."

He blinked. She was far too observant. Attuned, somehow, to his inner life despite their brief acquaintance.

Why not tell her? What harm could it do?

"They aren't nightmares. They're real."

A confused frown skittered across her features. "Real?"

"To me, everything I've ever experienced is as fresh and real now as it was when it happened. I remember everything I've ever seen or heard. I'm incapable of forgetting anything."

"Everything? How is that possible?"

He shrugged. "I don't know. What I do know is that I live with those two hundred seventy-eight men who died under my command in my head all the time. Awake or asleep, they're always with me." He reached up to cup her cheek in his hand.

"Or they were, until you came along. They aren't gone now, but for some reason, when I'm with you, they seem content to leave me in peace."

She released a long, slow breath of comprehension. "And that's why you had your nightmare? Because I left you alone?"

"I think so."

Her eyes glassy, she turned her face and pressed her lips into his palm. "I won't leave you alone again. I promise."

Only much later, after he had made love to her again with all the slow, elaborate precision he'd planned earlier, did he wonder what he would do when their week ended, and he returned to his estate in Wiltshire.

How in God's name would he live, much less sleep, without her?

9

For the next several days, Callie floated in a bubble of sensual euphoria. Though Jack left the brothel each afternoon shortly before lunch, he returned directly after dinner and led her upstairs to her room, where they would make love until the soft glow of dawn seeped around the curtains and they both fell into deep, dreamless sleep. Or so she assumed, for Jack's slumber seemed both sound and peaceful, unbroken by a return of the nightmare memory she had interrupted.

Today had begun like every other since she had made the mistake of leaving Jack alone. Harvey arrived shortly before eleven with their breakfast, which they consumed over the course of the next hour between brief, intense bouts of lovemaking. After thoroughly sating both appetites, they lounged for another hour in bed, managing somehow to talk about nothing and everything at the same time.

In the course of conversations like these, she had learned that he was the second son of an earl, that his father had passed on nearly a decade ago, that his older brother had been married for eight years but had thus far produced only two daughters, and that Mrs. Upshaw reminded him a bit of his mother, for both women shared an unfortunate penchant for garish colors and large hats. He had bought his army commission two years before Napoleon's incursion into Portugal, not because he had any strong soldierly inclinations to speak of, but because military careers were the stock in trade of the second sons of nobility. It could have been worse, however, for had he been a third son, he would have been destined for the church.

"Imagine me as a vicar, taking folks' confessions. I'd be carrying the sins of an entire parish about in my head for the rest of my days."

And after nearly a decade living primarily in France, he preferred brandy to whiskey, coffee to tea, and Molière to Shakespeare, though she must never let on about the last one. "Englishmen have been killed for less," he had explained with a grin, and she had laughed.

This morning, however, he leaned on one elbow, silently tracing an idle pattern over her upper arm and shoulder. "You've told me almost nothing about yourself."

Her stomach pitched sideways. "There's nothing to tell."

"Of course there is. A woman like you doesn't wind up in a place like this without good reason."

The hairs on the back of her neck vibrated at the implication of his words. "What do you mean?"

He recoiled slightly, his eyes narrowing with obvious puzzlement. "I mean that you are intelligent, educated, well-bred."

Irritation crawled up her skin. She wasn't ashamed of what she did, and she certainly wouldn't make excuses for her chosen profession to a man who had hired her. The hypocrisy galled her even more than the assumption that she must have been forced into the life she led.

"And intelligent, educated, well-bred women don't become whores unless they have to, is that it? No woman would fuck men for money if she had other options."

"Well, I—"

She rolled away, snatching her shift from the floor as she rose from the bed. "You know nothing about me. Nothing." Turning her back to him, she tugged the garment over her head and started toward the wardrobe.

Though she never heard him stir, his hands were suddenly on her arms, and he was spinning her around to face him. "I know. So tell me." She tried to look away, but he tipped her chin up so she couldn't avoid his smoky, persistent gaze. "Tell me all about plain Callie James."

Sweet Mary Magdalene, he had no idea just how "plain" she was. If he did . . . what would he think of her then? Would he still find her as worthy of his attentions as before?

Mrs. Upshaw always said a Cyprian's greatest assets were her air of mystery and aristocratic refinement, both powerful contrasts to her lack of sexual inhibition. Callie had never once been tempted to surrender her advantages, to dismantle her defenses by sharing her past with anyone. Until now.

Jack was wrong. He would have made a superb vicar. With his smoldering eyes and calmly authoritative manner, Jack could convince the devil himself to confess and renounce his sins.

What did it matter? Their week would be over in two short days. He would return to his life on the fringes of high society, and she would return to hers, pleasuring whichever man purchased her favors each evening and, yes, pleasuring herself in the process. Just because she had experienced five days of something that resembled love didn't mean she couldn't be satisfied with what she'd had before.

Besides, she wasn't ashamed of being a whore. Why, then, should she be ashamed of her parentage? They had done everything they could for her with their limited means and fore-shortened lives. And when they passed into the hereafter, they'd gone to their paupers' graves, missed and mourned by no one but their daughter.

Resentment curled in her breast like an angry snake. Jack might not be responsible for her parents' circumstances, but like most wealthy aristocrats, he was blind to it.

"My parents were just plain, hard-working people, Mr. Prescott. Poor people. Mostly, they made their living as ragpickers, though my father picked up odd jobs as a ratcatcher and my mother worked in the scullery of a brothel a bit like this one for a while. Neither of them knew how to read or write or cipher, and they certainly didn't have the wherewithal to educate me or teach me the finer points of deportment."

She stopped and waited for his reaction. The inevitable recoil.

It never came. Instead, he smoothed a stray strand of hair back from her cheek and tucked it behind her ear. "And yet, here you are."

"When I was fifteen, my mother convinced a gentleman she met to take me on as a scullery maid. By then, my father had already died of consumption and she knew she'd be close behind him." She pressed her fist to her mouth, suppressing a hiccuping sob at the memory of her mother, gaunt and hacking, waiting with patient resignation for death to take her.

Jack cupped the back of her head and drew her into his arms. "I'm sorry. I didn't know. I shouldn't have asked."

"No, you shouldn't have." She smiled wryly against the warm, bare skin of his chest. "But thank you for reminding me how fortunate I am that Mrs. Upshaw found me when she did."

He pulled back and looked down at her, arching an eyebrow. "How on earth did a scullery maid in a gentleman's household cross paths with a madam of Mrs. Upshaw's stature?"

"I wasn't a scullery maid."

His eyes crinkled with confusion. "But you said—"

"I said my mother got me a position as scullery maid. I didn't say I took it."

"So you weren't a scullery maid, then?"

She laughed. "I was. For about three days. I hated it. All that time scrubbing floors and pots and pans and peeling potatoes and so forth. 'Twas miserable. So, when the gentleman cornered me in the scullery on my fourth morning on the job, told me he found me beautiful, and begged me to suck his cock, I did. Within a week, he'd made me an upstairs maid, but instead of dusting and mopping and making beds, I took care of him in bed. Before long, I was also taking care of the butler and his son."

"And you didn't mind? They didn't hurt you?" His eyes searched hers, their turbulent gray sharpening with worry.

Callie shook her head. "Not at all. On the contrary, I was flattered by the attention and delighted to be relieved of my other duties. The three of them were very kind to me."

"They took advantage of you, you mean." A storm of emotion crossed his face. "I'd like to pummel every last one of them to a bloody pulp."

With a sigh, she extricated herself from his embrace and crossed to the fireplace. Bending down, she picked up another log and threw it on the fire. When she looked at him again, she could see he was still fuming with righteous indignation on her behalf. Touching, but terribly misguided.

If she told him the truth of matters, he might well find her repellent, debauched. But if she did not, he would labor under the misapprehension that she regretted her past, that she felt misused and mistreated. He would pity her.

And his pity would be far worse than his revulsion.

She looked at him for a long moment, committing to memory every jagged contour of his starkly handsome face, every smoothly muscled curve of his magnificent body. He had given her five days of bliss. Enough to last a lifetime.

"Do you remember your first time with a woman?" she asked when she had finally filled herself with him.

He blinked rapidly several times, as if startled by the question. "Yes, of course." The corners of his lips twitched as a smile fought for purchase on his face. "I expect that's a memory every man carries with him until the day he dies. Even if he isn't cursed with perfect recall."

"So, tell me, did she take advantage of you? Did you feel used or mistreated?"

His cheeks grew ruddy beneath the golden glow of his sun-ripened complexion. "I . . . um . . . well . . ."

She strode up to him and poked his chest with an index finger. "Precisely. I was no more taken advantage of than you were. It was the best thing that ever happened to me." Her jaw tightened with defiance. "I like fucking, Jack, and unlike most women, I'm not ashamed or embarrassed to admit it."

To her surprise, he grabbed her hand and pressed his mouth to the tip of her index finger. "You most certainly do. And you're definitely unlike any woman I've ever known." He chuckled softly, the rumble of his warm breath tickling her skin. "I suspect that's why I like you so well."

Relief made her dizzy and weak. And hopeful in a way she had no business being.

"You still haven't told me how you came to meet Mrs. Upshaw. Why did you leave your gentleman's employ to work here when you were so happy there?"

"Oh, that." A bitter cackle escaped her throat. "When the gentleman promoted me to 'upstairs maid,' he neglected to hire anyone to replace me in the scullery. The cook complained to the lady of the house, and before I could say 'mince pie,' I was tossed into the street without references."

Callie closed her eyes. She didn't like to think about those days.

She hadn't cared about the lack of references, of course—one wasn't usually asked for them when selling one's wares on a Picadilly street corner—but she had missed the money and roof over her head rather acutely. Sleeping in alleys had a way of making one rather less attractive to even the least discriminating members of the opposite sex. After a week on the streets, she'd been dirty and hungry and desperate.

Jack watched her expectantly, waiting for her to continue. But she couldn't tell him about the dark time. He would pity her, then. Believe she'd had no choices. When it was Mrs. Upshaw who'd given her the kind of freedom few women—rich or poor— ever dreamed of having.

"Though it's not common knowledge, Mrs. Upshaw doesn't run this brothel merely to line her own pockets. She believes our profession should be both safe and voluntary, but we all know for girls who work on the streets or in the cribs near the docks, 'tis neither. All of us here work in part to ensure that those who don't want to, don't have to. Mrs. Upshaw uses most of the house's profit to fund a halfway house. Girls who don't want to stay in the trade can live there free of charge while they study for other, respectable positions—maids and seamstresses and cooks and the like, but also nurses, governesses, and paid companions."

He arched an eyebrow. "Are you telling me my nieces' nurse might be a former prostitute?"

She laughed. " 'Tis a possibility, I suppose. At any rate, that's how I came to meet Mrs. Upshaw. She found me about a week after I lost my position and brought me to Harlowe House. That is where I learned to read and write and behave like a lady. She thought I'd make a fine governess or paid companion."

"And yet, you're here."

"Because this was the position I wanted." She lifted her shoulders in a self-deprecating shrug. "I am not vain, but I am realistic. No woman would hire me, and any man who did would have an entirely different position in mind. I would find myself back on the streets in a matter of weeks or months. Working here, I earn more in a few weeks than I could earn in years in a 'respectable' job. On my nights off, I can attend the opera or the theater or go to Vauxhall or just curl up in the library and read.

And I don't have to worry about being dismissed because the lady of the manor takes a disliking to me."

"All true," he said dryly. "But you know, you wouldn't have to worry about being dismissed by the lady of the manor if you *were* the lady of the manor."

10

Jack should have regretted the impulsive words the moment they left his lips. Strangely, he felt nothing but relief. And conviction.

Against every dictate of reason and respectability, Callie James was the woman he wanted—no, *needed* as his wife.

Her hand went to her throat and she stared at him with eyes the color of the heavens. She shook her head and laughed nervously. "You couldn't have meant that as it sounded."

Wheat-gold hair tumbled loosely around her shoulders, and her lips were still red and swollen from his kisses. Never had a woman looked more beautiful. Or more well-fucked. God, he wanted to wake up with her beside him, looking just like she did now, every morning for the rest of his life.

He reached out and wrapped a strand of that silky hair around his finger. "How did it sound?"

"As though you . . . no." She broke off, biting that ripe lower lip with her front teeth. "It's too preposterous even to think, much less to say aloud."

"What is preposterous about this?" He dropped to one knee and took her hand in his. "Callie James, will you do me the honor of becoming my wife?"

"What?" She snatched her hand back and whirled away, staggering to the chair and collapsing into it. "You must be mad," she whispered.

"So I've been told on more than one occasion, but I have never been saner in my life." He crossed the red and gold rug and kneeled in front of her again. "Marry me, Callie."

She stared down at her hands, which she clasped tightly in her lap. "You cannot be serious. But even if you were, which you are most certainly not, I could never accept."

An ironic grin twisted his mouth. "Would being married to me be that bad?"

Her eyes and cheeks were bright with emotion when she met his gaze. "No, I imagine it would be quite wonderful."

"Then say yes."

"I can't. Marrying me would destroy you with your family and friends." She reached out and touched his face, tracing an arc from his temple to his jaw. "What I do not understand is why you ask me to be your wife, not your mistress. I am hardly the sort of woman who requires the inducement of a ring and an exchange of vows."

He put his hand over hers and sighed. How could he explain what he didn't fully understand himself? His proposal had been so spontaneous, so unpremeditated, he hadn't thought it through at all. Asking her to be his mistress had simply not occurred to him. But as quickly as he considered the idea, he dismissed it.

Having her on the periphery of his life just wouldn't do. Her presence occupied his thoughts as no one else's could, quieting the chorus and dimming the visions that plagued him. In the hours they were apart, the noise in his head returned as fierce and chaotic as before.

"I won't have you by halves," he said at last. "I want all of you, or none. I want you by my side, day and night. I want to walk down the street with you, in broad daylight, and have everyone know you're the woman I hold above all others. Not just the woman I keep in a separate house and visit when I have a moment to spare. You deserve better than that. And so, I think, do I."

"It's impossible, Jack." She stood abruptly, forcing him to get to his feet as well or risk being knocked over as she walked by him. "You're the son of an earl. You can't marry a ragpicker's daughter from the Seven Dials. Especially not one who's worked in an expensive London brothel for the last six years."

Stopping at the fireplace, she stared into the fire. The orange-blue flames had just begun licking at the log she'd tossed onto the hearth a few moments earlier, tentatively, carefully, like a man exploring a woman's body for the first time. Tasting her skin, gauging her reactions, anticipating the slackening of limbs and acceleration of breath that would signal her complete surrender.

Callie wouldn't surrender easily. Life had made her tough, strong, wary, proud. And intensely loyal. So long as she felt her refusal would protect him, she wouldn't give in.

He walked up quietly behind her and wrapped his arms around her waist. "The past doesn't matter to me, only the future," he said as he nuzzled her neck, savoring her shiver of response. She could resist, but just like the log, she'd eventually succumb to the fire. "But I have to admit, it hadn't occurred to me to announce the truth of your past. You have the education and manners of a lady. If you claim to be the orphaned daughter of a gentleman and his wife, no one will suspect you are anyone but who you say you are."

She shook her head. "You don't understand. Do you have any idea how many men I've slept with?"

His brow furrowed. He had already accepted who she was, what she was. Why bring it up yet again?

"No, but you don't know how many women I've slept with, either. I fail to see what difference it makes."

"You don't understand. Those men are men like you. Wealthy aristocrats, politicians, military officers. The very people you must socialize with on a daily basis here in Town." She spun around and slid her arms up around his neck, her expression solemn. "If I were your wife, it would be only a matter of time until one of my former clients recognized me. How long after that happens do you suppose it would be before all of London learns who I really am? You would be ruined inside of a fortnight."

Him? Her concern for his reputation was poignant but ludicrous. He had no political aspirations and his brother held the family seat in Parliament. All he wanted to do was to retire to the country and live some semblance of a normal life.

His skepticism must have shown on his face, for she added, "Even if you don't care for your reputation, think of your family. How would they fare if it were known you married a whore?"

Ah, she had him there. He couldn't allow his mother or his sister-in-law to be dragged through such a scandal. His brother did a rather fine job on his own of embarrassing them with his many illicit but ill-concealed affairs. Jack wouldn't be responsible for increasing their burden. Fortunately, it would never have to come to that.

Self-satisfaction tugged one corner of his mouth up into a knowing half smile. "Then it is a very good thing I don't live in London."

She pulled backward, so abruptly and violently that he had to grab her wrists to keep her from toppling into the fire. "Of course, you live in London. At least during the Season. Everyone does."

"Not everyone," he said, chuckling. "The only people who have to be in London are those with parliamentary seats or other governmental positions, and I have neither. The rest are only here because it is fashionable and there are plenty of diversions to be had. But I am not the least bit interested in fashion, and my estate in Wiltshire—and you—are all the diversion I require."

"You have an estate in Wiltshire?"

"A small wheat-and-barley-producing property that passed from my mother's dowry to me upon my father's death. It's only good for about five hundred a year, but I have some ideas for improvement. I'm only in London this week and next to purchase equipment and to square my accounts. After that, I'm for Swallowcliffe parish, and I've no plans of returning any time soon."

The mere mention of the tiny village near Hayden Bridge Hall brought a smile to his face. Home to roughly two hundred souls, the town was as idyllic as its name, though the "cliff" part seemed a misnomer given that there wasn't much more than a low hillside to be found in the entire county. Soon those hillsides would spring to life, carpeted in every conceivable shade of green. He could almost smell the freshly turned earth, hear the songs of birds and crickets and the chatter of the creek that cut through his property. Life was everywhere in Swallowcliffe, and death nothing more than a path to renewal.

"So you see," he continued, drawing her back into his embrace, "you needn't worry about being recognized. I doubt most of the people who live in Swallowcliffe have been further afield than Salisbury, and the few gentlemen who have traveled to London probably did not also bring their custom to the Red Door. But even if they did, I cannot believe a one of them would make the connection between Mrs. Jack Prescott and a women they once met in a London brothel, nor would anyone be so impolite as to broach the subject."

She touched the tip of her tongue to her upper lip, a gesture that made him want to double over as if a fist had been delivered to his gut. From the softening of the worry lines around her eyes, he could tell she was halfway to accepting his offer, but something still held her back. He had to do something to push her over the edge. Only one thing came to mind.

Clasping her face between his hands, he kissed her, telling her with the touch of his lips what he couldn't tell her simply by moving them. That she was his heart. His breath. His life.

She responded with that mixture of innocence and experience that made him breathless. Though her hands explored his body with frank ease, confidently seeking and finding his pleasure points to heighten his arousal, her kiss remained hesitant, untutored. Raw and real.

"Marry me, Callie," he rasped against her mouth, fighting the flood of desire that threatened to drown his purpose. "Marry me and make me whole."

As he ravaged her lips, pulling her tighter against him, dragging her inexorably back toward the bed, he tasted salt. Startled, he raised his head to find tears streaming down her cheeks. Panic gripped him by the throat, shook him like a cat intent on killing its prey.

"Please don't say no," he whispered, swiping at her tears with his thumbs.

"I won't." A tremulous, watery smile curved her lips as she stroked his cheek with the back of her hand. "When it comes to you, it seems that word is not in my vocabulary."

Thank God. Perhaps He did exist, after all.

"Then why the tears?" he asked. They could be tears of joy, but intuition told him otherwise.

"Because I never wanted anything like this, but now that I have it, I am terrified of losing it. Of losing you."

Relief and jubilation exploded in his chest. "You won't. I promise."

Scooping her up in his arms, he carried her back to the bed and made love to her the way a man makes love to his wife—with deep adoration, fierce tenderness, and undying passion.

Later, he lay beside her while she slept and prayed she'd never have cause to regret her decision.

11

Callie stared blindly out the window as the carriage rumbled through the streets of London's most fashionable districts on its way to the Knightsbridge townhome of the Earl and Countess of Innesford. There, she would be introduced as Miss Caroline James, daughter of Mr. Reginald James, headmaster of a small school in Gutch Common, Wiltshire, and his wife, both of whom had tragically passed in a carriage accident a year ago. The orphaned Miss James, lacking prospects for employment in the small village of her birth, had recently traveled to London in search of gainful employment as a nurse or governess, where she and one Mr. Jack Prescott had reestablished an old acquaintance.

In the week since he had proposed, she and Jack had spent hours establishing and rehearsing the particulars of the fraudulent Miss James's unimpeachable background and upbringing, from her childhood preference of reading over sewing samplers and learning the pianoforte to their first chance meeting at an assembly in Tisbury shortly before Lieutenant Colonel Prescott had been called back to active duty upon Napoleon's return from exile on Elba. Callie knew every detail of her falsified past, almost better than she knew her real history, but she lived in terror of this meeting.

What if someone asked her a question she and Jack hadn't thought of? What if she misremembered the color of her parents' eyes or the name of their maid of all work or whether Tisbury lay to the north or the south of Gutch Common?

She closed her eyes, twisting her handkerchief tighter and tighter as she tried to calm her increasingly frayed nerves.

"Do cease fretting yourself, luv." Mrs. Albert patted Callie's knee reassuringly. One of Harlowe House's headmistresses, the stout, gray-haired matron was posing as Callie's governess-turned-chaperone. "Mr. Jack won't let anything go amiss."

Callie grimaced. "And you must cease referring to Mr. Prescott as Mr. Jack. He is not one of your students, you know."

Mrs. Albert waved her hand. "Don't you worry about me, luv. I'm an old hand at this game. I've been impersonating the Quality for years, and I know how it's done."

At least one of them did, Callie thought ruefully.

The carriage jolted to a halt, and a quick glance out the window confirmed her fears. They had pulled up in front of an imposing four-story building that faced on a well-manicured central square. With its elegant Doric columned porch and slate-roofed turret, it could only be the home of wealthy aristocrats.

They had arrived.

As they waited for footman to open the door and assist them to the ground, Callie could summon only two entirely unrelated thoughts.

First, Gutch Common lay ten miles south of Tisbury.

Second, if she threw up in the Innesfords' sitting room, she was likely to ruin a very expensive rug.

"I am sure I speak for all of us, Miss James, when I say how surprised we all were when Mr. Prescott announced his intention to marry." Lady Innesford smiled broadly as she spoke, an expression that did little to improve her appearance. A tall, lanky woman with a narrow face and a large overbite, the baring of her teeth only intensified her resemblance to a horse. And a rather unattractive one at that.

Ashamed of her uncharitable thoughts, Callie tried to focus on the countess's gown—a delicately brocaded ivory adorned with a peach-colored sash beneath the bosom and seed pearls sewn round the half-moon neckline. God may not have seen fit to bless the lady with much in the way of natural beauty, but he had certainly graced her with excellent taste and sufficient means to display it.

"Indeed," her husband agreed. "Didn't think my brother had it in him to settle down after all these years of bachelorhood."

What the countess lacked in good looks, the earl possessed in jaw-dropping abundance. Though the resemblance between Lord Innesford and his younger brother was plain enough— for they shared the same lean build, dark blond hair, and general facial shape—where Jack's features were roughly hewn and somewhat irregular, the earl's were smooth and symmetrical, almost too perfect to be believed.

But for all his physical beauty, Callie could not find him attractive. The frank, forward way his eyes—a deep, verdant green in contrast to Jack's stormy gray—assessed her from head to toe, as if she were a meal to be devoured at his leisure, made her shift uncomfortably in her chair. Had she not been convinced she would remember this man if she had ever seen him before, she would have imagined he knew exactly who and what she was. Instead, he appeared to be sizing her up for the role she had only recently abandoned. The irony might have amused her had he not been so blatantly contemplating the seduction of his brother's betrothed, and in full view of his own wife.

His behavior was nothing short of appalling. And this man was Jack's brother? No wonder he wanted to retire to Wiltshire.

If this man had been her brother, she certainly wouldn't have wished to live in proximity to him, either.

"I must say that I approve entirely of your taste in brides, Jack," Lord Innesford continued. "Where'd you say you met the delightful Miss James again?"

Callie's stomach twinged with alarm. Did the earl not believe their story? It had sounded a trifle forced to her ears, though neither the countess nor Jack's mother had appeared anything less than charmed by their tale of love at first sight, involuntary separation, and chance reunion a week before.

Jack, who perched on the arm of the chair beside her, gave her hand a gentle squeeze of reassurance before pinning his brother with a glare that brooked no argument. "As I said, we met in Tisbury two summers past. I should have asked Miss James to marry me then and there had I been free of my army commission." He smiled fondly at Callie. "In retrospect, that was a foolish error on my part. I am exceedingly grateful that circumstances drove us to cross paths again. This time, I am determined not to make the same mistake twice."

"Well, I think it's all terribly romantic," Mrs. Albert put in. "My poor Miss James has been pining for Lieutenant Colonel—pardon me, Mr. Prescott—something fierce since he was sent to France. Imagined he might even be dead, poor lamb, and with her parents gone so tragically, too."

Callie groaned silently. Mrs. Albert was laying it on a bit thick.

The dowager countess, who despite her silver hair appeared younger than her daughter-in-law, sighed wistfully. "I quite agree with you, Mrs. Albert. Though it all comes as quite a surprise, I cannot begin to tell you, Miss James, how delighted I am to welcome you to the family. I have often despaired for Jack's happiness—even as a child, he was a solemn, sober boy and kept too much to himself, I thought—but I can see you bring out the best in him.

"And I must confess," she continued, flicking a reproachful glance toward the earl and his wife before focusing again on Callie with eyes the same startling, stormy gray as her son's, "I am looking forward to having a few more grandchildren to dandle on my knees before I pass to the great hereafter."

Callie might have paused to contemplate the significance of that fleeting look if not for the apprehension that gripped her midsection at the mention of children. In the past six years, Callie had never once conceived a child. Despite the routine use of lemon-and-vinegar-soaked sponges and douches to reduce the likelihood of conception, pregnancy was a regular occurrence at the Red Door. Most of the girls had conceived at least once during the time Callie had worked there. That she had not suggested she was either freakishly lucky or—much more likely—barren.

Since the day Jack had asked her to marry him, she had had a hundred opportunities to tell him, but she hadn't. Instead, she offered herself excuses for not doing so. Her infertility might truly be the result of happenstance, after all, not actual incapacity. Until her interlude with Jack, she had been scrupulous in her efforts to prevent conception; perhaps the other girls were less so. Moreover, he had never once mentioned a desire to have children. Her barrenness might not matter one whit.

But the truth was that she was a coward. If she told him, she would surely lose him, for men of his position didn't want children. They *needed* them. Needed heirs for their properties and titles and bloodlines. Marrying a woman who was known to be barren might be an even greater social sin than marrying a former prostitute.

Jack grinned at his mother. "I don't believe we shall find accommodating your desires to be much of a hardship. Will we, darling?"

Callie nearly choked on her misery, but she laughed hollowly and nodded her agreement.

Her marriage was already based upon a stack of lies. What was one more?

The answer reverberated in her head over the sound of the earl's openly salacious chuckle.

This time, she wasn't lying to strangers to protect Jack. She was lying to Jack to protect herself.

12

————————

"Well, I must say I'm reconsidering the allure of country life since meeting you, Miss James," Harry remarked in the smooth, unctuous tone of voice he always used when addressing his latest conquest.

Jack clenched his fists, fighting the urge to plant his brother a facer. Although the resulting damage to Harry's too-pretty countenance might have a salient effect on his lecherous tendencies, the dinner table was hardly an appropriate venue for fisticuffs.

"Perhaps I shall have to come out and visit that quaint little place of yours, Jack." He lifted his wineglass from the table and twirled it between his fingers. "What's it called again, old chap?"

"Hayden Bridge Hall," Jack supplied through gritted teeth. Harry should know perfectly well what the place was called, but since he scarcely knew the names of the three estates that had come to him in the entail, his inability to remember might not be feigned.

"That's right," he said, snapping his fingers. "We went once or twice when we were children. Dreary dull place if you ask me, but then again, I was a bit young for the sorts of diversions I imagine I might encounter there now."

Callie, who sat to Harry's left, burst into a fit of coughing, while poor Lydia, seated to his right, could only smile wanly as if her husband's insulting ruminations amused her.

Harry reached over and smacked Callie sharply between the shoulder blades. "There now, Miss James, are you quite all right?" he asked after she'd stopped coughing.

Jack seethed at the familiar way his brother's hand lingered at the nape of Callie's bare neck. If Harry had been any other man, Jack would be calling him out for pistols at dawn.

"Yes, thank you," she responded, dabbing at her mouth with her serviette. "I am entirely recovered." When Harry failed to remove his hand, she leaned forward to retrieve her wineglass, forcing him to either withdraw politely or deliberately maintain the contact.

Even Harry knew when to exercise a degree of discretion, demonstrating a sudden, keen interest in his dinner fork, which he picked up and turned over several times as if searching for a spot.

Pity he didn't slip and poke himself in his constantly roving eye, thereby relieving Jack of the temptation.

"That's a right fine bit of tail you got there, brother," Harry said, jerking his head in the direction of the door through which the ladies had retired to the sitting room moments before.

Suspicion skittered down Jack's spine. "I beg your pardon."

"Miss James," his brother clarified, as he puffed on his cigar to light it. "Quite lovely. Though I can't fathom why you're so keen to marry her."

Jack quelled his rising alarm. Harry couldn't know. His damnably godlike face was unforgettable. If Callie had ever seen him before, she would have recognized him. He had to be guessing.

"I don't know what the hell you mean, but I don't appreciate the implication."

Harry shook the spill from which he'd lit his cigar to douse the flame and blew out a perfect ring of smoke. "Come now, brother, you don't seriously expect me to believe that girl is from the country. She's got city style, city manners. I doubt she's ever been outside London in her life. And she's no innocent. Virginal young ladies blush and look away when I rake them over, but she didn't bat an eyelash."

Hellfire and damnation, for a first-rate ass, his brother was remarkably observant. But Jack had no intention of going down without a fight. Harry's conjecture might be right, but he couldn't substantiate it. The only question was whether he was malicious enough to share his suspicions with his wife and their mother.

"You're grasping at straws to excuse your boorish behavior. What sort of gentleman ogles his brother's betrothed like that? I realize you're nearly incapable of keeping your eyes to yourself, let alone your hands and your cock, but she's going to be my wife, for God's sake."

"I am what I am. As are you. Harry the hell-raiser and Jack the immaculate." Harry grinned impudently, just as he had when they were boys and he'd been caught red-handed in some misdeed. No matter how grave his transgression, no matter how guilty he was of the crime, that gesture combined with his extraordinary good looks had always gotten him off with little more than verbal scolding and a promise to do better next time. Whereas Jack inevitably found himself out behind the woodshed for a good talking-to from the switch for the slightest misdemeanor.

"And that, dear brother, is what inflames my curiosity. Why, I ask myself, does my honest and dependable brother go to such great lengths to deceive his family about the identity of his future bride? And the only conclusion I can arrive at is that she wouldn't otherwise be fit to be his bride. What is she—an actress, a courtesan, or a just a good old-fashioned whore?" He leaned forward, his eyes wide and eager. "Whatever she is, she must be one bloody good shag."

Jack didn't stop to think. He stood up and slammed his fist into his brother's jaw, sending him sprawling from his chair to the floor. A bone-chilling fury coursed through his veins as he watched Harry struggle to a sitting position, wiping the back of his hand across his bloodied lip.

"That's one hell of a right cross you've got there, little brother," he said, as he got to his feet. "One would think you'd been sparring in the Pugilistic Club for the past two weeks instead of going the rounds with Miss James."

Glaring, Jack pulled back his arm, preparing to land another blow to his brother's much too pretty face.

Harry raised his palms in surrender. "Whoa, hold on there. I've no plans to spoil your little charade. If you wish to marry Miss James, I don't care whether she's bloody Harriette Wilson or some street doxy you picked up on the Thames. Mother and Lydia are completely taken with her and the pretty little fiction the two of you have concocted. As long as neither of you makes a major blunder, they'll never suspect she's anything but what you claim."

Jack dropped his hands to his sides, unable to formulate a suitable rejoinder. He could hardly thank Harry for his magnanimous offer to keep a secret Jack could never admit to having.

While he stood there dumbly trying to decide between a sharp denial and refusal to dignify his brother's supposition with a response of any kind, Harry came round and clapped him playfully on the shoulder. "All I ask is that, when you tire of her, you let me have a go at her."

"Why, you son of a b—"

This time, Harry ducked before Jack's fist connected. When Jack's eyes widened in surprise, his brother shrugged. "As it happens, I've been sparring with Gentleman Jackson quite a bit recently. One never knows when an aggrieved husband or father may come looking for satisfaction."

Jack sighed heavily, torn between rage and resignation. His brother was right. Harry would always be Harry—the hell-raiser, the rabble-rouser, the troublemaker. And Jack would always love him despite his flaws, worship him in the way only a younger brother could worship his mischievous, invincible older brother.

"One of these days, someone's going to come looking for satisfaction with more than his fists," Jack sighed, shaking his head.

"Maybe someone already has," Harry said with an enigmatic shrug.

Thick, nauseous apprehension settled in Jack's stomach, for beneath his brother's devil-may-care facade, Jack sensed real fear. "Are you in some kind of trouble, Harry?"

Harry bent over to retrieve his still-smoking cigar from where it lay on the floor near the back leg of his chair and grinned. "I'm always in some kind of trouble. It's nothing I can't handle."

"Then why are you doing this?"

"Doing what?" Harry asked blandly, settling back into his seat.

"You know what. Though you claim otherwise, you are trying to convince me not to marry Miss James, and I want to know why. Whom I choose to make my wife should be the least of your concerns."

His brother raised his eyebrows. "I beg to differ. A man has a vested interest in ensuring his heir marries well. And you are still my heir, you know. If anything should happen to me . . ."

Never once since their father's death six years ago had Harry made a point of Jack's status as next in line for the earldom. The possibility of Jack's inheriting the title had always seemed nonexistent to both of them, not merely because Harry was the halest and heartiest—if foolhardiest—of men, but because Jack's military career made it far likelier that he would predecease his older brother than the reverse.

Now, however, it was as though Harry was anticipating—and preparing for—his own death. Impossible. Unthinkable.

The sick sensation in Jack's stomach swelled painfully. "Nothing is going to happen to you, Harry. And Lydia is still young. She'll bear you a son very soon, I'm sure."

Harry stubbed out his cigar. "Even you in your perfection can't control everything, Jack." Pushing back his chair, he stood up. "If you are dead-set on marrying Miss James, I won't stand in your way. I only wanted you to realize what you might be inviting onto yourself, Miss James, and this family if anyone else sees through your ruse."

Jack opened his mouth to object, but Harry held up his hand.

"Let's rejoin the ladies. I imagine they're beginning to wonder what's become of us. Although this," he mused, touching his fat lip gingerly, "is going to be a bit of nuisance to explain. Did I have a run-in with a door frame or the mantel, do you suppose?"

How many times had they done this as boys, concocting some ridiculously implausible story to cover one of Harry's misdeeds? Except this time, they were covering for Jack's, and they both knew it.

"Door frame," Jack said decisively. "The mantel's too low."

"Sounds reasonable to me," said Harry, draping his arm over Jack's shoulder as they headed out of the dining room. "Let's see if it sounds reasonable to the ladies, shall we?"

As long as Harry did the telling, Jack was fairly certain there'd be no questions. He only wished he believed his brother's lie about being able to handle whatever trouble he was in.

13

Callie paced the floor of the luxuriously appointed sitting room that adjoined her bedchamber. Though it was well past two in the morning, she hadn't been able to settle her mind enough to consider sleeping.

Lord Innesford knew. She wasn't sure how he did or how much, but she was sure he didn't for one solitary moment believe that she was a gently reared young lady from a small village in Wiltshire. Any more than she believed he'd bloodied his lip by walking into a door frame. The earl might be a boor—though his behavior struck her more as posturing than genuine lechery—but he wasn't a clumsy oaf or a drunk.

She stopped in front of the fireplace and dug her toes into the thick, warm rug beneath her feet. Lady Innesford—or Lydia, as she preferred to be called—had told her the rich brown-and-umber colored carpet had been imported from Persia, as had the matching tapestries that adorned two of the four walls of the sitting room. Callie knew this was meant to impress her, and so she had oohed and aahed over the quality and expense of the room's furnishings, but in her heart she had felt a little sick.

Though she had always known the rich and aristocratic were different, she had never understood until today just how different.

How did they justify the expense, the extravagance? Their four-story house was home to mere four people—three if one took into account that Jack didn't normally reside here—while, in most of London, four families would have lived on each floor of a building this size. They ate four-course meals of oysters and roast beef and puffed potatoes and lemon ice while many of London's poor were lucky to have mutton broth and a crust of bread. What the Innesfords had paid for the one Persian rug in this room would no doubt house, feed, and clothe a family in the Seven Dials for a year, with enough to spare for a school tuition for one of the children.

How could she marry into such luxury when she knew so well that others were denied the barest of essentials? Perhaps the wealthy could be excused for their ignorance of what they did. They had never experienced poverty, couldn't comprehend what it meant to go to bed hungry and wake up hungrier. But Callie had lived it. She, more than anyone, understood that the comfort of the few depended on the misery of the many.

She shouldn't marry him. Shouldn't love him. But she couldn't bring herself to leave him. For however much he needed her to give him peace, she needed him to give her purpose.

She didn't flinch or turn her head when she heard the door open and close behind her. She'd been expecting him for some time now.

"You're still awake." Jack sounded surprised.

"I couldn't sleep," she admitted.

"Neither could I." He slipped his arms around her waist and nuzzled the nape of her neck. As usual, he had crossed the floor with catlike silence, his movements undetectable to the human ear. "But that should come as no surprise."

Callie ignored the traitorous tingle that spread through her midsection at his touch, at his familiar spicy scent. "Your brother knows, doesn't he?"

He lifted his head, but tightened his arms around her. Several seconds passed before he spoke. "Yes, but he has promised to keep his suppositions to himself."

"Lord Innesford doesn't strike me as a man who keeps much of anything to himself."

Jack snorted derisively. "That's true enough, but I believe he'll be the soul of discretion on this matter."

"Because you'll split his lip again if he doesn't?"

"You didn't believe the door frame story, then?"

She shook her head.

He chuckled. "You and my brother have a lot in common. You're both too observant by half."

She loosened his hands from her waist and turned to face him. A mistake. His stormy eyes surrounded her, embraced her, commanded her. Weakened her resolve. Fighting the desire to melt against him, she stiffened her spine and straightened her shoulders.

"I have nothing in common with your brother. Or with you." Pulling away, she gestured around the room. "Look at this place." A hysterical little giggle bubbled up in her throat. "You've been in my room at the brothel. Until today, I thought it was a veritable palace. Now, I see your world for what it really is, and I know I don't belong. Will never belong."

Jack smoothed back her hair, cradling the back of her head in her hands. "Please don't say that, think that. I can understand how this house must seem to you, how my family must seem to you. But Hayden Bridge Hall is nothing like this, and I am nothing like this. Hell, I spent the better part of the past fifteen years sleeping in barracks and in tents. I'm far more like you than I am like my family. I don't need or want all of these trappings." He tilted her face up toward his. "I only want you."

"I want you, too," she whispered, a chaotic jumble of emotions cracking her voice, "but not this way. I can't bear to lie, cheat, and steal to gain a life I was never meant to have."

"Then you shan't. I see now I should never have asked this of you." With a sad smile, he dropped his hands to his sides and turned away.

Sweet Mary Magdelene, what have I done?

The right thing, she assured herself. The only thing she could do and go on living with herself.

Then why would I rather die?

Jack faced her again as he collapsed onto the brown and gold brocaded sofa. "Tomorrow morning, I will tell my family the truth. Whole and unvarnished."

"What?" She stared him, aghast. Was he mad? "You can't mean that."

"I can and I do." His expression was perfectly sanguine, maddeningly calm.

"No, you mustn't." She rushed to the couch and kneeled in front of him. "You can't do that to them, especially to your mother."

He framed her face with his hands. "But I can't do this to you." Bending over, he brushed his lips against her forehead. "If my choice is between my mother's peace of mind and yours, I choose yours."

She wasn't aware of the tears streaming down her cheeks until the sobs broke out. Tears of joy and love and gratitude. And guilt.

Before he made himself a social pariah, she must tell him the truth about her barrenness. She couldn't let him throw away not only his good reputation, but his very bloodline.

"Don't cry, my love," he murmured against her cheek. "I was an idiot to even suggest we keep your past a secret. Tell me, have you ever heard of Elizabeth Armistead?"

"No," she said, swiping at her tears with her knuckles.

"She was married to Charles James Fox, a prominent Whig

politician who died about ten years ago. Before she married him, however, she was a renowned and wealthy courtesan. And before that, she worked in an exclusive brothel in St. James. Just like you."

Callie's eyes grew wide, and she shook her head dubiously. "You're bamming me."

Jack chuckled. "I most certainly am not. Moreover, marrying her didn't destroy Fox's reputation or career. He was even appointed Secretary of State almost ten years after their marriage became public."

He leaned back onto the sofa and drew her up into his lap. Cradling her in his arms, he stroked her hair as he continued, "I don't have any political aspirations, Callie. I have no title. If a man like Fox, who held audience with the king, could maintain his reputation after announcing his marriage to Mrs. Armistead, I am certain I can weather the rather minor scandal of marrying you."

Oh, she was tempted. Mortally tempted. Jack might as well be holding out the apple for her to take the first bite.

But even if what he told her about Mrs. Armistead and Mr. Fox was true, even if the scandal would eventually die down and allow them to lead a relatively normal life, there was the matter of children. Of his heirs.

"I have to tell you—"

"Shhhhh," he whispered. "No more arguments." He bent his head and licked her lips. "I have much more entertaining pursuits in mind."

Without preamble, his mouth came down on hers, hard and hungry as if she were the apple and he would devour her. Except she was as ravenous as he was, just as starved for the taste and scent of feel of him, her forbidden fruit. Would she ever get enough of his kisses, of his caresses, of the drag and glide of his cock between her legs? If they were to make love every night of their lives, would she ever tire of the way his fingers tugged at her nipples, swirled over her clitoris, stabbed into her pussy until she was writhing in his lap, begging for release?

Their clothes seemed to come undone of their own volition. Her bodice gaped away from her breasts, her skirts bunched around her waist, and through the open slit in her drawers, the smooth, velvety skin of his naked cock rubbed tantalizingly along the soft, swollen valley of her sex.

His hands teased her somehow bare nipples, making her arch and moan. He reached between their legs, grabbed his cock, and positioned the head at her opening.

"Ride me, sweetheart," he commanded hoarsely, his irises mercury and smoke, liquid and swirling around black pupils so wide and dark, she could fall into them and never find her way out.

She drove herself down on him, taking his astonishing length and thickness inside her in a single thrust. No other man had ever filled her senses so completely, stretching her in body and in spirit until the physical boundaries between them became blurred and indefinite.

"Yesssss," he hissed. "God, you're perfect."

Burying his face against her neck, he grabbed her around the waist and twisted his hips to grind his cock even deeper. Sparks of pleasure shot from where their bodies joined, and she shifted to intensify the sensation. Jack groaned as she began to move in small, undulating circles, then larger ones, dragging her swollen, pulsing clitoris across his flesh again and again. Catching on to her rhythm, he slowly increased the pace of his thrusts to match hers until she came in shuddering, jerking waves.

When she relaxed against him, limp and boneless, he slid his arm under her buttocks and rolled her onto her back. "I'm sorry, sweetheart," he muttered, "but I can't wait for you this time. Next time, I promise."

He drove into her with desperate urgency then, like a man possessed, like a man possessing *her*. His mouth found hers, his tongue stabbing greedily, hungrily between her lips, and his hands were on her arse, spreading her cheeks, sliding along her . . . She gasped in surprise as a finger pressed against, then slipped inside her rear entrance.

It was as if he had to be in her everywhere to be satisfied. To have, as he had once said, all of her or none of her. A flood of emotion swept through her, so primal and profound she feared her heart would swell until her rib cage cracked. She was shameless, for she knew now she would say anything, do anything, be anything to have this man's love.

He threw back his head, shouted her name, and came in deep, wrenching spurts, pouring his seed into her womb.

14

It was the wailing that woke him.

Except, Jack realized with a start, it wasn't his own voice that had wrenched him from sleep. No, he lay beside Callie in the oversized guest room bed, his limbs tangled in hers, his skin pleasantly warm and dry, not bathed in the cold sweat of his nightmares.

The cry rang out again, this time louder and closer. Someone—a woman, he thought—was coming up the stairwell, shrieking with . . . was it terror or grief? What the devil?

Callie stirred and stretched, then came awake with a gasp. "Are you . . ." she began, grabbing his arm, but then she too realized the sound came from outside the room. Her eyes snapped to his face. "Whatever is the matter?"

He shook his head. "I have no idea, but I intend to find out."

Swinging his legs from under the blankets, he sat up, rubbing his eyes. The weakness of the light visible between the small gap in the curtains suggested it was not much after dawn. He wasted several precious seconds searching for his breeches, which he eventually found in a small heap behind the bedside table.

During the time it took him to don them and button the fall, the footsteps in the hall had passed, and the cries had either dissipated into sobs or were so muffled he could no longer make them out.

Leaning over, he dropped a kiss on Callie's forehead. "I'll be back as soon as I can."

Although he supposed the point would soon be moot, he opened the door only a crack and peeked out into the hallway to ensure there would be no witnesses to his slipping out of Callie's room. Once in the corridor, he followed the sound of voices to the open door to his brother's room.

What he heard chilled his blood to the temperature and consistency of an alpine lake in January. Words he'd heard too many times before.

"I'm sorry, Lady Innesford, there's nothing I can do for him save make him as comfortable as possible."

Another wail of distress, followed by weeping. Lydia. "Oh, Harry, my poor Harry, what have you done?"

Jack broke into a run. His brother—oh bloody hell, his damnably reckless, thoroughly reprehensible, deeply beloved brother had gone and gotten himself killed.

When he turned the corner and entered his brother's bedchamber, his worst fears were realized. Harry lay on the bed, his eyes closed, his breathing shallow, his godlike features pale as wax. Were it not for the bloody, gaping wound in his gut, however, Jack might have been able to imagine his brother was merely sleeping off the after-effects of a night of heavy drinking.

God damn you, Harry, I asked if you were in trouble. How could you do this to me? To us?

Lydia lay prostrate across Harry's chest, her shoulders wracked with sobs. The surgeon, a round-faced gentleman with thick gray sideburns, stood beside her, packing his tools back into his black medical bag.

One more person occupied the room. A tall man in his thirties with reddish-brown hair and arresting azure eyes, he leaned against the wall in the far corner, his arms crossed over his chest. Jack had never seen him before, but he guessed the gentleman's identity.

"Lord Grenville?" Harry had written often in his letters of the marquess, with whom he had apparently shared a tendency toward wild and rakish behavior.

The other man nodded. "You are Innesford's brother?"

"Yes. Jack Prescott." He cocked his head toward the bed, biting back the tears that threatened to choke him. "What happened?"

Grenville closed and opened his eyes slowly, as if the mere thought pained him. "Thomas Wanamaker called him out last week. Pistols at dawn. Harry, the bloody fool, accepted. Wanamaker is a crack shot."

"You were his second," Jack stated flatly.

Grenville nodded again, his throat working miserably. "I'm sorry. I should have done more to prevent this. Should have talked him out of it."

"You couldn't have." Once Harry had made up his mind to do something, he never backed down, whether because he was stupendously pigheaded or because he believed in his own invincibility.

Jack looked back toward the bed. Harry's hand stroked Lydia's limp brown hair, which hung loosely around her shoulders. Tears prickled the corners of Jack's eyes. He couldn't bear to watch. His brother made no secret of the fact that he had married Lydia for her money and connections, but the tender, regretful way his fingers trailed through her tresses spoke of a deep fondness between them, if not love.

God bloody damn it. Harry was a damned fool, but Jack had known something wasn't right. Had suspected last night that Harry was grooming him to assume the earldom. And yet, when

Harry had assured Jack in that lackadaisical way of his that he could handle whatever trouble had come his way, Jack had believed him. Because, sod it all, he always believed Harry.

Now Harry's death was on his head. Number 279.

Jack slammed his fist into the wall beside him, half-wishing it was Harry's jaw and welcoming the physical pain as a salve to the crippling emotion that threatened to overwhelm him. Harry couldn't die, but Jack had seen this sort of wound too many times before. Men who were gut-shot inevitably died. The only question was whether they did so quickly and easily or slowly and painfully.

"How long?" he asked the doctor.

The man shrugged. "An hour. Maybe less."

Jack nodded.

"I'm intruding here," Grenville said from behind him. "If there's nothing more I can do . . ."

Jack turned and extended his hand. "Thank you for bringing him home to us, Lord Grenville."

The marquess shook Jack's hand, but his gaze drifted to the doorway. "Calliope?"

Bloody hell. Grenville knew Callie. Had known in her in the most intimate of ways.

Jealousy sliced through him like that bayonet blade a decade ago, laying him open and bleeding. Imagining her with this man— this handsome man—shredded his heart as surely as shrapnel from an exploding cannonball.

If things could get any worse, he couldn't imagine how.

15

Lord Innesford passed into the great hereafter at half past six in the morning. An unearthly quiet descended over the household, broken only by necessary comings and goings of the servants, the arrivals and departures of friends and associates who'd heard the news of the earl's death, and the occasional, muffled sounds of women weeping.

An outsider to the family's understandable shock and grief, Callie kept to her rooms for the better part of the morning so as to remain as inconspicuous as possible. After her disastrous decision to follow Jack to his brother's chambers, she couldn't run the risk of encountering yet another former client.

She didn't see Jack again until midmorning. When he entered her room, she was curled up in a chair in front of the fireplace, trying to read a book she had purloined from the library an hour before, sneaking down the servants' staircase and in the back way to avoid intruding.

"I came to make sure you've had something to eat," he said without preamble. "With everything that's happened this morning . . ."

She nodded, setting the book facedown on an end table. "Yes, one of the maids was kind enough to bring me breakfast a little while ago."

"Good, good." When he met her gaze, she could see that his normally storm-dark eyes had turned the translucent color of tears. Still, he held himself erect and impassive, every inch the commanding officer.

She should run and fling herself into his arms, comfort him, but she didn't. Not because he seemed in control of his emotions, though that was certainly true, but because she couldn't shake the memory of the look on his face when Lord Grenville had called her Calliope.

Though he claimed not to care how many men she had fucked or that she had fucked them for money, his expression said otherwise. He'd done his best to hide it, schooling his features almost instantly to bland indifference, but the emotion that flickered in his eyes and twisted his mouth into the briefest of grimaces had been unmistakable.

How could she be of comfort to him when she revolted him?

"I'll be occupied most of the day making arrangements for Harry's funeral." His throat worked convulsively, but his voice didn't waver. "Can you manage by yourself until I come back this evening?" He gestured toward the table, a hint of a smile playing on his lips. "I see you've found a book to read."

"Yes, I'll be fine. You do what you must." *As will I.*

A long, pregnant pause stretched between them. Callie's lungs felt as if they were filled with rubble, her breath pinned beneath the weight of his pain.

"Nothing has changed, Callie. But . . . we can't be married until my brother is buried and a suitable amount of time has passed. A few weeks, perhaps a month." He crossed to her chair and dropped a kiss on her forehead. "Nothing has changed."

And then, with a brisk, almost military bow, he was gone.

Callie choked back a sob. Everything had changed, and she wasn't fool enough to imagine otherwise.

Encountering Nathaniel Kent, one of her favorite—and most frequent—clients until he had fallen in love last month and stopped visiting the Red Door, had also brought her face to face with the full extent of her past's destructive power. If she married Jack, this morning's awkward reunion would be repeated again and again. In her six years as a Cyprian, she must have serviced upward of seventy different men. How long would it be before she chanced upon and was recognized by every last one of them? And how could a man love and respect his wife when he was constantly confronted with the evidence of her former harlotry?

The charming story of Mrs. Armistead and Mr. Fox notwithstanding, marrying Jack was absolutely out of the question now. There would be no quiet life in the country, away from the prying eyes and gossiping mouths of the London elite. Literally overnight, he had gone from being an army Lieutenant Colonel turned plain country gentleman to the ninth Earl of Innesford. A man with a title, a seat in Parliament, and a legacy to pass on to his heirs.

Heirs he would almost certainly never have if he married her.

Whatever ease she gave him from his horrific nightmares would be erased by the mockery marriage to her would make of his life, his future. The raw ache in her heart as she enumerated to herself everything he would toss away by tying himself to a woman who could never be accepted in polite society told her what she must do.

If she truly loved him, she would sacrifice her own selfish desires for the greater good. His good.

And most importantly, she must do it in a way that ensured

he would never have the opportunity to sway her, to change her mind. The break must be swift and brutal, so cruel that he would be too angry to come after her.

Her face was wet with tears as she packed her valise with the few personal items she could not do without. Brush, toothbrush, underthings. The gowns she had brought with her would have to stay. Mrs. Upshaw would buy new ones to replace them.

Calliope was going home. The only place she truly belonged.

16

The former Lieutenant Colonel in the Fourth Regiment of His Majesty's army and current Earl of Innesford was well on his way to getting drunk. Rip-roaring, falling-down, stinking, sodding drunk.

He tilted his empty brandy glass in the direction of the footman who hovered in the shadows near Jack's solitary table in the corner of White's, snorting in derision at the flicker of disapproval that crossed the man's face. The fellow's job was to serve the club's members as many drinks as they wanted, not pass judgment on the state of their sobriety.

It had been ten days since Harry's death, five since they had closed him up in the mausoleum at Ardesleigh.

And nine days, seventeen hours, and twenty-seven minutes since he'd returned from the most hellish day of his life—up to and including Waterloo—to find Callie gone. Without warning, without a note, without so much as a word of explanation.

The footman slid another tumbler of neat brandy across the table. Jack caught it and raised it to his lips, savoring the stinging bite of the liquor as it slid down his gullet and warmed his stomach. A shame his heart was as cold and dead as his brother. At least with sufficient alcohol in his system, he could expect to get a few hours of uninterrupted—if not particularly restorative—sleep.

"Evening, Innesford."

It took Jack three full heartbeats to remember that *he* was Innesford. The title had been his brother's and his father's before that. Jack had never imagined nor wanted it to be his.

The Marquess of Grenville, nattily attired in a dark green coat and buff breeches, stood beside the table. He indicated the chair across from Jack's. "Mind if I join you?"

Jack shrugged. "Suit yourself, my lord."

The marquess was apparently accustomed to doing just that, for he lowered his tall frame into the seat before Jack completed his grudging invitation.

"You look like hell," Grenville remarked conversationally after a few seconds of silence had elapsed.

Jack took another deep swallow of his brandy. Saints preserve him from the pontifications of strangers. "Good of you to notice."

"It would be hard to miss." The marquess extracted a cigar case from the inner breast pocket of his coat and flipped it open. "Care for one?" he asked, extending the box full of thin, elegantly wrapped cigars.

Jack shook his head. "No, thank you. I'm of the opinion that those things will kill you." He was fairly certain they had killed his father. The old man had smoked three or four a day, claiming they dried the unhealthful humors in the lungs. The doctors had diagnosed the earl's dry, hacking cough and shortness of breath as consumption, but Jack thought the cigars a more likely culprit.

"So will that swill if you drink enough of it," the other man said, gesturing toward Jack's brandy. He removed a cigar from the case and tapped one end against the table several times before setting it between his lips.

"That's my prerogative."

Grenville lit his cigar from the flame of the candle in the center of the table and blew out several puffs of smoke. "It most certainly is, and I won't keep you from it if that's your intention, but there is one thing I'd like to know before you succeed, if you wouldn't mind answering a question."

Jack shrugged. "Ask away." Given the marquess's flagrant air of entitlement, he'd ask anyway.

"How did the woman I know as Calliope from the Red Door come to be sleeping under your brother's roof?" One side of his mouth lifted in a lopsided grin that could only be described as admiring. "Not that I've any interest in accomplishing such a feat now that I'm a happily married man, you understand, but I have to confess to profound curiosity. Even at my most provocative, I wouldn't have dreamed of attempting anything so brash as to bring a who—"

Jack launched himself across the table, knocking his tumbler to the floor, and clenched his fist in the crisp silk of Grenville's cravat. "She is *not* a whore. She is—was," he corrected himself, "my betrothed."

The marquess's striking blue eyes widened, more with disbelief than fear. "The devil you say. I wouldn't have fancied Calliope as the sort of girl to pass herself off as a lady for a wedding ring."

"She didn't pass herself off," Jack responded through gritted teeth, shaking Grenville once by the throat before releasing him. "I knew. I asked her to marry me anyway. I didn't care. Don't care." He slumped back into his chair. "But it doesn't matter now. She left me. The same day Harry died."

"Wait a minute," Grenville said, readjusting his crumpled neckerchief. "You were prepared to marry her despite her . . . well, dubious past?"

Jack nodded morosely. Damn, he needed another drink. And another and another, until the knifing agony of her abandonment was reduced to a dull ache.

Grenville was silent for several long minutes. Then he rose from his chair. "Tell me something, Innesford. Do you love her?"

Did he love her? God help him, he couldn't not love her. Even when he hated her, he loved her.

If only she'd waited for him. He'd been brusque with her that morning, aching with grief and guilt over his brother's shocking death and still smarting with jealousy over the stark reality of meeting a man who'd held her, touched her, *known* her before he had.

If he had been gentler, less withdrawn, would she have left as she had? Or would she have given him a chance to convince her that the past truly didn't matter to him, that he could overcome his selfish wish that he could have been her first, her last, her only. Being her last would have to be enough. Was more than enough.

"Yes," he answered, "I love her."

Grenville dropped his hand onto Jack's right shoulder. "I love my wife, too. And I came damned close to losing her before I even had her because I was a stubborn fool. Go after her, man. Don't make the mistake I almost did."

Jack shook his head. "You don't understand. She left because she saw how I reacted when you recognized her. I wanted to tear you limb from limb. I told her the past didn't matter to me. But I lied. It does matter. Just not in the way she thinks."

"In what way does it matter?" Grenville asked gently.

"It matters because I know what those men will think when they see her, recognize her. What they'll tell their wives and sisters and mothers about her." He expelled a harsh, angry breath. "I didn't expect to inherit my brother's title. We were going to retire to Wiltshire, live quietly. And then Harry—" Jack slammed his fist on the table. "Goddamn him for getting himself killed and leaving me with the one thing I never wanted. And without the one person I truly need."

"You're afraid she'll be ostracized by Society, then? Whispered about behind her back? And miserable on account of it."

"I know she will be," Jack sighed. "I told her about Elizabeth Armistead and Fox. But I didn't tell her that Mrs. Armistead was never accepted by the ton."

Grenville made a low sound in his throat. It wasn't quite a chuckle, but it sounded oddly cheerful. "If that's the only thing that's stopping you, I believe I may have a solution to your problem."

17

Callie clipped roses in the small garden Mrs. Upshaw maintained behind the Red Door and her private apartments. She snipped the stems briskly and set the orange, yellow, and red blossoms in the basket beside her. The bright summer sunshine beat down her back, heating her skin through the white muslin gown, but the warmth was only superficial.

The chill that wrapped around her heart seemed permanent.

"You're a difficult woman to find."

Callie froze at the unmistakable sound of Jack's voice. She remembered, unbidden, what she'd thought the first time she heard him speak. Gravel and satin.

Had it only been a month since he had walked into her parlor and turned her entire existence on its ear? Controverted her every expectation from the moment he'd taken her upstairs and demanded she sleep with him? No, really *sleep* with him.

In her surprise, she accidentally sliced the head off a perfect red rose. She bent over to retrieve the decapitated bud.

"I didn't intend to be found. Or, more accurately, I didn't think you would come after me."

She felt him behind her more than she heard him, the heat from his body radiating like a roaring fire. And warming her, melting her as the sun couldn't. Her knees felt weak, wobbly.

His breath tingled against her neck. "You almost succeeded in keeping me away. I was angry and hurt by the way you left. I told myself it was better for both of us if I let you go. Fortunately, Lord Grenville brought me to my senses."

She whipped around to look at him. Sweet Mary Magdalene, he was beautiful. Not conventionally so, but the way she imagined mountains were beautiful—rough, jagged, and dangerous.

And those eyes, metallic and magnetic. There was no escaping them.

"L-lord Grenville?"

Jack grinned. "Perhaps you know him as Nathaniel Kent."

She thought her eyes might very well fall out of their sockets. "What did Nathaniel do?"

He gently removed the clippers from her hand and set them next to the basket. "He told me not to be a damn fool and lose the woman I love."

She gulped. "You . . . love me?"

Chuckling, he framed his face in her hands. "Why else would I ask you to marry me? Why else would you drive away my nightmares and give me peace? Why else would I have spent the past ten days drowning my memories of you in alcohol and failing miserably?"

"I—I—"

"Those were rhetorical questions. The only question I want you to answer is do you love me?"

"Oh, God, of course I do. Why do you think I left? Because I love you too much to—"

His mouth crushed down on hers—greedy, desperate, possessive. All her well-thought-out objections, all her noble self-sacrificing sentiments disintegrated beneath the sundering persuasiveness of his kiss. He tasted of love, longing, acceptance, and belonging.

How could she ever have thought her place was here? Since returning, she hadn't been able even to contemplate taking on a client. Mrs. Upshaw had set her to work greeting customers, gauging their preferences, and steering them toward whichever girl—or man—would best satisfy his needs. But the arrangement was temporary and soon, Callie would either have to return to her usual duties or find other employment.

Or neither.

She sighed and wrapped her arms around Jack's neck, returning his kiss with all the passion and conviction she possessed. The only place she belonged was right here, in Jack's arms. Home at last, home forever.

With a reluctant growl, Jack broke off the kiss. "Please tell me this means you'll marry me." He withdrew and reached into his breast pocket, extracting a folded sheet of parchment. "Preferably today. This is a special license and the vicar at St. George's is waiting for us."

Jubilation made her weak, shaky. *Just say yes. He loves you. You love him.* Her conscience held her back, pricking the bubble of her elation.

His lips twisted into a wry smile. "I know you're concerned about how we'll cope in London. How the ton will treat us, you. But you needn't be concerned." He caressed her cheek with the back of his hand. "You may not know it, but your friend Nathaniel Kent is a very powerful man. In addition to being a marquess, he is heir to one of the richest and oldest duchies in England. Though he has long had a decidedly lurid reputation, he's recently married, gone respectable. He has offered to have his wife and his sister sponsor you before the Queen. And once you have been presented, they will ease your entry into society. There will be a whispers and mild disapproval, but no one would dare to give the cut direct to a friend of the powerful Hardwycks."

Callie bit her lip, her eyes filling with tears. "I cannot believe you are willing to accept his help. Not after the way you looked at me when he recognized me outside your brother's room. You were . . . disgusted, revolted by me, by what you knew I had done with him and others."

"Disgusted by you?" he exclaimed. He drew her toward her chest, embracing her fiercely. "Oh, God, never. I'll admit, it isn't easy for me to accept that he has been your lover. I was jealous, pure and simple. And I can't promise I will never be jealous again should I come face-to-face with another of your former paramours. But I can promise that I will never hold my irrational feelings against you. I love you too much to lose you over what cannot be changed."

Despair threatened to choke her even as her admiration for him—his unbelievable generosity and magnaminity—grew like garden weeds. "And what about what can be changed?" she whispered. "What about your future?"

"My future?"

Miserable, she nodded. "Children. Heirs. You need them, now more than ever. And I am barren."

"Barren? How do you know? How can you be sure?"

She emitted a bitter laugh. "Breeding is a common hazard of my profession. Yet in six years, I have never once conceived. It is impossible to imagine I have simply been lucky. The only possible explanation is that I cannot conceive."

A long, painful silence stretched between them as Jack absorbed this information. Callie's heart crumbled like old, dry cheese. She held her breath, waiting for the inevitable end to a beautiful dream.

"I don't care." His tone was even, but his eyes swirled with emotion.

"You must. You are an earl now." She looked straight ahead at his chest, the brim of her straw bonnet shielding her from his powerful gaze. Ridiculously, she noticed for the first time that his cravat was rumpled and askew, donned in haste, and a half-sob, half-giggle burst from her lips.

He grasped her chin and tilted her head back, forcing her to look at him. Always the commander, always demanding the attention of his men. Or his woman.

"I didn't want this title, never expected to have it. Life conspired to give it to me despite my wishes." His features softened. "Life also conspired to give me you. To give me some measure of peace and contentment despite the past I can't forget. My own past. And I am willing to put my faith in life to give me what I need. If you are indeed barren, and we never have children, then so be it. I won't miss children I've never had. But I will miss you desperately, with every beat of my heart and breath of my lungs." He traced the arch of her eyebrow with the pad of his thumb. "As I have done every day for the past two weeks. And besides," he added with a lopsided grin, "I'm beginning to expect the things I least expect." His hand cupped the curve of her belly. "Perhaps I'm expecting it already."

"I am not with child," she assured him. "I have had recent evidence to the contrary."

He laughed and lifted her off the ground, twirling her around until she was dizzy, elated, and laughing herself. "Then we'll just have to try again. As soon as possible. Which means you had best marry me today, and avert the additional scandal of an eight-month baby."

"You are so certain, how can I say no?"

"You can't, thank God." His features alight with love and passion, he carried her to a bench shielded from the house by a thick hedgerow, and made good on his promise to try again.

By Callie's estimation, he was entirely successful.

SINFULLY EVER AFTER

1

Lady Jane St. Clair had been quietly, desperately in love with Gerard Everett, Earl of Chester, for more than half her life. When she was ten, her dewy-eyed devotion had seemed harmless enough, a childlike, uncomplicated emotion. In the ensuing eleven years, however, her innocent adoration had not dimmed, but instead matured into the full-blooded, full-bodied passion of a grown woman.

All the more reason she must not succumb to temptation and accept his proposal.

A gentle squeeze of her gloved hand brought her back to the present. Gerard—she supposed she ought to think of him as Lord Chester now that he had inherited his uncle's title, but it was difficult after so many years—sat beside her on the gold-and-mulberry-cushioned settee, his large, thick-lashed brown eyes bearing down on her with all their persuasive weight.

"Please, Jane, say you will make me the happiest of men."

What a ridiculously clichéd thing for him to say, Jane scoffed to herself, but her heart danced a jig anyway. He sounded so earnest, as though he really believed the words.

If only he weren't so handsome. So charming. So utterly incapable of fidelity.

She tore her gaze away from his face, from the sincerity of his expression. "Why?"

"Why?" Even with her eyes averted, she could see his eyebrows draw together and his lips crumple with confusion.

"Why would marrying me make you the happiest of men, my lord?" Her voice caught a little, strangled by thickness of her throat.

He caught her chin between his fingers and turned her head so that she had to look at him. Blast him, he was as practiced an actor as ever lived! Now he appeared not puzzled, but wounded.

"Jane, you are everything a man in my position could possibly want in a wife. It is always a pleasure to be in your company. You are kind, intelligent, well-read, and witty."

But not beautiful. Even when he intended to flatter her, Gerard couldn't bring himself to tell her she was beautiful.

He massaged her palm with his thumb. "In fact, I daresay you are my dearest friend," he continued, heedless of the terrible longing that swelled in her breast and belly at his touch. "There is no woman I admire and esteem more than you, Jane St. Clair, and no other woman I would rather have by my side for the rest of my life."

What of passion? she wanted to shout. *What of love?*

But she knew the answer. Aristocratic marriages were seldom based on passion or love. Those that were, like her brother's, incited more ridicule than respect. In truth, admiration, esteem, and friendship were a better foundation for a successful union than the financial and dynastic concerns that induced many couples to marry. Most would consider themselves lucky to have that much.

She could not blame Gerard for being a product of his station, any more than she could blame him for not loving her as she loved him. For not desiring her as she desired him. Why should he want "plain Jane" when he could have his pick of the loveliest wives and widows of the ton, of the most expensive actresses and courtesans? Like colorful flowers, the beautiful ladies beckoned him and he flitted from one to the next, never satisfied to light in one place for long, always in search of a brighter, prettier blossom.

But he did always come back to her. She *was* his dearest friend.

Every mistress he took, every light-skirt he slept with, was already a knife in her heart. Marrying him could do naught but deepen the wound. But if he married someone else, she would have no part of him at all, and that would cut her heart out altogether.

A tremulous smile formed on her lips and she nodded. "Yes, Gerard. Yes, I will marry you."

His beautifully sculpted features lit with pleasure and he pressed his lips, dry and chaste, to her cheek. "Thank you, Jane. You won't regret it."

Too late.

"I say, Chester, you look like the cat who drank the cream." The Earl of Holyfield rose from their customary table in the corner of Brooks' and extended his palm in greeting. "Which deserving gentleman have you cuckolded this week?"

Gerard clasped his friend's hand and grinned. "None yet, but then, 'tis only Tuesday." He nodded to the footman who stood a discreet distance away. The gray-haired servant responded with a bow before turning on his heels to fetch Gerard his drink.

"Hmmm," Holyfield murmured, his hawkish features sharpening with curiosity. "I've never seen you look pleased with yourself unless you were gloating over a new conquest."

"And who is to say I am not?" Gerard wiggled his eyebrows

as he took his seat, unable to stop grinning. He hadn't expected today's campaign to resolve quite so easily or satisfactorily as it had.

Holyfield raised his eyebrows skeptically. "Oh? And when do you plan to elucidate me as to your new light-o'-love's identity?" He settled into his chair and reached for his glass.

The footman appeared and set a tumbler on the table, then faded into the shadows. Gerard lifted the cut crystal and swirled the amber liquid beneath his nostrils. The rich, biting scent of his favorite French brandy was unmistakable.

He took a sip before giving his friend and cousin a mock frown. "Now, really, Holyfield, that's no way to speak of a man's future wife."

The earl's jaw dropped in a most gratifying fashion. "Wife? You?"

"Why not me? Marriage seems to agree with you well enough." That was an understatement. His cousin fairly exuded wedded bliss, as did the Marquess of Grenville, Lady Jane's elder brother, and really, *that* had been far from anyone's expectation given his sordid reputation.

Holyfield harrumphed noisily and then sighed. "Yes, why not you? Very well, then. You must tell me all about this paragon who has induced you to abandon your commitment to bachelorhood. It's far too early in the Season to be one of this year's crop of debutantes. A lovely, young widow, perchance? Or have you decided to make an honest woman of an opera singer and thereby drive my beloved aunt to an early grave?"

"Neither," came the gruff response.

Gerard didn't have to turn his head to know the source of the voice. *Grenville.* And he sounded none too pleased.

The marquess, a tall, elegant man who would have cut an imposing figure even if he weren't richer than Croesus and his family nearly as powerful as Prinny himself, ambled round the table and folded himself into the chair across from Gerard.

Though his expression was bland and his pose deliberately casual, Grenville exuded a predator's air of violence. And Gerard had a strong intuition that he was on the menu.

Holyfield looked from one man to the other in obvious confusion. "I'm sure one of you will enlighten me in due course."

Grenville folded his arms over his chest, crossed his legs at the ankles, and fixed Gerard with a hard blue stare. The challenge was both implicit and unequivocal.

With a shrug, Gerard turned toward his cousin. "This morning, I asked Lady Jane St. Clair to marry me." He chose to ignore Holyfield's visible recoil, and pressed cheerfully ahead. "And she has graciously agreed to make me the happiest of men."

The earl looked at the marquess, and something Gerard couldn't read passed between them. The two other men were of an age, had attended Eton and Oxford together, and remained the best of friends despite the fact that Holyfield had eloped with Grenville's intended bride and Grenville had subsequently married Holyfield's jilted betrothed.

Holyfield trained his shrewd green gaze on Gerard. "Lady Jane will make some lucky man an excellent wife. But you, my friend, will make her a lousy husband."

Gerard bristled at the implication. "You think I don't love her, don't you?" He narrowed his focus back to Grenville. "You, too, I suppose?"

Grenville raised a single eyebrow. "She may be my sister, but I am not blind, and neither are you. It will take more than a show of indignation to convince me you've fallen head over heels for her now when you've known her for years."

Gerard set his empty tumbler back on the table with a thud. "You sell your sister short, Grenville. What she lacks for beauty on the outside is more than compensated for by the depth of her mind and the quality of character."

"And you are certainly known for your pursuit of women with depth." Grenville snorted. "Deep pussies, mayhap, but scarcely deep minds. Can you look me in the eye and tell me you love my sister enough to be faithful to her?"

Gerard spun his glass between his fingers. He had to admire the marquess's candor. At the same time, the notion of fidelity in a ton marriage was ludicrous. No one expected it, and a married man who didn't keep an occasional mistress was suspected of being either impotent or on the verge of destitution.

Perhaps Grenville, married less than a year and to all appearances wildly smitten with his wife, could be forgiven for clinging to the delusion that he would never stray from her. Or she from him. After all, Society women were just as fickle and faithless as their male counterparts. And thank God for that, for the wives of his peers had provided him with many hours of pleasurable diversion.

But in the end, diversion was all they could provide. Passion was ephemeral. Once a woman's body had yielded its secrets, revealed where and how to touch for greatest effect, greatest mutual benefit, the thrill soon faded. The affair was best ended before monotony and boredom set in and killed any remaining esteem the partners might yet have for one another.

Gerard had been through it dozens of times. No woman, no matter how beautiful or skilled in bed, could hold his interest for more than a few months.

No woman except Lady Jane St. Clair. Her quick wit amused him. Her quiet intelligence daunted him. Her kindness soothed him. Though he felt nothing remotely like lust for her, he never tired of her company. She was the one woman to whom he had ever maintained any sort of constancy.

He marveled now that it had taken him so long to see the obvious. Though Jane did not possess the sort of beauty that drove a man to sonnets and frenzied passion, these were the qualities of a mistress. Gerard had no need of a mistress—they were as easily picked as daisies and just as short-lived. What he needed was a wife, a partner, a companion. A friend. And Jane was the only woman of his acquaintance who had ever fit that description.

Grenville and Holyfield both watched Gerard with stern, impatient gazes, awaiting his answer to the question of his commitment to fidelity. But it all depended on what it meant to be faithful, didn't it? He loved Jane. Not in the way that the two men staring him down believed they loved their wives, to be sure, but in an even more solid, more permanent one. Regardless of where he spent his lust, he would be always faithful to Jane in the only way that mattered—his heart.

Confident now that his response was no lie, he looked Grenville straight in the eyes. "I do," he said simply, honestly.

The marquess and earl exchanged another set of unreadable glances. After a few seconds, Holyfield shrugged and raised his eyebrows. Grenville scowled and shook his head before turning his attention back to Gerard.

"Damn me if I don't believe you're telling the truth, Chester." Grenville rose to his feet and extended his hand. "Welcome to the family."

Gerard stood and shook his future brother-in-law's hand. His eyes widened slightly when Grenville tightened his grip. The marquess pulled Gerard into what would appear to others to be a friendly embrace, but was in fact a threatening one.

"See that you start by breaking it off with your current mistress." Grenville whispered the words next to Gerard's ear. "I won't have my sister announcing her engagement to a man who is openly keeping another woman."

"Of course," Gerard responded easily. In truth, it would be no hardship. He'd been planning to end his association with Therese anyway. Although she had been his mistress a scant three weeks, she'd already begun to wear on him with her constant demands—for more of his time, for more of his money, for more of everything than he was willing to give.

"And while the banns are being read, you will attend my sister like a besotted man. Balls, the opera, phaeton rides on Rotten Row, the lot of it. Do I make myself quite clear?" Grenville bore down a bit harder on the hand he still clasped to emphasize his point.

Gerard tensed his fingers but held his ground. Despite the difference in their heights, Gerard had no doubt he could take the marquess in a fight. He had nothing to prove by arguing and everything to gain by acquiescence.

"You are far more conservative than your reputation would have me expect, Grenville." He kept his tone light. "A truly besotted man never waits."

A hand slapped his back. "Well, there's one thing you'd better wait for," Holyfield joked good-naturedly. "Grenville's downright old-fashioned when it comes to his sister's virtue."

Gerard gave a wry laugh. That was the one thing he felt reasonably sure he could wait for indefinitely.

2

Jane paced the gold and ivory carpet in short, sharp strides. With each abrupt turn as she reached the edge, her pale green muslin skirt whipped around her ankles.

"Saints preserve us, you're making me positively giddy. Do sit down with us and have a cup of tea." Jane's best friend and sister-in-law, Eleanor, adopted a cajoling tone as she patted the velvet seat cushion beside her.

"Heavens, yes." Lady Caroline Prescott, Countess of Innesford, agreed with an emphatic harrumph. "If you continue in that fashion, you shall wear a hole right through the floor and solve your problem in the most permanent and unpleasant way possible."

Although the idea of falling through a hole in the floor—or preferably, the earth—held a certain appeal at the moment, Jane had to smile at the image the words brought to mind. Where would she land? Probably smack in the middle of the formal sitting room where her mother and her friends were also taking tea this afternoon. That would be most humiliating indeed . . . and painful.

"Very well," she sighed at last, and plopped down onto the seat Eleanor had indicated. She looked from one woman to the other, and despair welled again in her throat.

They were both so beautiful, so feminine, and so utterly adored by their husbands. With their matching blonde hair, sparkling blue eyes, and delicate features, they could easily be mistaken for sisters, though nothing could be further from the truth. Caroline—or Callie, as she preferred to be called—had been born in the slums of London and then worked in the city's most exclusive brothel. Her marriage last summer to Lord Jack Prescott had been the scandal of the Season, far eclipsing the Earl of Holyfield's earlier elopement with Lady Louisa Bennett, whom Jane's brother had jilted at the altar only the week before.

It seemed everyone but Jane was destined for a happily ever after.

Though it was by rights Jane's duty as hostess, Eleanor lifted the elaborately carved silver teapot and poured a stream of steaming liquid into Jane's cup, then added a dollop of cream.

"I don't understand how you can fret yourself so," Eleanor said, pressing the cup into Jane's hand. "You have been besotted with Chester ever since I met you. You should be thrilled that he returns your affections."

Jane took a deep breath and released it slowly, determined not to weep in front of her friends. She had made her own bed, her eyes fully open, and she was now consigned to lie in it. "Surely you cannot believe a man like Lord Chester could be in love with someone like me. At least, not in the way my brother loves you or Lord Prescott loves Callie."

"Why ever not?" Callie's tone was brisk and no-nonsense, as was her wont.

Jane rolled her eyes. "I should think it would be obvious to anyone with functioning eyesight. How could a woman as plain as I possibly inspire passion in a man like Lord Chester?"

Callie released a short bark of laughter. "You are sadly misinformed about the character of men if you think the only thing that matters to them is a pretty face. I have seen you in your shift, Lady Jane, and you have more than ample," she paused, clearly casting for a suitable word, which could hardly be easy for a woman of her experience, "assets to attract a man of Chester's bent."

"Indeed," Eleanor added with a rueful smile, "Callie and I both have reason to envy certain of those assets." She tugged at the neckline of her bodice to emphasize her distinct lack of cleavage. "At least you have never been mistaken for a boy."

Jane shook her head, chuckling. She appreciated her friends' attempts to humor her, but she was far too practical in nature to be comforted by their words. Gerard could choose any woman he wanted to warm his bed. He needn't settle for a pretty face over a womanly figure or vice versa. Though Jane could admit that she had a rather fine bosom and a fashionably small waist that widened into softly rounded hips, she was certain Gerard had never noticed. He looked at her the way her brother did, as if she were twelve years old, evincing not the slightest interest in the curves the ensuing years had bestowed.

Callie was right about one thing, however. Jane was woefully ignorant in matters of the flesh, and deliberately so. A well-bred lady, she could plan an elaborate dinner party, play a complicated tune on the pianoforte, and produce stitches so even and fine they were scarcely visible to the naked eye. Nor had her parents neglected her intellectual education, for she had learnt Latin and French, and could converse in either language nearly as glibly as in English. In short, she was schooled to be the perfect wife in every regard but one.

The thought leapt to mind so abruptly, Jane had no time to examine its rationality before the words were out of her mouth.

"Perhaps if I knew what might please him, if I understood what a man desires when he takes a woman to his bed, I might have some chance of . . ." She trailed off, realizing how absurd this must sound.

She might have a chance of what? Ensuring his fidelity? Ensnaring him in the bonds of love? What utter claptrap. Any one of the ladies with whom he'd dallied in the past would surely have accomplished the task long ago if it were as simple as that.

But even as her cheeks flushed with humiliation at her foolishness, Eleanor and Callie exchanged shrewd glances, their silent communication both clear and completely unintelligible. Callie raised an eyebrow. Eleanor responded with a quirk of her lip and a small nod. A question asked and answered in the affirmative. But the question itself? Jane couldn't begin to guess, though it must have something to do with her ridiculous suggestion.

Both women smiled and turned nearly identical blue gazes on Jane. Eleanor spoke first.

"If you were marrying any man but Lord Chester, I would advise you to wait for your wedding night, but . . ." She trailed off, her cheeks pinkening as though finishing the thought aloud would embarrass her.

Callie, who had never suffered a moment's embarrassment when it came to carnal matters, picked up the thread after the minutest of pauses. "But with a man of Lord Chester's appetites, it would behoove you to know what's what in the bedroom. Your mother's speech isn't likely to do you any justice when the time comes."

Eleanor's cheeks grew redder still. "Not if it is anything like *my* mother's. And knowing yours, Jane, 'tis bound to be even less helpful."

Callie snorted. "Indeed, her Grace will probably tell you to lie back, let him do as he pleases, and then ask for more pin money when he's done."

Jane grimaced. That did rather sound like something her mother would say. The duchess was not precisely avaricious by nature, but she always expected her suffering to be recompensed. Jane's father had been paying off his transgressions in a lifetime's worth of gowns, jewelry, and other costly baubles. Judging by the state of her mother's wardrobe, she had suffered at her husband's hands nearly as much as her children had. At least she had something to show for it, Jane thought bitterly.

Not that she desired expensive gifts from Gerard Everett. Raised in lavish material opulence, Jane only wanted the one thing she'd never truly had—love. And sometimes, when they were together and his attention was focused on her as they discussed some matter of politics or art or literature, the prospect that he might one day come to love her, if only she could discover the proper inducement, seemed tantalizingly real.

Even so, the idea of learning "what was what" in the bedroom from her best friends—one of whom was married to her *brother*—made her more than a little uncomfortable. Did she really want to know what Eleanor got up to with Nathaniel in the privacy of their bedchamber? Jane was well aware that her brother had once possessed an unsavory reputation when it came to fleshly pursuits, but that didn't mean she wanted firsthand descriptions of all those pursuits might entail.

And then there was Callie, whose Biblical knowledge might be even greater than Nathaniel's. Jane had been apprised of Callie's past before they met for the first time, and though Jane knew precisely how shocking and scandalous her friend's former profession was, she had never given a great deal of thought to what, exactly, it meant to be a Cyprian in an expensive bordello. Nor was she entirely sure she wanted to find out directly from the source.

But if there was even the remotest hope that *this* was what would bring her fully into the affections of the one man who made her stomach twinge and her skin tingle and her heart flutter, then she would do it. Even if the thought made her queasy.

She drew a shaky breath. "Very well, then. If you think it is wise, I shall turn myself over to your tutelage."

Eleanor and Callie exchanged bewildered looks, then burst into peals of laughter. Jane watched, poised between irritation and embarrassment, as they giggled for nearly a full minute.

"Oh, no, we shan't be teaching you," Eleanor managed at last, pressing her palm between her breasts and panting for air as she spoke. "That wouldn't be at all proper."

Jane stifled a snort of disbelief. Could there be anyone— save a lady's husband, of course—for whom such a task *would* be proper? Propriety was quite out of the question at this point.

"Certainly not," Callie agreed, breathless with mirth. "We have someone else entirely in mind for the job."

Jane might have learnt precisely whom had a masculine voice not boomed from the doorway, "And what job might that be?"

Gerard's sweet, rich baritone was unmistakable, sending familiar swirls of heat curling from her chest down through her belly. She didn't have to turn her head to know he would look every bit as appealing as he sounded. From the top of his dark brown head to the tips of his booted toes, he would appear every inch the refined and respectable gentleman—combed, tailored, pressed, and knotted down to the minutest detail. But his eyes would tell another story, sparkling with that edge of mischief and fun that told even an innocent such as herself that out of his clothes, he would be anything but respectable.

Jane wasn't prone to swooning, but between her physical response to the sound of his voice and the terrifying prospect that he might have heard more of their conversation than his question implied, her head swam so fiercely, she thought she might well succumb to this embarrassingly female predilection.

Ah well. If she did, at least she had an empty plate to plant her face in.

3

Three startled pairs of eyes set in three guilty countenances fixed upon Gerard as he strolled into his betrothed's private sitting room on the third floor of the Duke of Hardwyck's vast and elaborate town house. The ladies sat around a small table laid with tea and cakes. Though their plates were empty and the tray in the center was still piled high with sweets, steam no longer rose from their cups, indicating they had been doing a great deal more talking—and, to judge by their expressions, plotting—than eating or drinking.

And his masculine intuition said whatever they were up to, he was the target. But then, when it came to scheming members of the fairer sex, he usually was.

To his admiration, Jane was the first of the three to gather her wits and find her voice. "Ger—Lord Ch—Chester," she stammered, her cheeks flushed, eyes bright. "Wh-what b—brings you here this morn?"

She looked, he thought with some surprise, downright pretty when she was caught off guard. It was a pleasant, if somewhat alarming, discovery. On the other hand, the mild tug of attraction that pulled at his groin would make his task of appearing the besotted bridegroom and thereby appeasing her brother that much easier.

He grinned and pressed his hand dramatically over his heart. "You wound me, my darling. Surely a man requires no motive to visit his future bride other than that he desires the pleasure of her company."

Ambling round to her side of the table, he knelt next to her and took her white-gloved hand in his. He raised it to his lips, the delicate scent of her lilac perfume teasing his nostrils and causing another unsettling twinge low in his belly. He did his best to ignore the sensation, which he had never before associated with Jane, and forged ahead with his performance.

Even though he was no longer entirely sure it *was* a performance.

"Or have you forgotten that you agreed only yesterday to be my bride? Must I propose again this morning before an audience so there may be witnesses to remind you?"

Jane snatched her hand back and swatted playfully at his. "Oh, do stop putting on, my lord. You know very well I haven't forgotten. It is only . . . I was not expecting you, and it *is* customary to have oneself introduced by a footman."

"You know I never learnt to stand on ceremony, what with being raised a poor relation. I suppose I shall have to rely on you to keep me in line now that you are to be my countess." He gave a careless shrug and leaned in a bit closer, unexpectedly entranced by this vantage on the rise and fall of her generous bosom. "Tell me, what other transgressions must I account for this day?" Aside from the almost overwhelming urge to bury his face in the hollow between her breasts and breathe in her tantalizing scent.

His cock gave an impatient twitch, and the fall of his breeches grew decidedly tight. Gerard realized that, should he come to his feet, his semiaroused state would be evident to all assembled.

"You mean aside from interrupting my private tea, failing to properly acknowledge my companions, and remaining on one knee for so long you are like to be stuck there?" Jane teased, her intelligent eyes sparkling with merriment. To his relief, she seemed blissfully unaware of his predicament, but he feared her ignorance was destined to be short-lived. "Do stand up, my lord, lest we require the assistance of a crane to restore you to your feet."

Think fast, Everett. And for the love of God, stop staring at her tits as if you'd never seen a pair before.

The self-admonition served to ease his budding erection just enough to allow him to stand without humiliating himself. If the ladies noticed at all, they'd likely think him a well-hung young stallion rather than a randy old stoat. With an exaggerated groan, he rose to his feet, then executed a deep bow toward Lady Jane's guests.

"Lady Grenville, Lady Innesford," he said, using the moment he was bent at the waist to make what he hoped would be an imperceptible adjustment to his nether parts to further disguise his dilemma. "I apologize for my earlier discourtesy, but I am afraid I was quite overwhelmed by my eagerness to see my betrothed."

Not to mention by the startling discovery that the emotion he'd thought to feign had somehow become real.

Lady Grenville waved a white-gloved hand. "Think nothing of it, Lord Chester. A man is entitled to be overcome in the presence of his beloved."

Jane coughed loudly. A surreptitious glance in her direction revealed she had narrowed a disapproving glare upon her friend. Clearly, he hadn't convinced her of his undying devotion with his show thus far.

Lady Grenville was not put off in the slightest by Jane's irritation, however. The marchioness smiled sweetly up at him, making her face even more angelically lovely than it already was, though that hardly seemed possible. Odd that her beauty, and that of the equally ethereal Lady Innesford, left him cold. Their cool, dainty blond looks held little appeal to him today.

Instead, his gaze kept sliding back to Jane, to her plain, round face surrounded by plain, round ringlets of plain, brown hair. And damn it, to her ample breasts and below, to where the light green fabric of her dress clung to the gentle inward curve of her waist and the outward flare of her hip. Hips that looked perfect in width and shape for a man to hold onto while he thrust his cock deep inside her tight, wet pussy.

Bloody hell. Sweat prickled at the back of his neck. He had to complete his performance and leave, before he truly *was* overcome by her presence. A reaction that made no sense whatsoever.

"Will you join us for tea, my lord?" Jane asked, eyeing him curiously.

Bloody hell, he was staring at her.

"I can have a footman bring in another chair," she offered.

Stay for tea? Not until he could gain control over his suddenly unpredictable prick.

He shook his head. "I'm afraid I'm expected in Parliament within the hour, my lady." An outright lie—the Lords were not in session today and he had no appointments—but she needn't know that. "I stopped by only to inquire as to your availability to join me, my mother, and my aunt at the opera tomorrow evening." Another lie. He'd intended to take her on a phaeton ride in Hyde Park, the first in the series of events he had planned to demonstrate his affections, but that was out of the question now.

"Yes, of course. I should be delighted."

"Excellent. We shall arrive to fetch you at seven o'clock sharp. And now, if you will excuse me, ladies, I shall leave you to your tea."

"Tomorrow night, you say?" The query came from Lady Innesford.

He nodded in response.

"Then you must fetch her at the Grenvilles', as she will be staying with them for the next few days so Lady Grenville may assist her in the preparation of her trousseau."

A series of sly glances passed between the ladies, and again he was aware of the niggling sense that they shared a guilty secret. One he would have been inclined to explore if he did not possess one of his own.

"Very well, then. Seven o'clock at the Grenvilles'."

He executed another bow and beat a hasty retreat from the sitting room. What on earth had come over him? he wondered as he took the two flights of stairs two at a time and practically flew out the front door of Hardwyck House, to the bemusement of the footman who'd let him in only moments before.

It must be the prospect of celibacy that made him respond as he had, he decided as he took the reins of his phaeton from another of the Hardwycks' impeccably liveried servants. Having broken it off with Therese, he'd thought to wait until after the wedding to take another woman, simply because he'd imagined it would make the task of bedding his wife both easier and more pleasurable—for both of them. Clearly, that wasn't necessary. If he waited that long to fuck a woman, he would fall upon his poor, virginal wife like a rutting beast and both frighten and hurt her.

No, it was best for both of them if he sated his lust elsewhere. And soon.

4

Jane wished fervently for a fan, but when she'd changed into one of the maid's costumes at Eleanor's behest, she'd quite forgot to tuck one into a pocket. And Lord knew she had plenty of pockets in the apron that covered the scratchy gray wool gown she wore.

Now, she suffered for the lapse, for between her burning cheeks and the heat simmering in her belly, she was in desperate need of any means by which to cool herself. Although perhaps that might not be such a good idea. The implement might only serve to fan the flames and cause her to go up in a pillar of fire.

When Callie and Eleanor had revealed their intention to send Jane to Mrs. Upshaw, the madam and owner of the Red Door, for instruction in the arts of the bedchamber, Jane's initial response had been strenuous objection. What if she were seen entering or exiting the brothel? And how would the madam teach her? Through practical experience? Inconceivable!

But her friends assured her she would only visit Mrs. Upshaw's private residence, not the brothel itself, and to ensure total discretion, in disguise as a housemaid. As to the second concern, the madam had an extensive library from which Jane could learn everything she needed to know. There was, in other words, nothing to fear with regard either to her reputation or her virtue.

Reassured, Jane had agreed to the plan, but now as she sat with the makeshift book of colorfully illustrated cards bound together by ribbons, she wasn't sure her virtue was not in quite as grave a danger here in the supposed safety of Mrs. Upshaw's library as it would be in the Sodom housed next door. Jane now understood the risk of too much knowledge, grasped the reason young ladies such as herself were kept ignorant of carnal matters. The threat of corruption came not from the outside, but from within. From the temptation not merely to look at and imagine but engage in and enjoy every sinful act, no matter how outrageous and unthinkable.

Take, for example, this final card, which depicted a man and a woman, both naked, their bodies entwined in the most shocking possible way. The woman straddled the man's face, and the pink tip of his tongue peeked out from between his lips and pressed up against her woman's flesh. As if that weren't scandalous enough, the woman leaned over him, the rosy tips of her nipples brushing his abdomen, and took his male appendage into her mouth. An appendage which appeared to be much larger and much . . . sturdier than she had ever seen on any male nude— and she had studied drawings of more than a few male nudes in the art books she purloined from the shelves in her brother's library.

Jane had thought she had a reasonable, if rudimentary, understanding of what passed between husbands and wives behind closed doors, but she had never in her most lurid fantasies imagined even half the acts depicted in the twenty or so cards that made up the madam's "primer." The first few had been relatively predictable. Couples embracing, kissing, caressing. Then scenes of copulation, the positions progressively more astonishing, more acrobatic. And finally, men and women using their lips, tongues, and fingers in the most amazing, inconceivable ways.

If this was the primer, what on earth was in the next book? And would she like it if Gerard did such things to her? Touched her in her most secret woman's place with his mouth?

The twinge in her belly and the rush of dampness from between her legs said she probably would, were it not the for the shame that threatened to melt her at the mere idea of Gerard—or any man—touching her in so intimate, so *wicked* a manner.

"Do you have any questions, my dear?"

Startled, Jane jerked her gaze from the makeshift book, her face growing hotter at the realization that Mrs. Upshaw knew precisely which image Jane had been scrutinizing with such fascination. She wasn't sure whether the madam's decidedly maternal appearance was comforting or distressing, for if Jane had been asked to conjure a mental image of the owner of a bawdyhouse, the woman who stood before her was the last picture she would have conjured. Setting aside the bright red rouge she wore on her wide lips, from the top of her feather-decked head to the matronly cut of her lavender satin gown to the tips of her sensible black dance slippers, Mrs. Upshaw resembled nothing so much as the mother of the bride at a Society wedding. The resulting clash between expectation and reality had initially eased Jane's anxiety, but now made her feel like a child caught filching an extra biscuit from the tea tray.

Swallowing hard as she met the madam's kindly but knowing gaze, she choked out the question at the forefront of her mind. "Do people . . . do they *truly* do such things?"

The corners of Mrs. Upshaw's mouth twitched as though she were trying to repress a peal of good-natured laughter. "Oh, my, yes! And a great deal more, though, of course, much of what takes place depends upon the tastes of the persons involved." She walked alongside Jane's chair and gestured toward the picture of the embracing couple. "For example, I regret to say that while I have encountered few gentlemen who do not enjoy it when a woman sucks their co . . . er . . ."

Mrs. Upshaw chewed on her lower lip for a second, and Jane had the distinct impression the madam had been about to use a coarse term but had thought better of it. A great pity, for Jane would have liked some other word for that part of a man's anatomy than "male appendage," much as she would like be able to refer to the soft, swollen, throbbing flesh between her thighs as something other than her "woman's place."

"Er . . . ," the older woman continued after a brief pause, "services them in such a manner, relatively few are willing to return the favor as shown there. 'Tis a shame, too, for it is quite as pleasurable for women as for men to be treated so." The madam patted Jane's shoulder and smiled. "I do hope your betrothed is one of those few, my lady. Every woman should be fortunate enough to have a man who sees to her pleasure as much as to his own."

Jane vacillated between disappointment and relief at the madam's words. Was Gerard the sort of man to put his face between a woman's thighs and lick her there? Would he be aroused or repulsed by the scent, the texture, the dampness of her woman's flesh? She couldn't begin to guess, since she was hardly sure how she felt about them herself.

But in the end, did it matter? She had come to learn how to please him, not herself.

Crushing the last of her maidenly reticence, Jane flipped back through the cards until she reached the one that depicted a woman kneeling before a man. His hands dug into her hair, and she appeared to engulf the entire length of him in her mouth.

Jane pointed bravely at the picture and looked up at the madam. "So, it is safe to assume that any man would be pleased if his wife were to do this for him?"

Mrs. Upshaw's light brown eyes sparkled with merriment,

but her expression was as solemn as a nun's at Jane's earnest query. "Oh, indeed, my lady, I have yet to encounter the man who is proof against that practice."

Jane studied the picture again, trying to imagine precisely what it was about being swallowed—and possibly bitten!—that would be remotely appealing. The idea struck her as more likely to be alarming given the extent to which men seemed keen to protect that particular portion of their anatomy from harm.

Nor could she quite fathom the mechanics of the entire operation. How long would the woman hold him in her mouth like that? The position looked, to Jane's eyes, decidedly uncomfortable. And did the woman remain perfectly still or did she *do* something? Though Jane couldn't begin to guess what . . .

Really, these motionless drawings were not as enlightening as one might have hoped!

The longer she contemplated the image, the more her eyebrows drew together and the more her lips puckered with confusion.

"Is aught amiss, my lady?"

Jane shook her head, but then changed her mind and nodded slowly. She could not afford to prevaricate if she had any hope of achieving her goal. Of keeping Gerard from straying from her bed as easily as her thick, unruly hair strayed from its pins. "It is only that, if I am to learn how to please Ger—my husband by doing this for him, I need to know *how* it is done. And I cannot quite understand from this picture what to *do* . . ."

The madam's pinched expression softened in understanding. "Yes, I quite see the difficulty. But I am not sure how to explain in words . . ." She rubbed her palm over her chin, her gaze becoming distant and thoughtful. "If the situation were different, I would . . . but no, Call—Lady Innesford would have my head if I did."

A small flutter of hope leapt in Jane's chest. "If you did what?"

The other woman worried her lower lip with her slightly

bucked teeth. "It would be a terrible breach of propriety . . . not to mention Lady Innesford's trust. You're a lady of quality, not a lady of the night."

Jane closed the book with a snap and set it on the table beside her. Rising to her feet, she clasped the madam's satin gloved hand with her bare one—an unsettling juxtaposition, for Jane had never before left home without gloves. She fixed the older woman with the same imploring, wide-eyed gaze that had once extracted sweets from even the strictest of nursemaids.

"Please, Mrs. Upshaw. My betrothed is well-known for his vast experience and varied appetites. To hold him, I must be both—a lady of quality *and* a lady of the night. And you are my only hope to achieve that. So if there is anything you can tell me, anything you can show me, that might assist me in making him—and myself—happy, I promise it shall be our secret."

The madam's mouth pressed into a thin, disapproving red line, and Jane feared she'd lost her plea, but then the older woman sighed and a wistful smile spread across her lips. "You're very much in love with your young man, aren't you, my lady?"

At the words "in love," Jane's heart pinched. Oh, how she wished she wasn't! How she wished she could have been sensible and fallen for any one of the half-dozen or so suitors who'd courted her since her coming-out three years ago.

Men who found her comely enough to flatter her by calling her, if not beautiful, then at least pretty. If she were truthful with herself, she would admit it was more than likely they found her dowry and bloodline more attractive than her face, but at least they desired those qualities enough to pretend otherwise. In truth, there had only been one thing wrong with them.

None of them were Gerard Everett.

"With every beat of my fool heart," she admitted sadly.

The soft, faraway look in the older woman's eyes said she, too, had once loved unwisely . . . and while it had not turned out well, she did not regret her folly. She squeezed Jane's hand gently and nodded. "Then we had best see to getting you a more thorough education. And while the best method is to learn by doing, the next best is to learn by watching."

"Watching?" Jane repeated the word stupidly, incredulously.

"Yes." Mrs. Upshaw dropped her hand and crossed to a cabinet on the opposite side of the library. From it, she withdrew a hooded cloak and a black mask, which she brought back and handed to Jane. "Put these on and come with me."

Jane knew she shouldn't. It was reckless and wicked. Unthinkable for a well-bred lady. But then, this entire enterprise was unthinkable for a well-bred lady. What did it matter now? *In for a penny, in for a pound.*

She donned the proffered items and followed the madam out of the large but cozy library and down a narrow, dimly lit corridor. At the end of the hallway, Mrs. Upshaw paused and opened a door, which swung inward. On the other side, Jane could make out a large landing with stairs leading in both directions. On the opposite side of the landing was a double doorway into a room from which the warm glow of large lamps shone. Jane knew, without being told, that the landing, the flight of stairs, and the room were inside the brothel.

The implications of what she was about to do hit her full-force. This was a mistake. If she were seen and recognized . . . She ought to beg off, ought to stop herself from committing the most grievous breach of propriety imaginable, but the peculiar blend of curiosity and excitement that had infected her since she'd first opened the book of cards propelled her forward.

As the madam turned and mounted the first stair, Jane caught a glimpse of a figure standing just inside the double doors. She paused in mid-step and squinted.

Surely it wasn't. Couldn't be.

But it was. The shock of recognition twisted in her gut and burned a path of acid up to her heart. She stared through the slitted eyeholes in the mask she wore, heedless of the possibility that he might turn away from the woman to whom he was speaking—a gorgeous, flame-haired creature wearing a diaphanous green gown whom Jane hated on sight—and see her standing there, watching him.

The woman ran her fingers under the lapel of his green jacket—the one that matched perfectly the cast of his eyes—and he covered her hand with his. He smiled and responded, saying something that made the redhead trill with laughter.

How *could* he? He had asked her to marry him only two days ago. And he had been at her house this very morning, claiming to be so overcome with desire to see her, he'd failed to wait for the footman to announce him. And yet here he was, hiring some strange woman—some strange, *beautiful* woman—to slake his lust.

How *dare* he?

An emphatic tug on Jane's arm drew her up short. Without conscious effort, she'd been walking toward the double doors, toward Gerard, though to what end, she didn't know. She knew only that seeing him here, with another woman—and knowing what they might do together—was more unbearable, more intolerable than any insult or injury she'd ever suffered.

"No, no, not in there. This way . . . why, what is it, my dear?"

Jane shook her head, despair and outrage thickening her throat. "Not what." Tears stung at her eyes, and she blinked to clear them as she turned to look at the older woman's kind, concerned face. "Who."

5

"You are every inch the man to play Apollo to my Daphne," the red-haired beauty simpered, fingering the lapel of his favorite bottle-green, superfine coat—never mind that it was his only bottle-green, superfine coat, though he had others in hues too innumerable to name.

He placed his hand over hers, if only to stop her from wrinkling—or worse, soiling—the fabric, and pasted his most convincing feigned smile on his face. "As I recall, Daphne ran away from Apollo."

Daphne, for that was undoubtedly her working name if not her real one, batted her lush eyelashes and emitted a flirtatious giggle. "If you'd like me to run, I'd be more than happy to oblige."

Gerard fought the urge to grimace. On any other occasion, he was certain he would have found this banter clever and amusing. Instead, the blatant artifice set his teeth on edge. But he played along anyway, quirking an eyebrow and smiling flirtatiously. "And who will play the part of your father by turning you into a laurel tree before I can catch you?"

She smoothed her hand down his chest to his abdomen, her expression sly. "Oh, I think we can dispense with that part of the story. I'm not the one who should be making wood, after all." Another giggle escaped her lips.

He chuckled in return, but the sound struck his ears as hollow and false.

What the hell was wrong with him? Normally, he preferred to take his time with women, to draw out the experience over a period of days—or at least hours—rather than minutes. The chase, even when the outcome was assured, was an essential element of the fun.

Usually. But not tonight.

Perhaps it was merely impatience. Lust had been riding him hard all afternoon and driven him to the Red Door much earlier in the evening than was fashionable. What he needed was a quick fuck to purge the specter of his unwelcome and inexplicable attraction to his future wife, not a long, leisurely romp.

His cock, which hadn't evinced the slightest interest in Daphne since his arrival, came awake and stretched at the mere thought of Jane. Plain, ordinary, unremarkable Jane. Except that parts of her were not as ordinary or unremarkable as he'd once believed.

How had he failed to notice before now? He'd known her for a decade.

Daphne slipped her palm over the fall of his breeches, over the growing evidence of his desire—for another woman. "Well, it would seem my request has already been granted. Would you like to chase me upstairs now?"

God, she was everything he should want in a woman. Lush, ripe, sensual, eager, and *available*. And yet, his body resisted his mind's logic. He didn't desire her.

Or any of the other equally lovely women who lounged on their respective divans, hoping to capture the interest of the next gentleman with a fat purse and heavy balls willing to part with the former in exchange for being relieved of the latter. For no accountable reason, however, the entire enterprise left a sour taste in his mouth. Good Lord, had he become so jaded and cynical that even jaded and cynical entertainments could no longer interest him?

He had all but decided to take his leave when a rapid swish of satin to his left caught his attention. He turned to find Mrs. Upshaw, owner and proprietress of this exclusive establishment, hurrying toward him and Daphne, the feathers atop her lavish hat bobbing wildly as evidence of her breakneck pace. She reached Gerard's elbow, puffing with exertion, her cheeks flushed.

A woman of Mrs. Upshaw's years—which he judged to be past fifty—and girth—which was ample if not downright expansive—did not undertake such a burst of energy without betraying the effort it cost her. Nor would she trouble herself in such a fashion without good cause. His innate curiosity engaged, Gerard anticipated her explanation with considerably more enthusiasm than he'd felt since his arrival.

"Pray forgive the intrusion," the madam huffed, "but I am in urgent need of this gentleman's assistance this evening." Her speech was directed toward Daphne, but her hand rested upon Gerard's upper arm in a peremptory gesture.

His assistance? Gerard recoiled. While he was certain Mrs. Upshaw had once been a fine figure of a woman, she was now a much finer figure of a grandmother or perhaps an aunt. It was all he could do not to shudder at the prospect.

His horror must have shown on his face, for Mrs. Upshaw burst into a rich peal of laughter. "Oh, my goodness, no," she said through her chuckles. "You've quite misapprehended me. I've a rather different proposition in mind than I expect you envision. I would, however, like to speak with you in private regarding my request."

Gerard exhaled his relief and inhaled intrigue. "I am your servant, dear lady."

"Excellent." She gave Daphne a brief glance and a nod, then wrapped her arm through the crook of his elbow. "I have a small office around the corner if you'll come this way."

The office was, indeed, small. In fact, he suspected it had once been a storage closet. Now, the eight-foot square room housed a small desk and two straight-backed wooden chairs. Hardly the sort of place to which one invited a gentleman of means, but then, Gerard had the distinct impression that such invitations were few and far between.

He settled into the chair nearer the door as Mrs. Upshaw rustled her way behind the desk and planted her satin-clad backside on the narrow wooden seat.

She rested her elbows on the desk, folded her hands together, and bent toward him, studying him through eyes that glittered with intelligence and keen assessment. She was taking his measure, though to what purpose, he had no idea.

"I sense you are not entirely displeased by my interruption now you are reassured I do not mean to have my wicked way with you."

Gerard's breath rushed out of him on an amused wheeze. "I am not normally so transparent."

"The usual entertainments have grown tiresome, then. Predictable, perhaps?"

He shook his head in wry admiration. She read him as easily as a playbill posted on a street lamp. "I daresay you have the right of it, Mrs. Upshaw."

She nodded, the brisk gesture of a woman whose intuition has been confirmed to her complete satisfaction. "It is as I hoped, then. I believe, sir, that we may be of service to one another."

Gerard arched an eyebrow. "And how is that? Pray do not keep me in suspense."

Mrs. Upshaw licked her brightly rouged lips, and just for a moment, he thought she hesitated, but then her features settled into calm resolve.

"I am considering a new girl for the house. Before I take her on, however, I must determine whether she has the proper . . . er . . . credentials for the job. I have been at odds with myself as to how to proceed with her, but I believe you may be the man to assist mc in assessing her suitability."

Gerard fingered the brim of his beaver. Had he heard aright? The madam was asking him to fuck one of her whores and then report back to her as to the adequacy of the girl's performance? In a day filled with odd events, this was surely the oddest. And yet, he had to admit, it was far from tiresome or predictable. The question hovered about his lips, but Mrs. Upshaw's next words forestalled it.

"I wish to make it clear, my lord," she continued, dropping the polite fiction that she did not know his identity, "that what I ask of you is unique. I have never asked this before, nor do I expect to do so again. If you feel you are not up to the challenge, then please tell me, for many—perhaps even most—gentlemen would balk at what I require."

Gerard's nostrils flared on a sharp intake of breath. It seemed the madam knew a great deal more about him than he'd previously imagined. She certainly knew his sore spot—one he could still feel in a faintly throbbing shoulder than woke him at night and reminded him of the days when he'd been an unwashed and unwelcome country boy thrust into a world he neither belonged in nor understood.

"I am not *most* gentlemen."

She smiled serenely. "Indeed, I am counting upon it." She raised her elbows from the desk, leaned back in her chair, and considered him with the slow, appraising eyes of a born businessperson. "As I am sure you know, for all my clients do, I never hire a girl unless I am certain she enjoys her work. Normally, this is not an issue, as they usually come to me with a certain amount of . . . shall we say . . . prior experience. But this girl is a virgin, and I wish that she remain that way as of the end of this evening."

The pronouncement struck Gerard wholly unprepared with the bone-jarring, breath-stealing force of a schoolboy jumping him from behind in a chilly Eton schoolyard. "What?"

Mrs. Upshaw's smile became a straight line of the utmost seriousness. "I agree, it is a singular situation, yet I am persuaded to give her the chance to prove herself. But to do that, I need the assistance of a man with sufficient expertise to rouse her passions and sufficient restraint to repress his own. The question is, are you that man?"

Gerard didn't need even a second to consider the question. Of course, he could exercise restraint—unlike some noblemen of his acquaintance. He exercised it every day of his life when he put on a polite face and pretended to believe the sly, subtle lies the "Quality" foisted upon one another in the name of gentility. When he pretended to like his peers, men who sold their tenants up the river every day in Parliament without a second thought, men who cheated at cards right before they cheated on their wives and still went home with a clean conscience.

At least he'd never be one of them. At least Jane would always know where she stood with him, never be one of the women who believed in her husband's fictional constancy. She knew better than that.

Mrs. Upshaw seemed to read his answer on his face. She clapped her hands together in obvious delight. "Excellent, my lord. I'm most pleased you're willing to assist me."

Gerard held up his hand. "Before I consent, I'd like to see her. Even an exceptional man requires an assurance that his restraint will be necessary."

The madam laughed aloud, a hearty, billowing sound. "Of course, of course. There is one more small thing, however."

He arched his eyebrow. He was coming to suspect that what Mrs. Upshaw terms "small" things were likely to loom rather large in his estimation. "Yes?"

"You must make your decision without the benefit of seeing her face. She is masked."

"Why?" he asked sharply, his neck tingling with the sudden premonition that something was altogether wrong here.

The older woman smiled back benignly. "So long as you never see her face, the girl has other choices in life. If her suit for employ with me is unsuccessful, she can safely return to the world on the other side of this door without prejudice, provided you cannot recognize her. It is but a small accommodation to preserve her privacy."

The prickles at his nape subsided at this perfectly reasonable explanation, and the lust that had troubled him all day rose up fresh in his loins. How refreshing, how delightful it would be to make love to—or at least do everything short of making love to, he amended—a woman he could never know well enough to tire of. To be able to pass her on the street one day and never know it was she with whom he had spent what was promising to be the least boring, most unpredictable night of his life.

She perched at the edge of the bed atop the signature red velvet coverlet employed in all the brothel's rooms. Her hands were folded in her lap as demurely as those of any debutante gracing the wall at her first ball, and her posture was as ramrod straight and regal as any duchess at tea. Except no debutante or duchess of Gerard's acquaintance engaged in either of these activities clad in naught but her skin and a black highwayman's mask.

The mask was Gerard's first surprise. It was not at all the feather-decked, jewel-encrusted affair he had envisaged when the madam mentioned it. Instead, a simple hood of black cloth secured at the back with a tie covered her head, obscuring all of her features save her mouth and chin. Neither of those attributes bore much notice, but as the madam had no doubt anticipated, it hardly mattered.

The girl had the body of Venus incarnate.

In the burnished orange glow of the firelight, she looked more like a pagan icon cast from gold than a living, breathing woman. Her flawless, buttery skin clung to the prettiest, roundest breasts he'd ever laid eyes upon, and they were tipped with aureolae and nipples so pale their slightly darker hue might have been represented by a nothing more than a sculptor's trick of drawing fine lines in molten gilt. Partial as Gerard was to large breasts, in his experience, tits as large as these were prone to sag when loosed from the confines of a robust pair of stays, yet Venus's did not, further evidence, it seemed, of the hand of Man improving upon the plans of Nature.

But it was the pure, poetic geometry of her form that most fired his imagination . . . and his blood. The molded outline of her rib cage extended down to the sweeping arc of her waist and soft curve of her belly punctuated by the tiny, puckered divot of her navel. Her long, tapered fingers, laced together in full view just above her mons, drew incongruous attention to the forbidden folds of flesh beneath. Flesh that would be soft, moist, and as perfectly formed to accommodate a man's cock as a wheel to an axle, a lock to its key.

She wasn't just Venus incarnate, she was the Golden Mean personified. How wise the ancients had been, not merely to discover the proportions most pleasing to the human eye, but to recognize the spiritual power of desire and embody it in Nature's most sumptuous creature: Woman. Oh, the clerics had done their level best to discredit and repudiate any passion—save the Christly variety, of course—but no matter how they inveighed against the sins of the flesh, men would always worship at the altar nestled between a woman's thighs.

He reached for the doorknob. Tonight, he would go where untold generations of men had gone before.

And, he thought with a possessive surge of triumph he refused to examine or acknowledge, none.

6

Jane had had plenty of time to reconsider the plan she and Mrs. Upshaw had hastily—and no doubt injudiciously—conceived. In any of the countless minutes that had stretched since she had disrobed and sat upon the edge of the velvet coverlet, she could have changed her mind. Could have gotten to her feet, clumsily recostumed herself, and slipped from the room with no one the wiser.

She hadn't.

For of all the things that could go dreadfully amiss in this room alone with Gerard, none could compare to the pain of knowing he was lying with another woman. Nor could the threat of discovery overshadow the thrill of knowing he would touch her tonight as a man touches a woman he desires, not the drab, dreary duckling with whom he must merely condescend to do his marital duty.

And now, as the doorknob turned, she no longer had the luxury of backing out.

Gerard's cheeks were flushed and his nostrils flared as he entered the room and shut the door behind him with a thud of finality. He strode toward her, his eyes dark with purpose and with . . . hunger.

Jane's heart lurched. Up, down, she wasn't sure which way. It hammered in her throat and pulsed between her thighs and pounded beneath her breastbone. Though how a single organ could possibly be housed in all three places at once, she couldn't fathom.

When he stood within a few paces of her, he extended his hand in a courtly gesture, like a gentleman offering to assist a lady from her seat and escort her to the dance floor. Almost by instinct, she placed her trembling—and shockingly uncovered— hand in his. How odd that she should focus on the impropriety of her bare palm resting in his gloved one when she was stark naked from head to toe. Or more accurately from toe to chin.

As if on cue, Jane's scalp grew hot and prickly beneath the black cloth. The fabric was thin enough and hadn't given her a speck of discomfort all evening long, but now it felt heavy and scratchy and altogether unpleasant.

"Ah, Venus rises," he breathed, his tone hushed, almost reverent.

Perplexed by his words, she tilted her head to one side in silent inquiry.

He chuckled hoarsely. "I half thought the madam was playing a rather cruel joke on me, and you were not a real woman at all, but a statue." He massaged her hand gently in his, as if assuring himself of the authenticity of her flesh. "I can still not quite persuade myself such perfection is possible in Nature. Perhaps you a really a clockwork woman, not the living, breathing sort that responds to a man's touch. Let's find out, shall we?"

He raised her fingers to his mouth and brushed his lips over her knuckles, a featherlight caress yet so sweetly erotic, she thought she might swoon. Her nipples, exposed to the air and his gaze, stiffened and swelled at the simple touch, and he sucked in a breath. "By Jove, perhaps you *are* cut out for this line of work."

He released her hand and slid his palm up to cup her breast. His fingers, despite being unreasonably long, could not encompass the entire globe, and he settled for holding its weight from beneath while he circled the engorged, aching tip with the gloved pad of his thumb. She gasped at the flood of sensation that pooled in her belly at the movement, a well of hot, liquid yearning she'd never dreamed could exist inside her.

With a harsh sound in his throat, he pulled away, leaving her cold and hot in the center of the floor. "I see it doesn't take much to get you hot and ready for a man you've only just laid eyes on. But then, I suppose it's only fair, since I'm hot and ready for you, and I've only just laid eyes on you."

Stupidly, she opened her mouth to protest, to say she most certainly hadn't only just laid eyes on him but had known him—and desired him—half her life, but to her great good fortune, he saved her by grabbing her wrist and forcing her hand down over the rock-solid bulge in his breeches.

Her eyes widened as he pressed her fingers to it, as thick and long as an axe handle, but alive and somehow yielding. Unable to restrain her curiosity, she ran her fingers around the edges, testing the width and length of it, wondering how the little dangly bits she'd seen in paintings and drawings could become this. When she had modeled male nudes in the past—quite in secret, of course, for her mother scarcely approved Jane's dabbling in such an unladylike pursuit as sculpting with clay, even when the subject matter was as banal as a flowerpot or as benign as a sheep—it had never occurred to her that the strange creatures she called men were so . . . changeable.

She was exploring lower down the ridge, trying to locate its source, when he growled—a pained rather than an angry sound—and reached down to the buttons of his fall. "You want to see my cock, sweet Venus? Touch it?"

Cock. The word echoed in her head like the striking of a clock tower. So that was what one called it!

She nodded, but she needn't have, for he was already working the buttons and loosening his drawstring, lowering the fabric until a velvety tip appeared and then, suddenly, the entire
length of it sprang free. As in the pictures she'd seen earlier in
the madam's library, the appendage stood away from his body
and pointed upward, almost as though it were a separate entity,
attached to him, yet quite apart from him.

Cock. It ought to be ridiculous, to use the same word for a
man's member as for a rooster, and yet, it made a perverse kind
of sense, for like a rooster, this organ was powerful and proud,
its upright posture a natural form of strutting and posing for female approval.

For no reason she could explain, she approved.

"Touch it, Venus," he said softly. "It won't bite."

She reached out and stroked the tip tentatively, half afraid of
what might happen when she did, for cocks were known for
pecking without warning. When nothing more sinister than a
chuckle emitted from Gerard, she became bolder and wrapped
her palm around the satiny shaft, sliding her hand up and down
its length to better revel in the curious contradiction of it. Hard,
yet soft. Dangerous, yet irresistible.

"Jesus," he muttered through clenched teeth. "You're a quick
study. Keep that up much longer and I won't be able to teach
you anything else for a good, long while."

She stopped what she was doing instantly, not wanting to do
anything that would end the lesson too soon. Not until she'd
learned the trick she'd seen in the pictures. The one Mrs. Upshaw
said no man could resist.

Dropping her hand to her side, she studied the jutting organ,
trying to fathom how she would accommodate the entire girth
and length in her mouth. Wouldn't she choke? And yet, she
found she wanted to taste it, to run her tongue along the silky
skin that seemed scarcely capable of containing the energy, the
vitality that thrummed beneath the surface.

He seemed to follow her gaze like a trail of bread crumbs straight to her thoughts. "Would you like to suck it, Venus? Take it in your mouth and taste it?"

She jerked her eyes away from his beautiful cock and up to his even more beautiful face. Tiny lines creased the corners of his mouth and eyes. She had never seen him look more attractive . . . or more pained. He wanted her to take him in her mouth, wanted it with a fierceness and need that made his voice rough and his hands tremble.

Her chest blossomed with delight. She was doing this to him, making him ache with the same longing that had plagued her, in different guises, for a decade. True, he didn't know it was she, but it didn't matter. Jane's face might not drive him mad, but her body did, and that was just as much a part of her as her eyes and nose and cheeks, wasn't it?

In answer to his question, she did the only reasonable thing. She dropped to her knees and opened her mouth as wide as she could. Just as she was on the verge of attempting to swallow him to the hilt in one dive, his hands clamped around the sides of her head and halted her forward progress.

"Now, now, perhaps you do need a bit of instruction, after all," he admonished with an indulgent chuckle. "Don't dive in on it, sweet. Take it slowly, a little at a time. Like this . . ."

In illustration, he thrust his hips forward until the head rested against her now slightly parted lips. Holding the back of her head in one palm, he fisted his cock with the other and rubbed the tip back and forth over her mouth. Of its own volition, her tongue snaked out and lapped up a small drop of moisture that pearled in the tiny crease at the very tip. It tasted of salt and sweet, earth and water.

He responded with a shudder and a muffled curse, but this time, he didn't discourage her attentions. Instead, he exerted a bit more pressure to the back of her skull. "Open up a little wider now," he instructed gruffly.

She did as he bid and he slipped the head up to the soft folds of flesh at its base beyond her lips. Marveling at the velvety smoothness, she pressed her tongue against the underside, causing the loosely gathered skin to slide back and forth.

"That's the way," he sighed with satisfaction.

Peering up at him from beneath the slits that passed for eyeholes in the mask, she saw that his eyes were closed and his head lolled to one side, his features drawn tight in an expression hovering between agony and bliss.

He released his cock and let one arm drop to his side. "Can you take more?"

Her head bobbed in assent. She would take whatever he had to give, whatever she could take to give him more of the exquisite pleasure she saw etched in his features, felt in the tense muscles of his fingers at the back of her scalp. The place between her legs throbbed anew, and she fought the desire to reach down and press her palm against the pulsing flesh to quell the ache.

"Good, because I can't hold back any longer. Relax your mouth and hold still, sweetheart. And if you want to stop, all you have to do is pull away. I won't force you."

He needn't have said so. She was lost at *sweetheart*. There was no question of force.

He pushed forward slowly, invading her mouth until the tip of his cock nearly touched the back of her throat. She feared she would gag, but then he withdrew and repeated the motion. Withdrew and repeated again, a little faster this time. A steady rhythm built between them, until she was drawing back when he withdrew and sliding forward when he pressed in.

And she understood, suddenly, what it was the women in the drawings were doing to the men. It was the motion, the friction, the rocking in and out that induced such frenzied, uncontrollable desire.

His breath came in increasingly ragged pants, and she sensed a tension coiling up inside him as his cock thrust into her mouth with increasing urgency. The knowledge created an answering pressure in her woman's place, and she couldn't prevent herself from cupping herself in a desperate effort to stem the rising tide. This was for him, not her.

But then he groaned harshly, "Yes, Venus, touch your pussy. Come with me."

More new words, but his meaning was clear. In the dark, in the privacy of her own room, she would sometimes pull up her night rail, spread her legs, and rub her fingers there. A thick, pleasurable sensation would grow as she rubbed, until at last it crested and broke like sweet, gentle ripples on a lake.

He wanted her to make that happen. To make herself *come.*

"Touch yourself, Venus," he urged softly, holding back now, easing the tempo of his thrusts. "I want to see you come."

She ought to have been mortified, but anonymity gave her courage. He need never know it was she with whom he'd spent this evening in the brothel, she who'd sucked his cock with wanton abandon, she who'd shamelessly touched herself in his presence. This was something she could never do as Lady Jane, the refined and proper daughter of a duke and someday wife of an earl.

But as Venus, she was becoming his creation, a woman without need either of modesty or shame, and she could do whatever he asked of her.

She slipped two fingers between the folds and found the spot, swollen and sensitive to the touch, yet eager.

"That's it, sweetheart," he encouraged, and the knowledge that he was watching her sent a thrill through her chest. As her fingers found a rhythm between her thighs, he reset the rhythm of his thrusts between her lips.

Time and place melted away, until there was nothing but the sounds and scents and sensations of two bodies working together to achieve release. Grunts and groans and gasps. The thick, wet *smack smack smack* of his cock in her mouth, of her fingers against her flesh. The musky, rich scent surrounding them like a haze. And the sweet-hot magic that swelled between them, making her fingers move faster, harder, wilder and his thrusts grow shorter, sharper, swifter.

His fingers tightened at the back of her head, twisting her hair so that she might have winced if she hadn't been so intent on the pleasure arcing up inside her pussy—his word, now hers—knowing she was on the precipice and unwilling to stop until she tumbled over. She was dimly aware of him trying to pull her head backward, away from his cock, but she wouldn't let him. Couldn't let him break the rhythm they'd established, which carried her along like a raging sea current toward the shore.

"Fuck, I'm going to come in your mouth if you don't let go." His words were pained, guttural, as if he were holding onto his control by the finest of threads. "I can't . . . not much longer . . . ahhh!"

The final utterance was torn from his throat at the same moment his cock jerked between her lips. A spurt of warm, thick liquid hit the roof of her mouth. Then another, and another, his shaft pulsing violently with each spurt. For just a second, she was immobilized by surprise, her concentration broken by this altogether unexpected turn of events, but reflex made her swallow, tentatively at first, then with increasing enthusiasm as the salty-sweet flavor rolled pleasantly over her tongue. He tasted like he smelled—of earth and ocean, rich and pungent, strong and vital.

"Didn't want to . . . make you swallow. Sorry." He groaned the apology, his fingers massaging her scalp as he continued to thrust and shudder. "But Mother of God, that's feels good. Don't stop."

Jubilation and triumph sang in her veins.

Nothing—not pictures, not lurid descriptions, not even watching the act—could have prepared her for this. Oh, for the simple mechanics of the act itself, perhaps. But not for this sudden, overwhelming hunger to consume him, subsume him, *become* him.

When it was over, he released her head, and she allowed his softening cock to slide from her mouth and sat back on her heels. A bead of sweat trickled down the back of her neck, her skin felt flushed and tingly, and the place between her legs still vibrated with the need for the release she hadn't quite achieved.

It didn't matter, though. The thrill of giving Gerard such deep and powerful satisfaction was enough. To wish for more would be greedy. And if Jane had learned anything in her twenty-one years of life, it was that it never paid to expect anyone else to fulfill one's desires.

She focused on the shiny black uppers of his boots while he went about tucking himself back into his drawers and closing up his breeches. This was no time to become maudlin. She had gotten precisely what she wanted; when they were married, she would know how to please him and perhaps keep him in her bed a few weeks—who was she fooling? days—longer than she might otherwise. And, if nothing else, she knew he would not find her body unappealing to couple with, even if he found nothing to recommend her face.

An ungloved hand appeared suddenly appeared in her line of vision. "The goddess should not kneel before the man. Stand up, sweet Venus, and let me do the kneeling."

7

Venus—for Gerard could no longer think of her by any other name—slipped her hand into his. Slowly. Shyly.

Gone was the wanton sex goddess who sucked cock and touched herself like a born harlot, replaced by a delicate creature who moved with the demure, elegant grace of a lady of the manor. As he helped her to her feet, he wondered at her circumstances. Her hands—soft and dewy as rose petals and beautifully manicured—had certainly never seen so much as a day's labor. Her carriage was of the variety found only in those schooled to perfect posture and gait by a severe governess and a heavy book.

Who was she? And what could have induced her to such a radical decision? It was one thing for a lady of quality who had already squandered both her virtue and her fortune to take up the life of a Cyprian, but quite another for one whose virginity was still intact. A respectable young lady of little means could make a decent living as a governess or paid companion. And if she wished for greater opulence, a woman as beautiful as Venus could surely find a nobleman willing to set her up as his mistress.

Hell, *he* would set her up as his mistress.

Like a fast-growing and pernicious weed, the idea flourished the instant it planted itself, never mind that only this morning he had sworn not to take another mistress until after he and Jane had been married for several months. That noble intention fled, replaced by the fantasy of having Venus as his own, of teaching her not just the rudiments of mutual masturbation, but of every carnal enterprise imaginable.

He would buy her a lovely little house in Chelsea and surround her with a bevy of servants to see to her every need. She would have the most opulent, most fashionable wardrobe of any woman in London, designed by the cleverest milliners to showcase her magnificent figure. When he escorted her about Town, he would be the envy of his peers. "Where did you find such a prize, you lucky devil?" they'd say as they slapped him on the shoulder.

Yes, he would see to her every material need, but more, to her every physical desire.

Starting now.

She had been close to coming before he'd distracted her, and her arousal hadn't diminished in the intervening moments. Her breasts rose and fell in tempo with her erratic respiration, and her neck and shoulders were flushed a dusky pink. Her nearly translucent nipples remained puckered and erect, and the musky scent of her cunt teased his nostrils.

For some fool reason, she thought whoring was her only option. But he'd show her she could do better.

She could be his.

"Go to the bed," he instructed.

She glanced at the bed and then back at him, worrying her lower lip between her teeth. He knew what she was thinking.

"I promise I won't relieve you of your virginity." *Not tonight, at any rate.* "Trust me, Venus. I only want to give you pleasure, as you gave me."

Her lip stayed between her teeth, but after a brief hesitation, she nodded and walked to the bed. He followed, watching the generous curve of her arse sway deliciously in front of him. Was there any part of this woman Nature hadn't fashioned to perfectly suit him? He only wished he could complete the picture by removing her mask, freeing the thick hair that was tucked up beneath it, and revealing the face that accompanied her glorious form.

But that, like their first fuck, could wait. Right now, he just wanted to give her so much pleasure, she'd never again consider giving herself to another man.

He gestured toward the bed. "Sit where you were when I came in."

She took up the same position as before, right down to the hands clasped over her mons.

Chuckling to himself, he knelt before her, separated her hands, and pushed them to her sides. "Lean back on them to support yourself if you like. And spread your legs."

Her skin flushed a brighter shade of pink, but her pulse jumped in her throat at the command. *Good.* Shy or not, embarrassed or not, she was with him. She parted her thighs.

"More. A little more," he coaxed, his own heartbeat accelerating as she obeyed and the glistening, velvety lips of her pussy came into full view. With her legs spread so wide, he could clearly see the hooded peak of her clitoris peeping out from between the soft folds of her labia.

Lovely, just like every other inch of her.

Gerard brushed one thumb over the exposed bud, the lightest of caresses meant to gauge her arousal. Her hips bucked and she whimpered brokenly, the sound suspended midway between ecstasy and anguish. So responsive, so sensitive. It would take little effort to bring her to completion, but he would have to

254 / *Jackie Barbosa*

exercise restraint and go carefully and tenderly or risk over-stimulating her nearly overloaded senses.

To say nothing of his own. Just the thought of tasting her was making his cock hard and his balls tight again. After the orgasm he'd just experienced, he ought to be spent for twenty minutes or more, not less than five. He shook his head. She had him randy as a virgin on the verge of tupping his first whore. Ironic that *she* was the virgin . . . and the whore.

But not if he could convince her otherwise.

He bent down and pressed his mouth to the spot where her slit began, just above her swollen clitoris. The muscles in her legs clenched at the contact, and he braced his palms on her thighs to prevent her from slamming them shut. He needn't have bothered, however, for when he flicked her with his tongue, she relaxed beneath him with a shuddery "Ohhh" of pleasure.

It was the closest she'd come to uttering an intelligible word, and he found himself wanting to hear her voice almost as much as he wanted to see her face. He licked her a second time, more purposefully, then a third, and her flesh pulsed beneath his tongue.

Resisting the urge to bury his face in her spicy-sweet cunt and take her straight to paradise, he kept his strokes light and soft, purposely holding her at the edge of release until he got what he wanted. She clutched at the coverlet beneath her hands, gathering fistfuls that flowed from her finger like red velvet water. Her hips arched and twisted in a vain attempt to increase the pressure he exerted.

Damn, but she tasted better than the finest Scotch whisky, and her scent more intoxicating. The woman was a living, breathing aphrodisiac, and he couldn't get enough of her.

"Please," she whispered, breaking her silence at last. "So close."

The words were barely audible, delivered in husky, breathless tones. Even so, he could make out the clipped consonants and rounded vowels of a cultured English speaker. Familiarity tickled his consciousness, but surely it must be a trick of his imagination. If any lady of his acquaintance possessed a body like this, he surely would have noticed her long ago.

Removing his hand from its resting place on her inner thigh, he spread her labia with two fingers and blew gently on her clitoris before suckling it between his lips. Her stomach muscles clenched. He tweaked the bud with his tongue one more time, and a fierce surge of exultation swept through him as the first spasms wracked her body. She came like a storm sweeping in from the sea, dark and chaotic, without delicacy or reservation. Mixed in with her sobs and gasps of pleasure, he heard one intelligible word.

"Gerard."

8

Oh God, what have I done?

Even in the midst of the indescribable splendor of release,
Jane recognized her mistake the second his name crossed her
lips. Stupid, foolish Jane. In a matter of minutes, her deception
would be revealed.

There was no question in her mind what discovery would
bring. She would be a fallen woman in his eyes, her sin unfor-
giveable. He would denounce her, renounce her, and break their
engagement. Worst of all, she would lose his friendship.

Her throat thickened with misery even as the waning tremors
of pleasure left her limbs tingling and languid. She braced herself for the inevitable loss of the very thing she'd set out to win.

He raised his dark head from between her legs. His mouth
glistened with her juices, and he licked his lips slowly, reverently, as though he wished to savor the taste of her just a little
longer.

A fresh pang of yearning twisted in her belly despite her
wretchedness. If someone had told her this afternoon she would
spread her legs and allow a man to touch her most intimate flesh

with his mouth, she would have scoffed at the absurdity of such a suggestion. But even had she credited the notion, she would not have imagined that she would like it. How such a shockingly immodest act would fill her with dark, uncontrollable desire and bring her such rapture.

A rapture she'd never feel again. Unless . . .

She studied his face. He didn't seem angry. Perhaps he hadn't heard her. Maybe she hadn't said his name as clearly as she thought. She had been making rather of a lot of decidedly unladylike and wholly unintelligible noises.

He tipped his head to one side and raised an eyebrow. "Well, you're certainly full of surprises, sweet Venus. Tell me, how do you come to know my Christian name?"

Relief lightened Jane's chest like hot air filling a balloon. He'd heard her, but he hadn't recognized her voice. She might yet salvage the situation . . . and preserve her secret. If only she could prevent him from hearing Jane when Venus spoke.

Venus's voice would be nothing like Jane's. It must be deeper, throatier. Sultry, like the woman herself.

Jane took a long, slow breath, and when she exhaled, she was Venus.

"Come now, Lord Chester," she teased, tracing the folds of his crisp, white cravat with her fingers, "you are well aware you are a man of no small reputation. Indeed, it is said you court notoriety with greater zeal than you court favor with the ladies, and you do that with more than adequate enthusiasm."

Gerard frowned slightly before gently removing her fingers from the starched linen, and Jane had to stifle a giggle. Perhaps she should have mentioned his obsession with his wardrobe. The man could have set Beau Brummell in his heyday to shame.

"Then we have not met before?" He peered at her masked face with a sharp, penetrating gaze, as if he hoped he could make out her features if only he stared long enough.

Though she knew such a thing was quite impossible, Jane's

stomach twisted with anxiety, and she fought to maintain her composure. Detaching her mind from her body, she answered the question with a casual shrug and a shake of the head. "I assure you, my lord, we have never been formally introduced."

It was easy to state this fact with firm conviction, for it was entirely true. The first time Jane met Gerard was at a summer house party at his uncle's. It was the summer she was ten, and their acquaintance had been made when he discovered her in his wardrobe.

She had hidden in it one morning to escape the taunts of the other children in attendance. The hiding place had worked exceptionally well, but for one small hitch: she couldn't get out, for the latch operated only from the outside. He found her there near dinnertime, her knuckles raw and her voice hoarse from her vain attempts to call attention to her location. When he opened the door, she was huddled in one corner, stiff and exhausted and convinced no one had even missed her in the hours she'd been gone. No one ever missed Plain, Dull Jane.

He was so much older than she—near twenty—and so terribly elegant and handsome, she expected him to laugh at her or reproach her for her stupidity or scold her for ruining his clothes. Instead, he'd been unbearably kind, smoothing her hair as she sobbed out the story of her torment at the hands of her peers and reassuring her that he knew exactly what she suffered. Even though she'd known this to be a bald-faced lie—he was far too good-looking and sophisticated to ever have been the butt of anyone's jokes—she had been comforted nonetheless. And when he had sworn he'd bring about an end to the relentless teasing she'd endured all week, he had been as good as his word.

She'd fallen in love with him that very day.

The sensation of his lips brushing her fingers pulled her back to the present.

"Our lack of acquaintance is purely a shame, mademoiselle, for I am quite certain if we had met before now, you would not be here." With a slight groan, he rose from his knees and sat beside her.

The contrast between her naked body and his fully clothed one caused heat to rise to the surface of her skin. She wasn't sure whether it was embarrassment or desire that warmed her, but neither one would get her to safety. Casting a longing glance toward her shift, which lay over the back of a wing chair in front of the fireplace, she turned her attention back to playing her role.

"And how is that, my lord? Would you have hired me as your scullery maid? Or perhaps to a higher position as a parlor maid?"

"A maid? Don't be absurd, sweet Venus. There is only one position I would dream of offering you, and though I admit to envisioning you on your knees from time to time," he grinned at her, causing her heart to careen wildly, "I can promise you shan't be scrubbing anything."

She stared at him, dumbfounded. Her blood roared in her ears, making her dizzy and a little queasy. Was he really asking her to . . .

"Be my mistress, Venus." He clasped her hands in his, and his soft brown eyes implored her to say yes.

Reality splintered and then fractured into a thousand tiny pieces. Gerard wanted her to be his mistress! Not forty-eight hours after asking her to be his wife, less than twenty-four after declaring the depths of his esteem for her, he was asking another woman to be his mistress.

Hysterical laughter bubbled up in her throat while hot tears collected in the corner of her eyes. Jealousy burned her chest, hardening her heart and lungs like hollow clay pots fired in her kiln.

Dear God, she was jealous of herself. The irony of what she had done could not have been more acute if she had indeed managed to cut off her own nose to spite her face. If the situation weren't so awful, it would be hilariously funny.

The laughter, when it burst forth, sounded more like a witch's ominous cackle than amusement and once it began, she couldn't hold it back. She laughed and laughed, so hard her sides ached and the eye-slits of her mask were soaked with tears. And all the time, Gerard said nothing, but stared at her, mouth agape, as if she'd gone quite mad. Which likely she had.

Slowly, his expression converted from one of abject puzzlement to one of hurt and anger.

As the fit of hilarity—or insanity—at last began to subside, he stood up, retrieved his hat from where it lay discarded on the floor, and stalked toward the door. "I had no idea you'd find the idea of being my mistress so damned amusing." He turned to look at her, his eyes narrowing to dark, black slits. "Clearly, I misread your response to me this evening. I was under the impression you enjoyed what transpired between us. That you were as . . ." He paused, clearing his throat. ". . . moved as I was. Apparently, I was mistaken. I apologize for offering you the opportunity to live a life of luxury when you'd clearly prefer to be a whore." He spat the last word like the invective it was.

She should have let him go. Should have let it end there. Her identity was safe, and she had gotten what she wanted from their encounter. In spades.

But she couldn't bear the hurt-little-boy expression on his face. She thought again of their first meeting all those years ago, of the way he'd comforted her by telling her he, too, had once suffered his peers' disdain. She hadn't believed it then, but she found herself believing it now. The pain reflected in his eyes was fresh, but it wasn't new. She, better than anyone, knew the difference.

She couldn't let him leave believing what he did. Just couldn't.

She shot to her feet and raced to the door, grabbing a fistful of sleeve to halt him.

"It's not that," she whispered.

He spun to face her. "Then what?"

Jane had never considered herself particularly quick-witted. She had her talents, but being able to say the right thing at precisely the right time had never been one of them. But from necessity sprang invention.

"It is said the longest you have ever kept a mistress is two months. I am afraid of being yet another in a long string of paramours you soon forget. I would rather be, as you say, a whore than come to care for you only to lose you to your next flight of fancy in a matter of weeks."

The dark cloud lifted from his features. Soberly, he cupped her chin and tilted her head up. A frisson of anxiety raced down her spine. At this angle and in this light, he could make out the color of her eyes clearly. Would he recognize her now?

"What must I do to prove I can be constant, Venus?"

Her stomach plummeted like a stone, coming to rest somewhere near her knees. Gerard Everett promising to demonstrate constancy? She would have been less shocked if he had promised to fly her to the moon.

But of course, he wouldn't be able to do it, would he? He'd never accomplished it before.

A small, sly smile curved her lips. "You wish to prove you can be constant, my lord? Very well. Visit me here every night for a month."

"That is no great hardship, sweeting." His gaze roamed over her body the way a hungry child might survey a bowl of sweets left temptingly in reach. "In fact, I believe I shall enjoy it immensely."

"Ah, but the rules shall be the same as tonight. I shall continue to wear my mask and retain my virginity, for I have not entirely resolved myself to taking up a Cyprian's life."

He blinked and drew back. "For the entire month?"

She nodded, her smile growing wider. She had him. He would give up within a se'nnight.

Slowly, he licked his lips, considering, and a spike of heat stabbed her belly as she recalled what he had done with that marvelous tongue just a short time ago. What he might do again if she permitted it.

"And if I succeed, you will be my mistress for however long I desire?"

Suffocation seeming imminent, Jane gulped for air, but nodded. "For as long as you require."

"I believe, sweet Venus, that we have a bargain." He grabbed her by the upper arms, pulled her toward him, and crushed his lips to hers in a brief but breathtaking kiss. "Until tomorrow night." Then he straightened his beaver and strolled out the door.

He had been gone for a full five minutes before she recalled that she was to accompany him to the opera tomorrow night.

9

Of all operas, why did tonight's offering have to be *The Marriage of Figaro?*

Gerard stole a covert glance at Jane, who leaned on the ledge of his private box, her eyes riveted to the action on the stage. She laughed as the final scene with its twists and turns of mistaken identity unfolded. But then, she could enjoy the story's sardonic send-up of marital infidelity without suffering pangs of conscience.

As she fanned herself, a thick tendril of brown hair slipped from her elegant coiffure and over her nose. She pursed her lips and blew at the offending lock, and Gerard sucked in his breath as if she'd kicked him in the gut. He dragged his gaze from her mouth only to have it snare on the tight valley between her breasts. His cock stirred, and he shifted in his seat as the singers reached the crescendo of their final aria.

Sod it all. After spending the entire day fixated upon his impending assignation with Venus, his body was achy and confused. Every time his gaze slid Jane's way, he found himself imagining her heavy brown tresses spread out across Venus's pillow and her intelligent brown eyes peering out from behind Venus's black mask. Whenever she laughed or frowned or shook her head at the performers' onstage antics—which was frequently—he itched to wrap his arm about her shoulder, pull her close, and kiss her hard on the lips, the way he'd kissed Venus before leaving her last night. Only this time, in his imagination, she kissed back, sweet and passionate and loose-limbed.

He gave himself a mental douse of cold water. Impending matrimony clearly did not agree with him if it so befuddled his senses he could no longer distinguish his modest, mousy bride-to-be from the voluptuous, uninhibited beauty he wanted to fuck in every indecent way known to man.

For the innumerable time, he extracted his pocket watch from his waistcoat and flipped open the elaborately decorated gold cover. Eleven-forty. Exactly five minutes had elapsed since the last time he'd looked. At this rate, he wouldn't arrive at the brothel until well after one in the morning.

Would she still be waiting for him? Or would she believe he'd reneged on his promise to come to her tonight? And if she had given up on him, how could he convince her that his lapse had been the unavoidable result of an oversight, not the deliberate act of a man incapable of keeping his commitments?

As he shoved the timepiece back into its pouch, his mother shot him a hoary-eyed glare. She had noticed his preoccupation with the hour and was serving him notice that she would take him to task for the transgression at her earliest opportunity. He gave her his most winning smile and an apologetic shrug, hoping to blunt her irritation sufficiently to prevent her from lambasting him in Jane's presence. The last thing he wanted was for his betrothed to be made aware of his impatience to be quit of her company.

Not that Jane's company was in any way objectionable. On the contrary, were it not for his runaway libido and his overactive sense of guilt, he would have enjoyed their evening together immensely. In contrast to the other aristocratic theatergoers in attendance, who came primarily to see and be seen by their peers, Jane took a marked interest in the performance, and a pure, unabashed delight in her surroundings. If she cared what anyone made of her presence in his family's box or of the elegant but unadorned blue velvet gown she'd chosen to wear, she showed no sign of it, even though the titters from the surrounding boxes when they'd taken their seats had been swift and audible and clearly unfavorable.

Lord, how he admired her for knowing she was being disparaged and not caring.

The curtain fell and applause swelled to a wild crescendo. As if any of them had paid any attention whatever to the performance, he thought with disgust. A few of the nearby boxes were already vacant, and he rose to his feet, anxious to depart before it became impossible to navigate through the crush of bodies in the exterior hallway.

His mother narrowed her eyes at him, but followed suit, tucking her opera glasses into the pouch hanging from her waist. His aunt, however, waved her hand dismissively.

"Don't rush me, dear. When I come to the opera, I like to take my time enjoying the scenery." She raised her own opera glasses back to her eyes, but when Gerard followed their trajectory, he realized she was gazing neither at the stage nor at the theater's rich embellishments, but at a tall, dark-haired gentleman in a box across the way.

Gerard could not see the man well enough at this distance to make out his features or identify him, but if he knew anything about his aunt, the chap must be young, fit, and very handsome. His uncle's second and much younger wife, the countess was a decade older than Gerard but looked much younger. Pretty, vivacious, and tethered by neither matrimony nor maternity, she was far from ready to follow her husband to the grave.

His mother turned her censorious gaze from him to his aunt.

Though she did her best to keep her opinions to herself, it was clear that she didn't approve of her sister-in-law's dubious observance of mourning—the countess had shed her widow's weeds with notable alacrity—and fast ways. She didn't approve of *his* fast ways, either, despite his many attempts to explain to her that things were different in London. With her country-born and country-bred concept of honesty and integrity, she just couldn't grasp the subtleties and complexities of ton life.

"Now, Marianne, you've had four hours in which to 'enjoy the scenery.' Surely you've had more than your fill by now. And in any event," she continued, jerking her thumb in Gerard's direction, "I believe my son has another engagement for which he is already frightfully late."

Bloody hell. He was going to strangle her later. Didn't she realize she was destroying him in Jane's eyes?

But of course, she did. She was shaming him apurpose.

To his surprise, Jane laid her hand on the inside of her elbow. "Then we had certainly best be on our way. I shouldn't like to keep Ge—Lord Chester from meeting his obligations." She tugged on his coat sleeve, all but dragging him toward the exit.

Too astonished to object or wonder why she might be in as great a hurry to leave as he was, he fell in step beside her as they walked out into the hall outside the box. His mother and aunt followed close on their heels. As they threaded their way through the growing throng, Gerard tried to think of some safe topic of conversation. Anything that would steer them far from the dangerous territory of marriage and infidelity.

But his wits were far too slow and addled, for Jane was already saying, "The music and singing were lovely and the costumes quite grand, but I can't say I think much of the plot."

He sucked in a pained breath, knowing what she would say next. The Countess, Rosina, was a fool to forgive her husband's attempted seduction of Susanna. The story would be infinitely more believable if, instead of ending happily, Rosina demanded the Count's immediate castration.

Guilt stabbed at his gut, for he was no better than the despicable Count.

She looked up at him, her brown eyes wide and guileless, and said something else entirely than he expected. "I simply cannot credit a husband failing to recognize his wife merely because she is wearing another woman's clothes. We are not yet married, yet I am quite certain I could recognize at a hundred paces even if you were clothed in beggar's rags."

He was so relieved, he would have kissed her then and there if they hadn't been making such good progress through the narrow passageways that led to the street outside the theater. Instead, he chuckled. "As I am sure that I would recognize you no matter your costume."

She tipped her head to one side and arched an eyebrow. "Do you really think so, my lord?"

He nodded sagely. How could he fail when he had known her more than half her life?

She grinned. "Well, perhaps we should put our mutual certainty to the test, then."

"Oh? What do you have in mind, my lady?"

"My parents will certainly insist upon hosting a ball to celebrate our engagement as soon as the first banns have been read. What do you say to the proposition we hold a masque, and that we do not reveal ourselves to one another before the party begins? Whoever correctly identities the other first wins."

Once again, Gerard was reminded of why he had chosen Jane as his wife. She might not be the most beautiful lady of the ton, but she was far and away the cleverest. Not only would the game provide a small, amusing diversion for the two of them, but her suggestion would render their engagement ball much more entertaining for their guests than most. In his experience, engagement

balls were uniformly dreary affairs at which Married and Unmarried alike were unpleasantly reminded of their present marital state and spent most of the evening either bemoaning it or
doing their best to alter it, in one fashion or another.

Before he could respond, however, a large group of finely attired ladies and gentlemen filed slowly from one of the boxes
and right into their path. Loath to lose any time, he placed his
hand over Jane's and steered her to the far side of the glittering
hallway. As they passed, however, he recognized the doddering
Marquess of Darby.

Damn and blast! On any other night, he would have ignored
the elderly gentleman, but Gerard desperately needed the old
chap's support for a bill he was sponsoring in Parliament. Gerard
been trying all week to speak to Darby about the bill, but for a
gouty old man who could scarcely walk with the assistance of a
cane, the marquess was remarkably difficult to catch up with. A
brief word with the gentleman tonight could mean all the difference in next week's negotiations.

Gerard slowed his steps and turned to Jane regretfully. "My
apologies, Lady Jane, but I must pay my respects to Lord Darby.
I'll be but a minute."

Jane smiled up at him. "Of course. Take as long as you require."

His cock and balls tightened. *As long as you require.* Jane
may have spoken the words, but he heard them in Venus's rich,
sultry tones.

Damn. Any length of time with the marquess was far too
long to suit him when Venus was waiting.

10

As Gerard strode purposefully toward his quarry, Jane leaned against the outside wall, admiring his long, muscular limbs and easy, loose-limbed gait. He looked especially smart tonight, she thought with an unwarranted surge of pride, garbed in an exquisitely tailored black frock coat, black breeches, white shirt, and white cravat. The rich green brocade of his waistcoat provided the only splash of color to the otherwise sober ensemble, but it was all the more eye-catching and effective for its lack of pretension, especially by contrast to the garish display of many of the other men who passed by as she waited. If they hoped to attract peahens, of course, their costumes would be entirely effective. Otherwise . . .

Her future mother-in-law, Mrs. Everett, and Lady Chester, noting that Gerard was now engaged with Lord Darby, drew up short and began speaking to each other. Jane couldn't make out their conversation over the buzz of conversation and hum of foot traffic, but she could tell they were arguing about something. Probably Lady Chester's unseemly interest in younger men.

She didn't want to know what the woman she would soon be expected to call "Mother" would say if she knew what Jane planned to do later tonight with her son.

Jane knees grew wobbly at the thought, and she sagged against the wall for support. It was madness to meet him at the Red Door. Throughout the performance, guilt and anxiety had besieged her. The plot of the opera, laced with marital infidelity and disguises, had done nothing to settle her nerves.

If she were wise, she would return to her brother's house tonight and go to bed. Gerard would believe that Venus had either changed her mind or grown tired of waiting for him and that would be the end of it. He would be disappointed, perhaps even hurt, but he would recover swiftly enough—she knew him well enough to be certain his heart would remain intact. Her identity and reputation would remain safe, for he clearly hadn't recognized her in her guise as Venus.

But wisdom had nothing to do with the burning ache between her thighs or the fluttery sensation in her belly or with the fierce, undeniable compulsion to touch him—and be touched by him. Not as plain, undesirable Lady Jane but as Venus, the embodiment of his every erotic fantasy.

Last night, for the first time in her life, she had felt beautiful and *wanted*. And she couldn't—wouldn't—deprive herself of the chance to experience that feeling again . . . for however long she could have it and despite the risk of discovery.

"I told you it was Lady Jane."

Jane started at the sound of a high-pitched, slightly whiny voice to her left. She'd recognize it anywhere . . . unfortunately. Lady Victoria Tremaine, daughter of the Earl and Countess of Stratleigh, and one of Jane's most relentless childhood tormenters. Even after the party at the Chesters, Victoria had made no secret of her disdain for the Duke of Hardwyck's pitifully unpretty daughter.

Victoria was everything Jane was not—pretty, popular, and

perfect. The only thing the two of them had in common was that after three Seasons, both were still on the shelf.

Or had been. Until now.

Jane fought back an uncharitable burst of glee at the sudden realization that she—plain Jane—would precede Victoria to the altar, and pasted a friendly smile on her face. When she turned, Victoria, elaborately gowned in an ivory satin dress embellished with a surfeit of ruffles and ribbons, and her two favorite accomplices, Miss Josephine Merriweather and Miss Elizabeth Alcott, were bearing down on her with the speed and reckless abandon of a runaway horse cart.

"What a pleasure to run into you this evening, Lady Victoria. Miss Merriweather. Miss Alcott." The acknowledgments forced their way from between teeth Jane had to make a concerted effort not to grit, but they sounded polite enough.

Victoria's full, rosy lips pulled upward into a tight, thin smile. "Yes, a pleasure. And a surprise." She jerked her head in Miss Merriweather's direction. "Josie swore I was mistaken when I said 'twas you in the box with Lord Chester this evening. Didn't you, Jo?"

Miss Merriweather, cursed with coloring so fair she bordered on translucent, had the good grace to turn a deep shade of crimson when she nodded in answer to her friend's question.

Jane's stomach curdled with unease. "Are you asking if I accompanied Lord Chester's family this evening?"

Victoria patted her ebony curls and shrugged. "No, I'm not asking if you accompanied them. I know that, darling."

Jane stiffened as the memory of a hundred past taunts rolled over her. Victoria always called her victims *darling* right before she thrust her petty but well-sharpened knife between their ribs.

"What I am perishing to know," Victoria continued, "is whether the rumors are true."

"And what rumors are those?" Jane countered, though in a sick part of her belly, she already knew.

Victoria clucked her tongue in false sympathy. "Of course, you'd be the last to hear such things, wouldn't you, dear? People are saying that Lord Chester's aunt has demanded he take a wife who won't—oh my, how can I put this delicately?—outshine her in Society."

Jane closed her eyes briefly as pain stabbed her heart. She had been prepared to be slighted, to be told to her face she was unattractive and undesirable, the moment she laid eyes on Lady Victoria. But this . . . this was a thousand times worse. Because for all it was being told to her out of spite and ill will, it might very well be true.

Why else had Gerard suddenly decided to marry her, of all people, after she had been out for three Seasons? Lady Chester was still young and lovely and enjoyed being the center of masculine attention, especially at the Chesters' own ball. The last thing she would want would be for her nephew to marry a woman who might rival her at such events.

Oh, she had been a stupid, wishful girl to believe he cared for her in any way, that he wanted to marry her because he admired her for her skills and intellect if not for her appearance! And though she hated to show any weakness before Victoria and her vindictive little band, Jane's throat thickened with tears and she leaned back against the wall, wishing she could melt into it and disappear.

"It is a shame, is it not, Lady Victoria, that rumor is so terribly unreliable?"

Jane's eyelids flew open at the sound of Gerard's voice, its tenor low, even, and . . . deadly calm. He stood just behind Lady Victoria and Miss Alcott, and as all three ladies turned to gape at him, he ambled to Jane's side and slipped his arm around her waist. A delicious heat followed the path of his hand as it settled on her opposite hip.

Gerard narrowed his eyes on Lady Victoria. "Since I am confident that you, of all people, would not wish to be in the embarrassing position of spreading false news, let me assure you that Lady Chester's wishes have nothing whatsoever to do with my choice in a bride." He turned his gaze to Jane, his hard expression softening with an emotion that looked for all the world like adoration. "I asked Lady Jane to marry me because I admire and esteem her and wish her to be my countess, and for no other reason. She is everything I could wish for in a wife, and more, she is my dearest friend."

He pulled her tighter to his side, a gesture of reassurance, and Jane found herself believing him. Again. Her heart swelled with joy so fierce, it hurt nearly as much as her previous anguish.

She was already giddy when he leaned down and brushed his mouth over hers. Soft and insubstantial as a flower petal, the kiss was intended to demonstrate the authenticity of his affections to their attentive audience, but the slow, sweet contact so captivated Jane's senses, she quite forgot they were surrounded by no fewer than a hundred spectators. She angled her head and parted her lips, an instinctive attempt to deepen the connection and prolong the moment. He twitched in response, the muscles in his arms and torso going rigid at the same time hers grew soft and pliable as fresh clay, ready to be shaped to the artist's whim.

Emitting a low, throaty exhalation that was more vibration than sound, he crushed her to his chest. No longer restrained or gentle, his lips explored hers—sucked, teased, nibbled. He tasted faintly of mint and citrus, more strongly of fervent hopes and secret longings.

Or maybe that was her.

Jane clung to his shoulders and did her best to follow his lead in this mysterious new dance of lips and mouths and tongues that was as dizzying as a waltz, as thrilling as twirling in circles across a crowded dance floor . . .

Crowded.

She gasped when Gerard broke the kiss abruptly and recalled, in staccato bursts of perception, that they were in the exterior hall of the theater, that they were being watched, that the only audible noise was her own ragged breathing and the distant hum of faraway voices. Cheeks flaming, she turned to find their audience gaping at them. For the first time in her life, Jane wished she were prone to fainting spells.

"Chin up," Gerard whispered, his lips almost touching her ear. His hot, spicy breath so close to her ear raised gooseflesh along her neck. "Nothing like a betrothed couple losing their heads in public to silence the naysayers."

Jane nodded dumbly, self-doubt curdling her stomach. Had he truly been lost in the moment, as she had? Or had he kissed her so passionately for the sole purpose of making his point to Lady Victoria and her cronies?

When she noted that Gerard had already returned his attention to Lady Victoria, his breathing as smooth as Jane's was ragged, she had her answer. How could she have forgotten what an accomplished performer he could be?

One thing was certain, however. His irritation with Jane's most persistent tormenter was far from feigned. He smiled at Lady Victoria, but no one would mistake his expression for a friendly one. If anything, it was more menacing than a scowl would have been.

"Anyone who suggests my esteem for my bride is anything less than genuine and wholehearted will answer to me, and the consequences will not be pleasant. I do hope we understand one another."

The pretty, petty young woman blanched. "Yes, of course, my lord. That is, 'twas only what I had heard and I didn't believe it, mind you, not for a minute, but you understand, I wanted Lady Jane to . . ."

Gerard held up his hand. "That will do, Lady Victoria. And as to the rest of you," he continued, addressing himself to the stunned crowd, "if you'd like a repeat performance, you'll just have to attend the wedding. Now, if you'll excuse us . . ."

With that, he tucked her hand back into the crook of her arm and swept her through the hallway and down the stairs. The rumble of scandalized conversation followed them.

Her wedding—and marriage—had just become the talk of the ton. And Jane knew with sick certainty what the rumor mill would do to her when the inevitable happened.

She would be the laughingstock of London. But then, that would be nothing new.

She had waited for him.

Gerard exhaled heavily, uncertain whether the fierce sensation exploding in his chest was relief or guilt.

Relief that Venus had stayed so far into the night; she had fallen asleep atop the red satin coverlet, one hand tucked beneath her cheek, the other dangling off the edge of the bed. Or guilt that his impatience and forgetfulness had made such forbearance necessary.

Relief that she had trusted him enough to believe he would keep his word despite every indication to the contrary. Or guilt that by doing so, he was making a mockery of his declaration of devotion to his future wife in front of more than a hundred gawking witnesses, not to mention the unaccountably ardent kiss that had accompanied his claim.

He didn't know what the devil had come over him tonight, had come over him since he'd proposed to Jane—was it only two days ago?—except that his senses were profoundly muddled. Holding Jane in his arms, kissing her, he'd been inexplicably reminded of the woman who lay in all her naked splendor on the bed in front of him. He'd remembered every unholy caress of Venus's lips and tongue last night and in his mind's eye, it had become Jane kneeling before him, Jane taking his cock into her mouth, Jane swallowing his seed as if it were honeyed wine.

At the same time, he'd imagined as he kissed Jane that it was Venus whose mouth opened so invitingly beneath his, Venus whose tongue snaked out to caress his, Venus whose lips nibbled and suckled at his. It would be Venus he made love to on his wedding night, Venus whose hot, wet cunt he'd pound until she came, sobbing with rapture and gasping his name.

Madness, that's what it was, and there was only one way to dispel it.

He strode toward the bed, his cock growing heavy at the sight of the generous swell of her breasts and the soft curve of her hips. Surely there'd never been a woman with a finer arse. Tossing his hat onto the chair in front of the fireplace, he lowered himself to the edge of the bed and leaned down until his mouth touched her neck.

She smelled of plain lye soap and beneath that, of earth and woman and desire. Familiar scents, to be sure, but did they belong to Jane or to Venus? The two women had become so intertwined in his memories, he couldn't be sure.

Not until Venus had a face of her own.

Jane awoke to the sweet, disorienting sensation of a warm lips and stubble-roughened skin traversing her throat to the tender spot just beneath her ear to her jawline to her mouth. Still half asleep, she parted her lips with a sigh and turned to accept his . . .

Kiss? No!

She jerked away, banging her head against Gerard's chin as she came abruptly to full consciousness. Blinking against the sudden intrusion of light, she scrambled across the bed and away from Gerard, her heart pounding with alarm at her near disastrous error.

If he kissed her, he would know!

She could cover her hair, cover her face, remove her clothing, disguise her voice, and scrub off her perfume, but the taste of her mouth, the feel of her lips would give her away.

"Please, my lord, you mustn't kiss me."

Gerard rubbed his bludgeoned jaw with one hand. He would likely have a bruise come daylight, as she would no doubt have a lump on one side of her head. "Why not?" he demanded, his eyes narrowing.

Her stomach twinged with alarm. He was suspicious.

She chewed her lower lip, casting desperately for a believable answer. "It's too . . . familiar. Too intimate."

He raised an eyebrow. "So, if I bury my face in your pussy and lick you until you come, that's not too intimate? Interesting." One corner of his mouth quirked upward in amused skepticism.

A wave of hot longing flooded the very place he spoke of. And put that way, her answer certainly seemed ridiculous. He had been more intimate, more familiar with her last night than when he'd kissed her at the opera house. And yet . . .

"Kissing is what people do when they love one another. Or are falling in love."

He dropped his hand from his chin and slid closer, crowding her into the corner. "What is wrong with falling in love, my goddess?"

"Nothing, but I—I told you I did not want to come to care for you only to lose you because another woman takes your fancy."

"Hmmmm." Gerard patted his face gingerly where she'd smacked him and regarded her thoughtfully. "So now I can neither fuck nor kiss you for an entire month? That seems a rather poor way to convince me I should take you as my mistress. Why should I accede to your demands when there are plenty of other women who'll allow me to do both . . . including my future wife?"

Jane's heart pounded so furiously, she imagined it might hammer its way out of her chest. *He knows, he knows, he knows.*

But if he didn't, she would be a fool to give up now.

She gave him a sultry smile and reached out to lay her palm upon his chest. "I am sure she won't allow you to do a great many things until after you're married, however." Sliding her hand down toward the waistband of his pantaloons, she kept her gaze on his face and noted that his eyes were growing dark and unfocused as her fingers trailed over his abdomen. "As for other women," she continued, her voice now firmly in Venus's husky register, "I am sure they will cost you a great deal more than I."

When her fingers reached the first button of his fall, the harsh, hooded expression on his face gave her courage. Glancing down, she saw the sharply defined ridge of his hardened shaft and knew that, whatever his suspicions, he wanted her to continue with what she was doing. Her blood sang in her veins at the power she had over him. As Venus, she could touch him and do magic.

As Venus, she might even make him love her.

Confident now, she flipped open the first button, "You have only to agree to my terms, and I will do anything and everything else you ask of me."

He moved so quickly, she could only let out a small squeak of surprise as he grabbed her wrists and flipped her onto the bed beneath him. "Anything?" he asked, planting himself between her legs. The fine wool fabric of his pantaloons felt rough and tantalizing against the delicate flesh of her inner thighs.

A tiny flutter of alarm at the undercurrent of danger in his tone made her pause as she wondered briefly what "anything" might include once kissing and copulation were excluded, but since she could think of no way in which Gerard could touch her to which she would object, she shrugged and nodded. "Anything."

His mouth curved into a hungry, wolfish grin that made her belly tingle and her toes curl. "Excellent." As swiftly as he had pinned her beneath him, he rolled over until she straddled him. Throwing his arms out to the side, he waggled his eyebrows with fiendish amusement. "You can begin by undressing me."

It was all she could do to keep from throwing back her head and laughing. If *this* was what he meant to threaten her with, he was sorely misguided. She had been undressing him in her mind for years, had been putting form to those images in terracotta for nearly as long. What would he think if he came upon her hidden cache of nudes, each bearing his face upon a different body type—on an approximation of Michelangelo's David here, of Praxiteles' Hermes or Bernini's Apollo there? Would he be flattered or horrified or . . . perhaps worst, amused?

Silly Jane and her peculiar little hobby. Ladies who wished to dabble in art painted pretty watercolors of flowers and landscapes. They did *not* dirty themselves by playing with mud and pretending to be *sculptors*.

"I recommend starting with the cravat," Gerard prompted. "I've found it's remarkably difficult to remove the shirt with the blessed thing on."

Jane's cheeks flushed hot, and she was grateful for the camouflage the mask provided. Once again, she'd been off making a daisy chain of her own maudlin thoughts instead of attending to the moment.

"I did wonder whether 'twould be best to begin with the coat or the cravat," she replied as airily as she could muster, "as I expect the shirt will not come off so long as you wear either of them."

"An astute observation. Coat first, then?"

She nodded. "I think so."

Grasping the collar of his wool coat—the same elegant black one he'd worn to the opera—she peeled the fabric back toward his shoulders. He rose obligingly to a sitting position, but as he did so, his head came level with her chest. While she struggled to push the sleeves down his arms, his warm breath blew across her nipples, bringing them to hard, aching points. She had almost managed to divest him of the garment when he drew one of the pebbled peaks into his mouth and suckled.

Gasping, she arched her back involuntarily as bright, fiery sensation ignited like a torch inside her. Each pull of his lips, each scrape of his teeth, each flick of his tongue upon her breast added fuel to the restless need that burned between her legs and extinguished all rational thought. She squirmed impatiently, seeking release from the delicious torment he inflicted. Didn't he realize she couldn't speak, couldn't think, couldn't do anything but *feel* when he touched her this way?

Gerard lifted his head. "I'm sorry, my goddess. Am I distracting you?" he teased.

He knew exactly what he was doing, the scoundrel, and she saw now it was part of the game. She must undress him while he did his best to divert her from the task. But the rough edge to his voice and the ragged tempo of his breathing told her that doing so would cost him no small effort in restraint.

In other words, she could play the very same game. She grinned at the thought.

Whether she won or lost, she'd have what she wanted soon enough—the man she loved, naked and at her mercy.

12

In the end, Gerard let her win. Not merely because it was the gentlemanly thing to do, but because every feathery caress of her fingertips as she explored his body made him shiver with near ecstasy. She seemed fascinated by the hair on his chest and by his small, flat nipples, lingering over them as though she had never seen a nude man in the flesh, let alone touched one, before.

But then, perhaps she hadn't. He hadn't removed a stitch of clothing save his hat last night. Recalling the way she'd kneeled before him then, nude and wanton, and sucked him while he remained fully dressed, seemed to cause his cock to stretch to even greater dimension. When her hand brushed across the front of his pantaloons, he had to grit his teeth to keep from yanking open the fall to release his aching shaft from its uncomfortable confinement. There was only one place he wanted his prick confined now, and it sure as hell wasn't in his own drawers.

When she had to turn her back on him to remove his shoes, treating him to an unobstructed view of the most beautiful arse he'd ever laid eyes on, however, he could no longer restrain him-

self. As she leaned forward to yank off the first one, he moistened his index finger and slid it along the cleft between her buttocks until he found the small orifice he sought. He pressed
gently inward even as he heard her sharp intake of breath.

"What are you doing?" Her tone was scandalized, but the
rapid rhythm of her respiration and the slight relaxation of the
sphincter as he seated his finger up to the first knuckle told him
she didn't entirely object to what he was doing.

"As I recall, you did say you would let me do anything I
wanted."

"Oh." A quick, uncertain exhalation followed by silence.

He twisted his hand and slipped another of his fingers inside
her pussy. She was hot and tight and incredibly slick with arousal.
There could be no doubt she wanted him every bit as much as
he wanted her.

Nonetheless, she jerked away at the second penetration. "You
can't . . . you mustn't . . ."

He guessed the reason for her objection immediately. "Don't
worry. It takes something rather larger than a finger to break a
woman's maidenhead." In fact, as he slipped his finger further
into her channel, he could feel the thin membrane that indicated
she was, in fact, as virginal as she claimed. He hadn't, until this
moment, quite believed it.

"Oh," she breathed again, longer and more sustained this
time. Her muscles clenched and released, and she wiggled her
arse experimentally, as if she couldn't decide whether to attempt escape or to encourage further liberties.

If she kept moving around in that fashion, however, the outcome was hardly in question. That was, if he could wait long
enough to satisfy the ever-expanding ache in his loins. He must
remove the rest of his clothing now, or risk ruining his finest
pair of pantaloons.

Slowly, carefully, he withdrew his fingers, and smiled to himself when she whimpered in obvious frustration. "Never fear,

my goddess. I'm far from finished with what I have in mind for you." He caressed the ample curve of her backside, reveling in the smooth, silken texture of her flesh beneath the calloused palms he normally hid beneath his gloves. He'd never developed a liking for idle hands, and his work-roughened skin betrayed his lack of gentlemanly restraint in that regard.

With a gentle shove, he lifted her off his legs and rolled out from beneath her. Pushing himself to a sitting position on the edge of the bed, he kicked off his shoes and shucked his pantaloons and drawers, leaving them in a crumpled heap on the floor alongside the articles of clothing Venus had already removed. His best silk cravat would probably never be the same again, but he couldn't bring himself to care.

Wrinkles be damned. He would deny himself—and her—no longer.

13

In other circumstances, Jane might have spent hours exploring, studying, and mapping every detail of the exquisite male physique stretched out beside her. Everything about Gerard's body fascinated her, from the tiny pinpricks of his nipples poking through the dusting of wiry, russet-colored hair on his chest to the sharply defined ridges of his abdominal muscles to the thick, proud shaft rising from the nest of curls at the juncture of his thighs.

But she couldn't think about anything but the need pulsing between her thighs and the incredible, exquisite pleasure she had experienced when he put his fingers inside her down there. Such a sense of fullness and fulfillment . . . almost as strong as when he'd made her come with his mouth. In fact, she'd imagined if he thrust a bit further, for a tiny bit longer, she might have come again, then and there.

"Come here." Reclining comfortably against a red velvet pillow, he beckoned with a crook of his finger. A wicked tendril of desire twisted in her gut as she wondered if that was the finger he had used earlier.

She made to lie down beside him, but he shook his head.

"Turn around so that your back is toward me. Like before. Yes, that's the way," he encouraged as she clambered gingerly atop him, his cock brushing against her abdomen as she did. "Now—" He grabbed her hips. "—scoot back up here." His voice roughened, sending tingles over her skin. "I would taste you again."

Feeling awkward and shy but wildly aroused, she complied, crawling backward until she straddled his face, her nether parts open and exposed to him as never before. Her face grew hot at the thought of him looking at her there, touching her there with his fingers and his tongue. The reserved, gently bred, ladylike part of her wanted to shrink away, to hide. But the larger, wicked, wanton part of her craved every sinful moment of what was to come.

As if he read her thoughts, sensed her moment of uncertainty, his brushed his fingers almost reverently over the folds of her flesh. "You're so beautiful here. Ripe and sweet. And so responsive." He stroked her slowly, like a favored pet. "You almost came earlier, didn't you? When I fucked you with my fingers?"

Jane bit her lower lip and nodded. "Yes," she whispered.

"I wonder . . . would you come for any man who touched you the right way, or just for me?" As he mused, one digit slipped inside her pussy, and her muscles leapt in response. Unconsciously, she rocked backward, forcing his finger deeper and intensifying the sensation.

"Just you. Only you," she gasped as his tongue snaked across the axis of her need.

Though he could never know why, she spoke the purest truth. She couldn't imagine allowing another man to touch her this way, see her this way. She would die of humiliation. Only for Gerard, the man she seemed to have been born to love, could she make herself so vulnerable, so defenseless.

He made a low, skeptical sound in his throat. "But why me? You hardly know me."

But I have known you forever, since before I was flesh and blood and bone. All I needed was to find you to know I would always belong to you. And you to me, even if you never accepted or believed it.

"I don't know," she answered, lying through her teeth. How she hated lying to him, and yet, she had left herself no other choice.

"It doesn't matter," he answered roughly. "I've known you only a day, but I've never wanted to lose myself in a woman this way. My cock . . . God, I burn to get inside you, Venus. Will you let me love you tonight? In a way that, I swear, will not compromise your maidenhead."

And what way could that be? She couldn't begin to fathom what he had in mind, but then she jumped as she felt his tongue between her buttocks, probing the same rear entrance he'd penetrated with his finger earlier. Her head swam at the overwhelmingly erotic sensation, her mind not quite capable of compassing what she thought he must be telling her.

"You can't mean—"

"You like this," he muttered, his lips moving against her flesh and making her giddier than ever. "Your pussy is gets wetter, readier, every time I touch your arsehole."

She couldn't deny it. But the very idea . . . it was so terribly foreign, so utterly wicked. And yet, that very wickedness seemed to heighten her arousal.

"I'm not sure . . ." Her voice sounded vague and distant to her own ears, as if she were speaking from very far away.

"I promise I'll stop if you ask me to."

But she couldn't fathom that, or think clearly at all, for already he was doing magical and alarming things with his tongue. And with his fingers, which he thrust into her pussy and her arse, first one, then two, stretching her, filling her, claiming her. Her respiration became erratic, wild, and she found herself working with him, rocking her pelvis in rhythm with him, teetering precariously on the edge of release.

Her legs trembled, and she leaned forward to brace herself on her arms lest she collapse on top of him. As she did, she became instantly aware of a benefit of the position into which he'd maneuvered her: she could touch him in the same way he touched her.

Arrested by the thought, she ran her fingers over the velvety length of his cock. So foreign and outlandish, this bit of male flesh that could undergo such remarkable metamorphosis, from slack and unobtrusive to such conspicuous rigidity. And even when erect and uncompromising, the organ was a study in contrasts—hard as steel within, soft and smooth as silk on the outside.

As she pondered this dichotomy, a droplet appeared in the slit at the tip. Recalling the salty, bitter-sweetness of his seed, she ran her tongue along the underside of the head and up to capture the tiny bit of fluid. He groaned and jerked, the rhythm of his fingers and tongue momentarily interrupted.

An impish notion struck her. "I'm sorry," she said innocently. "Am I distracting you?"

"You know you are," he muttered, his voice muffled as his lips brushed distractingly over her flesh, "but I can cope."

She might have laughed then, but he redoubled his efforts, skillfully increasing the pressure and speed of his tongue and fingers. He slipped a third finger inside her rear entrance, filling her almost unbearably. The sensation was so intensely erotic, she couldn't speak, couldn't think, couldn't even breathe. Couldn't do anything but close her eyes as his tongue and hands wreaked further havoc on her sensitized flesh. Could only stiffen and cry out and then come, wave after wave of violent, outrageous pleasure crashing over her.

When at last he withdrew his mouth and fingers from her body and rolled her gently off him and onto her back, she was too languid and sated to object to or worry about what might happen next.

Pressing his palms to the backs of her thighs, he lifted and spread her legs. The head of his cock, slick with her saliva, pressed into the narrow channel his fingers had recently vacated. She whimpered at the invasion, the sensation of her muscles stretching and contracting in both acceptance and denial.

"Am I hurting you?"

She shook her head. Judging from his taut, almost anguished expression, she was hurting him, not the other way around. He braced himself on his arms now, his corded biceps trembling with effort.

"If I do, make me stop," he groaned.

Never. As he eased inside of her, little by little, she marveled at the odd dichotomy of feelings—she was so full, too full, and it did almost hurt, and yet the pain itself was a kind of pleasure. Did it feel the same to him? So painful, it was agonizingly pleasurable? No wonder his face was etched with torment.

When his cock was fully sheathed, he began to move inside her. Slow, easy thrusts, dragging across nerve endings so raw and sensitized, she couldn't bear for him to continue, couldn't bear for him to stop. Her pussy throbbed with need, and she reached between her legs, pressing the heel of her palm there to quell the frantic pulsing of her flesh.

Gerard shifted his weight onto one arm and placed his hand over hers. "Do it. I want to feel you come while I fuck you." His passion-dark eyes bored into hers. "Please."

Shy but emboldened by his plea, she swirled her fingers experimentally over her swollen flesh. Liquid fire exploded, stealing her breath with its speed and ferocity. The pace of his thrusts increased, his breathing grew harsher and more ragged. She heard herself moan, heard the mattress creaking, heard the repeated *smack smack smack* of their coupling. Everything else faded, her entire being concentrated between her thighs, on the erotic intensity of what he did to her, of what she did to herself. The realization of just how completely she had surrendered herself to him toppled her over the edge into a bone-jarring, beautiful climax.

"God, yes," he hissed.

He closed his eyes and threw back his head, his features drawn in what appeared to be anguish as the first tremor seized him. With one last thrust, he buried his cock to the hilt inside her and came with a shout, spilling his seed deep inside her in spasms as tangible and elemental as the pulsing of her own blood. And every bit as vital to her survival.

Collapsing atop her, he withdrew and gathered her up in his arms. His lips brushed against her ear and said something, so softly, she could scarcely make out his words. Even when she did, she couldn't believe she'd heard them right.

"I love you. As God is my witness, I have fallen at last."

Joy and despair leapt and twined in her breast like snakes. She had what she had thought she wanted for more than a decade. His passion, his desire, his love. But now she was greedy. She wanted his love not for the nameless, faceless whore he thought her to be.

There was no time to consider the wisdom or consequences of her actions. She simply did what her heart told her she must.

"And I love you, Gerard Everett," she whispered, and reached up to remove her mask.

14

Shock. Disbelief. Outrage. Panic. Betrayal.

Words couldn't adequately capture Gerard's churning emotions.

Venus was Jane. Jane was Venus.

In the space of the time it took for her rich, russet-colored hair—the dazzling color of which he'd never appreciated before because it was always tortured into stiff curls and tight chignons or stuffed beneath bonnets and hats, though he had noticed that it regularly attempted to escape—to unfurl down her back until it reached just below her shoulder blades, he cursed himself a hundred different ways.

He should have *known*. Had known all along, if he were honest with himself. All the clues—subtle and not so subtle—that he'd dismissed because carrying them to their rational conclusion seemed impossible. Her posture as she waited for him the first night, as poised and graceful as a duchess yet exuding an innocence wholly incompatible with her nudity. He'd thought her voice sounded familiar, hadn't he? Not the register, but the way she formed her consonants and vowels. Not to mention the implausibility of an educated, intelligent, and virginal young lady contemplating a career as a whore who was still so determined to shield her identity that she insisted upon wearing a mask. Finally, there was his response to their kiss in the opera house combined with her refusal to allow him to kiss her later. She must have known she could disguise her voice and her scent, but not the taste of her mouth.

No wonder he'd lost his head and imagined the woman he held in his arms, the woman whose lips parted and responded so feverishly to his touch, was not Jane, but Venus. Because, against all logic and probability, it was. His body, it seemed, was smarter than his brain.

No wonder he'd been so bloody confused the past two days. He hadn't been falling in love with two women, as he'd feared. He'd been falling in love with one.

The one woman he didn't want to love in this fierce, primal way. This dirty, carnal way that made him want to bury his cock in her and fuck her like a whore.

He closed his eyes, sick to his very soul.

Hell and brimstone, he *had* just fucked her like a whore. Had just *sodomized* his future wife, for Christ's sake. His *wife*. The mother of his children. The one woman he was called upon by his status as a gentleman and a peer to hold in the highest honor and respect.

Yet he had just fucked her in the arse.

His mind shied away from his body's instant reaction to that thought. Because it wasn't disgust or horror at debauching and defiling her that he felt.

It was the desire to do it again. And again. And again.

Dear God, he was the most unremitting degenerate on earth. Every bit as low and common as his boyhood tormentors had claimed. Son of a simple country girl and the second son of a second son, undeserving of his title and position.

"Gerard?" Her timid query, accompanied by the light touch of her palm on his arm, drew him back from his recriminations. She was watching him with wide, anxious gray-green eyes, her lips pressed together in a tight line of worry and apprehension.

Damn her! What the hell had she been thinking? Why on earth had she come to a brothel and offered herself up to him like a common prostitute?

Another, more horrifying thought occurred to him. Would she have offered herself up to the first man who'd come along? Allowed that man to suckle her tits, lick her cunt, fuck her arse? Indeed, how could he imagine she wouldn't have? She couldn't have known he'd be at the brothel last night. It had been sheer, dumb luck that Mrs. Upshaw had enlisted him to the task of educating her latest recruit. And in the ultimate twist of irony, he had made a cuckold of himself.

Red-hot rage blazed in his chest as he remembered his intrusion on her little tea party with her friends yesterday. One of whom, he recalled bitterly, had once worked in this very house and the other of whom was married to Jane's famously profligate brother. Dear God, the cause of their startled glances and guilty expressions when he'd appeared was clear now. He had stumbled upon them plotting Jane's carnal education.

He couldn't decide which was worse—that she might have intended to give herself to another man, any man who happened along, or that, once she'd discovered he was the man who would be responsible for her "training," she had thought him so gullible, so much a slave to his physical urges, that he wouldn't see through her disguise. Christ, she'd even rubbed his face in his inability to recognize her when she'd suggested they have a masquerade ball.

Fury surged through him. He grasped her roughly by the shoulders, but stanched the impulse to shake her until her teeth shattered.

"Get dressed. I'm taking you home." He issued the terse order impassively, afraid that if he allowed even a fraction of the caustic emotions churning inside him to come out, he would lose all control of them. And if he did, he couldn't guarantee whether he would roar with anger or whimper with despair.

"Please, Gerard, I can—"

"Explain?" He shook his head. "There is no adequate explanation for what you've done here, my lady. Or should I say, my whore?"

Her face and lips went pale and bloodless at his scathing words. "I never meant . . . that is, I only wanted y—"

He clapped his hand over her mouth. "Don't utter another word tonight, or I shan't be responsible for what I might do." Shoving her away, he pointed toward the screen behind which he was certain her clothing was hidden. "Go. Now. Before I do something I regret."

Her eyes shone with tears, and but to his relief, she didn't shed them. Instead, she rose from the bed and scurried for the screen, as if she'd suddenly become modest.

Hah! The woman clearly hadn't a modest bone in her body.

He snatched his drawers and pantaloons off the floor and yanked them on, fastening the buttons of his fall with trembling fingers.

Not five minutes ago, he'd told her he loved her. And he'd meant it. Three words he'd never said—never even contemplated saying—to any other woman other than his mother and . . . well, Jane herself.

But that was different. A safe, reliable kind of love. Not the wild, uncontrollable sort that led a man to make mad, impossible promises, like undying passion and eternal fidelity. As if that were even possible!

He jerked his shirt on over his head, muttering a muffled curse as he noted the deep creases in the ruffled front of the starched linen. His cravat, equally crumpled, lay nearby. He retrieved it and began his attempt to knot it around his neck, then tossed it on the bed in disgust.

Falling in love with Venus had been unexpected, even astonishing, but not objectionable. When the emotion ran its course, they could safely part ways and go on with their lives.

But loving Jane this way? Dread made him dizzy.

"I am ready."

Lost in his thoughts, he turned his head in Jane's direction. She stepped out from behind the screen, wearing the same, simple blue velvet gown she'd worn to the opera. Except now her hair fell down her back like thick autumn leaves and he knew what lay beneath the confines of her dress. Velvet-skinned breasts, slender waist, perfectly rounded hips, and a glistening, pink pussy he wanted to bury his tongue and fingers and cock in over and over until neither of them could walk or talk or think.

Damn, what a rich joke her maker had played upon them all. All the men who thought her plain face a disqualification to beauty, including him. Little did they know what untold riches that unassuming exterior concealed.

And he was bad as the rest of them. He had known her for nearly a dozen years, looked at her a thousand times . . . and looked right through her. Had never really seen her for who she was.

Perhaps *that* was why she had come here. To prove to herself before she married him that she was worthy of passion, of desire.

But that didn't excuse what she'd done. Nothing could. And he would spend the rest of their lives holding her to account for it.

He grabbed his waistcoat and coat and threw them over his arm. "Shall I take you to your brother's house or your parents'?" Her answer could very well indicate how much her sister-in-law knew.

She swallowed visibly. "My brother's." It sounded more like a question than an answer.

"I see." His suspicion confirmed, he gestured toward the door. "After you, my lady."

Lady Grenville was in for some hard questions. And his bride was in for something much, much harder.

15

Jane peered out the window of the front door to her brother's townhome until Gerard's coach was safely out of sight. After another two minutes had passed, she turned the handle quietly and slipped out onto the stoop. The dim, watery glow of pre-dawn lit the eastern sky.

Pulling her cloak tighter over her head to conceal her identity, she descended the stairs to the cobbled sidewalk. A few carts rumbled through the streets, but she needed a hackney, and one would be hard to come by at this hour. She walked toward the corner of the square before she spotted something that made her heart pound with relief.

A hackney sat at the curb just across the street, its driver huddled in the high seat behind the cab, a tattered blanket wrapped about his shoulders. She rushed to it, pulling her coin purse from her cloak pocket when she stood alongside the stout roan mare hitched to the coach.

"Good morning to you, sir."

He stirred and blinked sleepily. "And to you, lady."

Opening the small velvet pouch, she took out the sovereign

she carried and displayed it to the coachman. His eyes widened instantly and he appeared considerably more alert.

"In exchange for this, I would like you to drive me about town for an hour or so, until full daylight, then deliver to me to address I specify. Do we have a bargain?"

"An hour's drive, ye say?"

"Thereabouts. Until about eight in the morning."

"And if I do that, I get yer sovereign?" The avaricious expression on this flat-nosed face said he was more than interested, but hoped she might be desperate enough for the unusual service she was requesting that he could extort an even grander sum from her.

Well, she was indeed desperate to avoid returning home so early as to raise her parents' suspicions as to her whereabouts, but he couldn't induce her to pay more. The sovereign was the last coin she had in her possession.

"Yes."

He rubbed his chin, clearly undecided as to whether to accept her offer or demand more money.

"If you are not interested, I am sure I can find another coachman who will be." She made a show of tucking the coin back into its pouch. "Good day to you, sir."

"Nay, nay," he called out as she pivoted on her heel. "I'm more'n pleased to be of service." To demonstrate his willingness, he leapt down from his perch and opened the cab door.

She took his hand and stepped inside, arranging her cloak and skirts as she settled onto the thinly padded seat. The coachman closed the door behind her, and the hackney rocked slightly as he climbed back up to his perch.

When the coach lurched forward at the crack of a whip, Jane leaned her head back against the squib and sighed. Her backside wouldn't take kindly to this hour-long jaunt through the bumpy streets of London, especially not combined with the residual soreness from her encounter with Gerard.

Heaven help her, had she really permitted him to . . . She broke off mid-thought, unable to form the words for what they had done together, even in the privacy of her own mind. She flushed hot at the memory of him thrusting his hard, thick length inside her in that most shocking of orifices, but it wasn't the heat of embarrassment. No, it was the heat of arousal, accompanied by the familiar rush of moisture between her thighs.

She clamped her legs tight together in an attempt to squelch the wholly inappropriate sensation. One she had no business feeling, not when she had no idea what he planned to do next.

Her stomach roiled at the damning list of almost endless possibilities, each more awful than the last. Would he call off the betrothal? Reveal her iniquity to her brother and Eleanor? To her parents? To the world?

But ten times more distressing than the potential ruination of her reputation was the harm her cruel masquerade had done to the friendship she'd once shared with Gerard, and to the future they might have had if she had only been more patient, less needy.

Why had she removed her mask? *Stupid, stupid Jane.* But worse, why had she done it in the first place? Why had she allowed her jealousy of another woman—a woman he would have fucked and forgotten—to move her to such a reckless endeavor?

Tears stung the corners of her eyes and blurred her vision. Her ill-considered plan had miscarried in the most spectacular way imaginable. Through it, she had learned that handsome, dashing, sought-after Gerard Everett could fall in love with Jane St. Clair, the plain, dull little wallflower pitied and ridiculed by the entire ton. And through it, she had assured his love was the one thing she would never, ever have.

"I thought you were staying at Grenville's for the week."

Jane flinched at her mother's shrill, censorious tone, but schooled her features to utter calm before looking up from her plate of coddled eggs and sausages. "I missed my studio," she replied, then forked another bite into her mouth before she could make the mistake of justifying herself any further.

Lady Hardwyck emitted her characteristic long-suffering, put-upon sigh and dropped into her chair, snapping her fingers at the footman as she did so. "I do wish you'd give up that . . . that vulgar pursuit. You'll be required to soon enough, you know, as I hardly think Chester will be quite so indulgent as your father and I have been."

Jane tucked further into her breakfast to avoid making a scornful face. One could hardly call her parents' treatment of her hobby indulgent. They permitted it because, short of denying her pin money, they couldn't prevent her from purchasing clay and the other supplies she needed, nor could they keep her from using her antechamber as a workshop.

Her eggs tasted like sawdust as she considered her mother's assertion. Though it pained Jane to admit it, the duchess was probably right. Earls didn't have wives who spent their free time sculpting nude men. Not that Lady Hardwyck knew about those. If she did, Jane's pin money and studio would have been gone long ago.

But it hardly mattered, did it? In all likelihood, Gerard would arrive this morning to break their betrothal and reveal her perfidy to her parents. She would probably be banished to Yorkshire, where it would rain ten months of the year and mist the rest of the time, and there would be no place to purchase her supplies even if she were permitted to have the pin money with which she might buy them.

"So," her mother said briskly as the footman placed a plate piled high with not only eggs and sausages but kippers and scones, "have you given any thought to your engagement ball? We must put on a suitably grand affair—"

Jane's blood thundered in her ears, muffling the duchess's words until she heard them not at all. Oh God, the engagement ball. The one she'd suggested holding as a masquerade. A throbbing ache built in her chest, so dense and painful she became light-headed from lack of air. What had she done? To herself and to Gerard? He would never forgive her, but how could she forgive herself?

"I said, 'What do you think?'"

The impatient question dragged Jane back to her senses like a sharp kick to the stomach. "I'm sorry, Mother, but I was out quite late last night at the opera and got up rather early to come home. Can we discuss this another time? I believe I need to go upstairs and lie down."

"Suit yourself." Her mother popped another kipper into her mouth, chewed, and swallowed. "But Chester will be by later today to discuss the details. A note to that effect was waiting for me when I came downstairs. I expect him shortly after one."

It was all Jane could do to wipe her face, rise to her feet, and stumble blindly from the dining room. Every hope, every dream, every aspiration she'd ever had, save one, destroyed by her own hand.

Only one thing could soothe the wound and give her the strength to carry on.

She must *create*.

16

"How may I assist you this morning, Lord Chester?"

At the lilting, female voice behind him, Gerard swiveled his head away from the blazing fire he'd been staring at since the Grenvilles' disgruntled footman showed him in nearly twenty minutes ago. The marchioness floated through the arched doorway to the sitting room, appearing so ethereal and lovely in her sprigged white muslin morning gown that she needed only wings to complete the image.

His mouth twisted. How ironic that this veritable picture of purity should have played a pivotal role in another's corruption. But then, she had married the man many in the ton had once considered the likely spawn of the devil.

"I am a bit puzzled as to the cause of your visit," Lady Grenville continued, "as you took Lady Jane home to Hardwyck House last night."

What?

"I did n—" Gerard broke off before he completed the thought aloud. He had most certainly not taken Jane to her parents' home last night; he *had* brought her here, not once, but twice!

But the marchioness, while young, was not stupid. Of that he was quite certain. And only a stupid woman would make such a patently false claim to the one person who would surely know it was untrue.

It would seem he had made at least one inaccurate assumption. Lady Grenville had not known where Jane was last night. But that didn't mean she was as innocent as she looked.

"I did not come to see Jane, my lady," he amended. "I came to see you."

She raised an eyebrow in obvious skepticism, but gestured toward one of the large wingback chairs that dominated the room. "Then, please, have a seat."

He shook his head. "I prefer to stand."

Lady Grenville was unusually tall for a woman, but he maintained a slight advantage in height as long as they remained standing. Sitting, he would lose his edge.

"Very well. What did you wish to discuss, my lord?"

"The Red Door."

A pretty pink blush rose high in her cheeks. "I'm afraid I haven't the slightest notion what you mean."

"The devil you don't." He strode toward her, using all of his considerable presence to convince her that continued subterfuge would be both futile and foolish. "Tell me, whose idea was it for Jane to learn the ways of the world in a whorehouse? Yours or Lady Innesford's? Because I would lay odds that it could not have been hers."

Her color drained slowly away, but she met his gaze with defiance sparkling in her china blue eyes. "Anything Callie and I did, we did because we care for Jane's happiness. And because she loves you, likely more than you deserve."

Bloody hell! Was the woman actually trying to make this *his* fault? He wasn't the one who sent an innocent to a brothel to test out her wares on unsuspecting men. And how on earth did they imagine that fitting him with a pair of horns before he'd even married her could constitute a demonstration of her love?

But then, of course, it all came down to what he deserved—or didn't—in the eyes of the ton. Unlike Lady Grenville, who traced her roots to royalty, or Jane herself, who descended from a long line of nobility going back as far as William the Conqueror, Gerard had unfairly inherited his title by accident—the second son of a second son who came into his position only because his great-uncle's third young wife, like the first two, failed to produce offspring.

And they would never let him forget it. No matter how charming, how sophisticated, how fashionable, how rich he might be or might become, he would never be one of them.

A shame he'd nearly forgotten that himself.

"I see. So, giving my unworthiness, you saw no harm in her engaging in a little prenuptial slap and tickle with any man wealthy enough to afford the Red Door's exorbitant prices?"

Lady Grenville's eyes widened. She clapped her hand over her mouth and staggered backward, swaying a little. "What . . . I don't understand. We never suggested such a thing." She turned away and whispered almost inaudibly, "Oh God, Jane, what have you done?"

The woman was either a very practiced liar, or she was telling the truth. Still, she had essentially admitted to having done something. And he was determined to find out exactly what that something was.

"The question, my lady, is what have you done?"

She spun back around and glared at him. "Whatever I did, I did because I love Jane. Can you say the same?"

There it was again. As if he were somehow to blame for this situation. "That is hardly the issue, madam."

Stepping forward, she poked a finger into the center of his chest, hard. "Is it not? Tell me then, what were *you* doing at the Red Door?"

Indignation flared in his chest. "I assure you, that is none of your concern."

"On the contrary, it is entirely my concern when where you choose to put your prick is a direct source of injury to my dearest friend."

Gerard couldn't have been more shocked if she sprouted the angelic wings he'd briefly fancied upon her back and summoned a heavenly choir. In fact, he'd have found that considerably less outlandish.

He opened his mouth to answer, then shut it again, unable to compose a single, sensible response to such a remarkable statement. Was still unable to believe he'd actually heard her correctly.

"Jane loves you, Lord Chester. Has loved you for as long as I have known her and, I suspect, much longer than that. She deserves to be loved in return. And whatever she's done to you could not, I think, be worse than what you would do to her without a second thought, over and over again, for the rest of your lives." She fell silent, studying him with hard, piercing eyes that seemed fashioned from shards of blue Venetian glass before she added the final words to cut him to shreds. "Perhaps you should consider the beam in your own eye, my lord, before you think to condemn the speck in hers."

17

By twenty minutes after the hour, Gerard had had enough of being stuffed into sitting rooms to idly await the pleasure of his hosts' company. Mohammed might be willing to wait for the mountain to come to him. Gerard was not.

He needed to see Jane. Now. Whether she was disposed to his visit or not.

Having spent the better part of the morning contemplating the painful accuracy of Lady Grenville's pointed observations, he had to admit his own culpability, even as a part of his mind tried to excuse it.

He was a man, after all. And the rules were different for men. Society neither expected nor demanded his fidelity. That reality had been clear to him all his life, just as it had to have been clear to Jane that her purity and fidelity, at least before she married and produced an heir, was essential.

Except, of course, she hadn't been unfaithful to him. Or more accurately, she'd been unfaithful to him with *him*, which made no sense and yet he couldn't shake his sense of outrage. And she had done things to him, with him, for him that he would never have dreamed a respectable woman would even consider, let alone participate in with such obvious enthusiasm.

Damn, but the memory of her beneath him last night, long legs spread wide, pussy damp and swollen with desire while he filled her willing arse with his cock had his pulse quickening and his balls tightening with lust. She'd been hotter, sweeter, more uninhibited and responsive than any woman he'd ever known. And he'd known plenty in the Biblical sense of the word.

He frowned. He was still far from certain he could forgive or forget what she had done, let alone accept that the mousy, slightly shy girl he'd once found huddled in a wardrobe had blossomed into the gorgeous wanton he'd taken to bed these past two nights. But until he could see her, talk with her, understand why she had taken her masquerade to such risky, hurtful extremes, he couldn't decide.

He looked up and down the hallway, verifying that no one would be arriving to greet him within the next few seconds, before heading up the staircase to the third floor. When he reached Jane's private parlor, he found the door open and the room empty. Undeterred, he entered and walked through the double doors into her bedchamber.

This room, too, was empty but for its furnishings, including a massive four-poster bed decked in an incongruously delicate buttercup yellow spread with dark pink roses embroidered upon it. A bed, he noted, more than large enough for two.

Where the devil was she? The footman had told him Jane was home but not disposed to see anyone just yet. Gerard had assumed that meant she had only recently risen from her bed, and given the hour at which she must have arrived at home, that was no great wonder.

He was about to give up and search elsewhere—though he hadn't the first notion where elsewhere might be—when he heard a faint clattering noise come from the opposite side of the room. Seeking the source of the sound, he located a small door, half-hidden from view by the large oak wardrobe to its right. Unlike the others he'd encountered, it was closed.

And he'd place a bet with the devil that his quarry was on the other side of it.

He opened the door without knocking, but without making any particular effort to be silent.

She stood with her back to him, bent slightly over a waist-high table, a white smock covering the plain, dark blue gown she wore. Her concentration in her task was evident not only in her failure to notice his entry into the room, but also in the tightly corded muscles of her slender, elegant neck and her apparent disregard to the many thick tresses of hair escaping from her loosely knotted chignon.

The scent of earth—no, of clay—assailed his nostrils as the other contents of the small room, originally intended to be used as a dressing chamber, impinged upon his consciousness. The potter's wheel. The shelves, laden with a variety of pots and vases and sculptures in various stages of production—some glazed and fired, some not. And all of them very, very beautiful.

"You're a sculptor?" The awestruck question escaped before he considered its likely effect.

Predictably, since she wasn't aware of his presence, she startled violently, bumping the table and causing whatever she had been working on to teeter precariously. She caught and steadied it, muttering something under her breath that sounded suspiciously like "damn." When she turned to face him, she stood directly in front of what he was now fairly certain was a statue of some sort, and crossed her arms over her chest.

An action that thrust her breasts upward until they nearly overspilled the confines of her gown, the cut and sizing of which suggested it was several seasons old. Lust stirred in his loins, astonishing him with its speed and fierceness. Last night should have taken the edge off his desire for her. And yet, if anything, his need to have her, to hold her, to *love* her, seemed stronger than before.

This sudden, almost violent need to break every boundary between them and lose himself in her filled him with uneasiness, even dread. Such an emotion couldn't last. And that should please him, for its unpredictability was driving him mad. Instead, all he could think was how bereft and lonely he would be when the feeling passed, and life became as empty and meaningless as before.

Her chin tilted upward in defiance. "I am." Her tone asked whether he wanted to make an issue of it.

He did, but not in the way she thought. Taking two steps, he reached the nearest of the shelves and lifted a small vase with a long, elegant neck. A neck that reminded him instantly of hers. He ran his fingers admiringly over the smooth, shiny black glaze.

From the corner of his eye, he saw that she flinched, but also that she moved slightly to her left. For some reason, she was hiding her latest project from him.

"You're very talented," he said, hoping to diffuse her wariness. "And you've obviously been doing this for a long time. Why didn't you tell me?"

Her features scrunched into an expression of disgust. "Playing in the mud is hardly a ladylike pursuit. And therefore, hardly something the daughter of a duke should advertise."

Gerard set the vase gently back on the shelf. "That's absurd. Lots of ladies paint—and most of them rather badly, I might add. I've had to compliment some fair horrors in my time simply to be polite." He gestured around the room, every nook and cranny of which exhibited her artistic skill. "Your 'mud,' by contrast, is inspired."

The statuary was particularly impressive. Horses, dogs, and birds as well as mythical creatures like griffins and dragons and, of course, the odd human figure, all exhibiting a grace and delicacy of form he'd rarely encountered, even in the expansive art collections of the finest homes and museums. He stroked the graceful neck of a particularly lovely swan, then the incredibly lifelike tail of a prancing horse.

He wasn't aware of walking from one shelf to the next as he perused each item in turn until he reached the back of the room and realized that what appeared to be a drapery covering a window was actually a heavy cloth concealing another shelf.

"What's behind this?" he mused, reaching up to draw it aside.

"No, please." Jane's urgent plea halted his hand, but it was too late. The cloth, anchored at the top only by means of two light paperweights, fell to the ground.

Gerard's eyes widened and his jaw dropped. Male nudes. *Dozens* of them, most modeled on familiar Classical or Renaissance sculptures, but each with a unique feature.

His face.

He spun around. Jane's face was white as fish in cream sauce.

She had also moved away from the table, no doubt in an attempt to reach him before the cloth fell away, and he could now see the project she was working on. Another male nude, but this one wasn't modeled on anything he'd ever seen in a museum. Not only was the musculature clearly recognizable as his own, but the appendage at the apex of the statue's legs bore no resemblance to the limp, fig-leaf-covered penises favored by artists since ancient times.

No, the cock on this nude was flagrantly, hugely erect.

He stared from her to the statue, unable to comprehend what he was seeing. His supposedly sweet, innocent bride was a . . . Damn, he couldn't find an accurate word.

There was no doubt she'd been making these statues for years. Modeled his face on various body types, as if putting form to her imaginings of what he might look like without his clothing. And now, she was sculpting him exactly as she'd seen him . . . hard and thick and ready to fuck her into oblivion.

The statue was indecent, obscene, and yet, strangely beautiful. Arousing.

He was shocked. He was horrified. He was ... flattered.

And well on his way to emulating his likeness in every conceivable way.

18

Jane's heart sank lower and lower into her belly as Gerard continued to look from her to the unfinished sculpture behind her, his expression wavering between shock and disbelief. There would be no averting the inevitable now. By this time tomorrow, she would be denounced and disgraced, her reputation thoroughly and utterly obliterated. Not even the chimney sweep would have her to wife after this got out, her flawless pedigree and enormous dowry notwithstanding.

She turned back to the table and picked up the flat-ended wooden tool she had been using to add the finishing touches to her statue. This might well be the last sculpture she ever created, and she would be damned if she would stop before it was exactly as she'd envisioned it.

Her tribute to the masculine beauty and power of the man she loved.

Her vision blurred with hot, stinging tears, but she blinked them furiously away as she teased the clay to form hair on the top of the figure's head—thick, silken hair that fell in waves to the nape of his neck, tucked up around his ears and over his forehead in impudent curls. Hair she wanted to bury her fingers in . . .

Warm, strong hands circled her waist, and hot breath tickled the back of her neck. "Wouldn't you rather have the real thing?"

Although her fingers trembled and a traitorous tingle spread along her nerves, she continued her task. "No," she lied, determined not to fall into his trap. After what she had done to him, how could she expect him not to take his revenge?

His palms slid up her rib cage, and his lips pressed warm and firm against the sensitive spot beneath her ears. She bit her lip to keep from melting into him. There was nothing she could do, however, to stop her breath from hitching or her nipples from hardening to taut, tense peaks.

"Your body says otherwise," he murmured.

"My body is mistaken." Her body was stupid. It ached for him. Begged for every caress, every kiss, every gesture of love and desire he might bestow, like the slavish dog whose master has offered a table scrap.

But her mind was smart. And she wouldn't take scraps. Not any longer.

His thumbs brushed over her nipples. Despite the layers between them—chemise, stays, dress, and smock—a tremor shook her, causing her to lose her grip on the tool she was using. It clattered to the table.

He spun her to face him. His handsome features were dark, hard, and his brown eyes glittered like hot embers. "Tell me you don't want me, and I'll leave."

She closed her eyes, unable to bear the intensity of his gaze. "You'll leave anyway," she whispered, her throat thickening painfully.

He gave her a shake, rough but somehow tender. "But I always come back, don't I?" His breath hitched oddly, and then he let out a long, slow exhalation. "My God, it's always been you."

Jane's eyes fluttered open. "What?"

His thumb caressed her jawline, rubbed a dried smudge of clay from her cheek. "You've always known, haven't you?"

"Always known what?"

"That I was born to love you, but that I'd never see the truth of it unless you showed me." He smiled softly. "That is why you went to the brothel, isn't it?"

Her mouth dropped open for a second. Was that why she had gone? "No, I—"

"Shhhhh." He pressed two fingers over her lips. "Lady Grenville and Lady Innesford sent you only for advice on matters of the marriage bed. You sought to learn how you might please me."

Now, her mouth gaped so wide, someone might mistake her for a suckling pig and stuff an apple in it. Or, she thought with a sudden twinge of longing, a cock. "How did you—?"

He brushed a thick column of hair that had escaped its hastily fastened bindings of her forehead. "I'm not as mutton-headed as I look."

"You do *not* look mutton-headed," she objected reflexively.

He chuckled, a rueful grin twisting his beautiful lips. "I wasn't always the dapper, insouciant fellow you see before you today, you know. And I have been called a great deal worse than mutton-headed." Lowering his head, he pressed a gentle kiss to her temple. "What I don't understand is how you wound up in that room, waiting for me. Because you were waiting for *me*, I know that now."

Jane took a long, steadying breath. How could she explain the series of events and emotions that had led her to toss out every rule, every code of conduct, every shred of respectability and dignity she'd ever been taught? Even now, she could hardly understand it herself.

"I . . . Mrs. Upshaw showed me some cards. With drawings on them." She felt a blush stain her cheeks.

Gerard nodded, encouraging her to continue.

"There was one. A woman with a man's—" She hesitated, not quite able to say the word *cock* aloud. She settled for "organ in her mouth." Her ears now flamed along with her face. "I was . . . curious because Mrs. Upshaw told me it was something men like very much."

"So it is," Gerard rumbled, amusement and arousal tingeing his voice.

"I couldn't understand why, though. From a still picture. I didn't know what a man would find so appealing. So Mrs. Upshaw offered to show me." The words tumbled out now, fast and furious. "But when we entered the brothel from her apartment, I saw you. Talking to a beautiful woman with red hair." At the memory, her throat began to burn with the same caustic jealousy she'd felt then. "I couldn't bear the thought of you going upstairs with her. To do with her the things I'd seen on those cards. Things I wanted you to do only with me. I'm sorry. I never meant to deceive you. But once I'd started, I didn't know how to stop."

"Ahhh, sweetheart." He cupped the back of her head in his palm, kneading the taut flesh beneath her hair with just the right pressure to ease the tension that had built there. "It is I who should be sorry. The only person who deceived me was me. When I saw you sitting on that bed, somewhere in the back of my mind, I knew it was you. I just couldn't allow myself to believe it. So I convinced myself to disregard what my senses told me."

She frowned. "But you couldn't have known. The mask. And I changed my voice."

He shook his head. "You were right after the opera last night. When you observed that no one could truly mistake his beloved for another—or another for his beloved."

His fingers slipped to the back of her neck, easing the knots of worry she hadn't even realized were there. She closed her eyes and sighed with pleasure.

"There is one more thing," he murmured near her ear.

Her eyes fluttered open. "What is that?"

"I wouldn't have gone upstairs with her. Wouldn't have slept with her."

"Her?" Jane asked vaguely, her limbs weakening with every caress of his fingers. Much more of this and she might collapse into a heap on the floor like the first clay statue she'd ever attempted, before she'd learned to build armatures.

"The woman at the Red Door. The one you saw me with. I'd decided to leave before Mrs. Upshaw approached me."

Jane looked at him sharply. "You wouldn't have? Why not?"

"Because, I only wanted one woman that night," he said softly as he drew his fingers down over her lips. "You."

"Oh?" She breathed the question because words escaped her.

He traced her bottom lip with his thumb. "Now, no more talking. Or thinking. Only feeling."

And then his fingers were replaced by his mouth, hot and seductive and dangerous, making her forget all the uncertainties between them in the raw, heady magic of his kiss. Pulling her flush to his body, he spun her around, backing her into the table on which she kept her tools and pottery glazes. With one sweep of his arm, everything crashed to the floor and suddenly, she was sitting atop the hard, sturdy surface, her skirts bunched up to her hips with her legs spread wide and the ridge of Gerard's cock pressing against her damp, unmistakably willing pussy.

His hands glided up the insides of her thighs, sending gooseflesh down her legs and shivers up her spine. If she'd known what his touch would do to her, if she'd had any inkling of the true pleasures of the marriage bed, she wouldn't have waited three long years since her debut to accost him in a whorehouse. Three long, wasted years that could have been filled with this . . . this joy.

His lips trailed liquid fire from her mouth to her neck to her breast, which he'd somehow cleverly slipped from its too tight confinement in her bodice, and his fingers parted the slit in her drawers and delved into her soft, wet flesh.

Releasing her nipple from his mouth, he gazed up at her with a simmering intensity that seemed to suck the breath from her lungs the way a fire draws air from a room. "I want to make love to you, Jane. Properly. Here." He thrust two fingers inside her pussy by way of illustration, causing her to gasp audibly.

"Here?" she squeaked. "Now?"

He grinned. "Well, we could move to the bed in the other room, but I think it would spoil our claim to have gotten carried away, should anyone find out later. And besides," he added with a quick glance over his shoulder and a conspiratorial wink, "I've always wanted to do it with myself as an audience."

"I don't know . . ." she murmured, but his fingers were doing something quite singular now, his thumb brushing over her clitoris until her whole being seemed centered between her legs and . . .

Release crashed over her, and she had to wind her arms about his neck to keep from collapsing back onto the table as the spasms took her.

"I'll take that as a yes," he said, swiftly undoing the buttons to free his cock from the confines of his breeches.

Taking the shaft in his hand, he guided the soft, rounded tip to where his fingers had been just moments ago. When had he removed them? She hadn't time to consider the idle question, however, because he took her mouth in a searing kiss as he pushed the head of his cock a short way inside, just to the point where she could feel the resistance of her maidenhead blocking his path.

He hesitated, his respiration labored, his features taut with concentration. "Stop me if I hurt you."

She threaded her fingers in his hair and smiled. "Just kiss me. I can't feel pain when you do."

318 / Jackie Barbosa

His mouth swooped down on hers, his tongue sweeping past her lips to stroke and pet and tease. Oh yes, *this* was what she needed. What she'd desperately missed last night. The difference between fucking—between bodies joining for nothing more than physical satisfaction—and loving.

When she was quivering with need, he grabbed her hips and did it. With a single smooth, sure thrust, he shattered the last barrier between them.

And they were one.

As perhaps they had always been.

19

Gerard rested his forehead against Jane's, taking rapid, shallow breaths in a desperate attempt to restore his control. If he didn't, he'd come before he'd even begun.

Her pussy gripped him, tighter than her mouth, wetter and more yielding than her arse. He gritted his teeth as his balls drew tight against his body with threatened climax.

Not yet.

"Did I hurt you, my goddess?" he asked, lifting his head and studying her expression for any outward signs of discomfort.

"Only a little. And only for a second." She wiggled her hips beneath his hands, causing him to nearly lose his grip, both on her and on reality.

Damn and blast, but the way her cunt squeezed his cock, she would milk him to orgasm without moving at all.

"I like the way you feel inside me here," she said, still doing whatever it was with her inner muscles that made him want to throw back his head and roar while he spilled his seed into her womb. "It's different than last night," she went on.

Of course, she had to remind him of that. His knees almost

gave way at the memory of how magnificently erotic, how deeply satisfying it had been to fuck her arse. God, she'd been so willing, so receptive, so giving. She'd never doubted him for a minute, had trusted him completely and without reservation.

No wonder he loved her.

"Not better, exactly, but different. More . . . real."

He smiled at the description. Real. Yes, this was real. So real it ought to terrify him and yet, he was strangely at peace. Because, somehow, he knew that this would last. No matter how many times they made love, no matter how many ways, this woman—this body and mind and soul—could never bore him. She was the only woman he would ever need, now and forever.

"Gerard?" The gentle question drew him from his ruminations.

"Yes, my love?"

"I would like for you to fuck me now. That is, if you have no objections?"

Lust blazed back to life. "None at all."

A cheeky grin spread across her lips, and he wondered why he'd ever thought her plain. She was without a doubt the most beautiful woman in the world.

"Then get on with i—"

She broke off with a squeak as he dragged his cock slowly, agonizingly out, then plunged back in. And almost fainted at the heady sensation of her cunt stretching for him, squeezing him, drawing him back inside. Lightheaded as more blood rushed from his head to his groin, he nonetheless managed to maintain enough awareness to adjust the angle of penetration to maximize her pleasure.

He started with a slow, easy pace, but she was having none of it. Wrapping her legs around his hips, she dug her feet into his buttocks and urged him to increase his rhythm. "Please . . . faster . . . harder . . . more," she begged between panting breaths. "I'm so close."

Humankind had never conspired to invent a more potent

aphrodisiac than the pleas of a woman impaled on a man's cock. Gerard doubled, then tripled his tempo, pounding into her until the wet, smacking sounds of copulation created an almost symphonic accompaniment to the music of her little moans and sobs of pleasure and the rapid, heavy drumbeat of his heart.

Anticipating the approach of her climax and his own, he released her hips, took her face between his hands, and forced her to meet his gaze. Her eyes were glazed with passion and he wasn't sure she would understand a word he said, but he had to tell her now, before he buried himself in her one last time and came so hard, he forgot even his own name.

"Only you, Jane. I love you. Always and forever."

She surprised him by whispering back, "And I love you, Gerard. Beyond forever."

Then she arched her back, and the first spasm wracked her. He couldn't hold out any longer as her cunt grabbed and released, grabbed and released, milking his cock in long, voluptuous waves. He lowered his mouth and kissed her as his release overtook him in a burst as bright as sunshine, shaking him to his bones, wrenching his seed from him in thick, visceral bursts until it seemed he had lost his entire being within her. And he never wanted to leave.

It was some time before either of them had the will to speak or move. When at last they pulled apart and straightened their clothes, an awkward moment of silence descended. Having just declared his undying love for her and relieved her of her virginity, there could be no question of his intentions. And yet, he sensed uncertainty in her averted gaze.

She was the first, however, to break the silence. "I suppose I shall have to give it up."

Gerard frowned. "Give what up?"

She gestured around the room and sighed. "This. But especially this," she said, running her hand tenderly over the statue she had been sculpting when he arrived.

The lewd, indecent, exquisite likeness of him she'd created with such skill. And love.

He wrapped his arms around her and pulled her into his embrace. "Never, my goddess."

She blinked up at him. "But surely you cannot approve of your wife doing something as wicked, as sinful as sculpting men in the nude."

A slow smile spread across his lips, then burgeoned into laughter which he ruthlessly suppressed. The last thing he wanted was for her to think he found her art amusing or less than worthwhile. "You're entirely right, my darling. It is a most sinful avocation for a wife, to say nothing of a lady and a countess. But as long as the only man you sculpt is me, I believe I can bear it."

She threw her arms around his neck and peppered his face with kisses. "Oh, thank you, Gerard. I can't thank you enough."

"No need to thank me. I want your happiness above all else."

"In that case," she said, a sudden twinkle of mischief lighting her eyes. "I have a small request."

He raised his eyebrows warily. "And what is that, my love?"

"Will you sit for me?"

Now he threw back his head and laughed, before nodding toward the patently aroused statue. "If you plan to get me in that state before we begin, I shall sit for you any time you like. As long as you're prepared for the consequences."

She slid her hand down to the fall of his breeches, caressing him, teasing him, making his eyes roll back in his head. "Always and forever. I suppose, my lord, that we shall live sinfully ever after."

Author's Note

Over the centuries, many fabled poets have tried their hands at translating Classical poetry into English verse, among them Dryden, Marlowe, Pope, and Longfellow. Up until the early twentieth century, the defining characteristic of English poetry was the fact that it rhymed, and so all translators until that time attempted to reproduce the sense of the original Latin or Greek poem in rhymed English verse. Needless to say, translations of a single poem could vary widely, depending upon what words and phrases the translator imported to the text in order to produce the elegant rhyming couplets or stanzas the poet was aiming to achieve.

The two poems in this book—the first from Ovid's *Amores* and the second a well-known fragment of Sappho's lyric poetry—are not nineteenth-century translations, but my own creations. I started with fairly literal, free-verse translations of the poems done by A. S. Kline, which I reworked significantly to arrive at the rhyming couplets provided here. This turned out to be both difficult and rewarding, and the exercise gave me a real appreciation for the greatness of those poets of bygone eras.

You can find Kline's work online at http://www.tonykline.co.uk/. To see several different modern translations of the same Sappho poem used in this story, go to http://www.sappho.com/poetry/sappho2.html. For examples of earlier translations of Ovid's work by John Dryden and others, see http://classics.mit.edu/Ovid/metam.html.